GW00702127

VERTICAL CHALLENGE

A Harrier Encounter

By the same author

Time To Act: A Mercenary Tale – Published by
Minerva Press 2000

VERTICAL CHALLENGE

A Harrier Encounter

Anthony J Broughton

Book Guild Publishing
Sussex, England

First published in Great Britain in 2007 by
The Book Guild Ltd
Pavilion View
19 New Road
Brighton, BN1 1UF

Copyright © Anthony J Broughton 2007

The right of Anthony J Broughton to be identified as the author
of this work has been asserted by him in accordance with the
Copyright, Designs and Patents Act 1988.

All rights reserved. No part of this publication may be
reproduced, transmitted, or stored in a retrieval system, in any
form or by any means, without permission in writing from the
publisher or the author, nor be otherwise circulated in any form
of binding or cover other than that in which it is published and
without a similar condition being imposed on the subsequent
purchaser.

All characters in this publication are fictitious and any
resemblance to real people, alive or dead, is purely coincidental.

Typesetting in Baskerville by
IML Typographers, Merseyside

Printed in Great Britain by
CPI Antony Rowe

A catalogue record for this book is available from
The British Library.

ISBN 978 1 84624 170 3

Contents

CONTENTS

Acknowledgements

I would like to thank Graham Tomlinson, who was the Harrier Chief Test Pilot at the British Aerospace site in Dunsfold, for his help and advice about flying Harrier Jump Jets. I would also like to thank Joseph Roake, who was Engineering Manager of Design at BAE Systems in Farnborough, for the encouragement and support that he gave me. I would also like to thank BAE Systems Intellectual Property Department for allowing me to quote details of Harrier Jump Jets and Dunsfold Aerodrome in Surrey.

Characters

SUZIE DRAKE (MISS OCHRE), ex-mercenary, now co-owns SMJ boatyard

MIKE RANDLE, ex-soldier and mercenary, now co-owns SMJ boatyard, partner of Suzie Drake

SIR JOSEPH STERLING, diplomat troubleshooter in the Foreign Office for security matters

DETECTIVE INSPECTOR COLIN BROOKE, Special Branch

JIM and JENNY STERLING, son and daughter-in-law of Sir Joseph Sterling, co-owners of SMJ boatyard

RYALL, hired thief, boss of a group of small-time crooks

ALEX KIRBY, killer and crook, Ryall's partner in crime

TAFFY, member of Ryall's gang

PHIL, member of Ryall's gang

MR BLACK, once a Metropolitan Police Inspector, now turned to crime

TANYA GIBSON (MISS LILAC), ex-RAF pilot recruited by Mr Black

CHARACTERS

PAULA HARDCASTLE (MISS PINK), RAF trainee pilot recruited by Mr Black, and a former partner of Mike Randle

MR GREEN, computer expert in the employ of Mr Black

MR BROWN, MR GREY, MR WHITE, MR BLUE, TERRY, associates in the employ of Mr Black

AHMED DINASHAR, emissary for the People's Liberation Organisation of Yalon (PLOY)

ABID ALI-KHAN, a fence for stolen goods

HARRY MORTIMORE, works in the Records Department at the Foreign Office

1

Robbery

The security guard looked up from his newspaper and glanced across at the five monitors stacked on the side of his desk. The views on the screens before him covered the factory compound, loading bay, main entrance and large car park. Not that there was much to see, especially in the gloom at this time of night. Most of the area was covered by bulkhead lights and showed little beyond the pool of glow that emitted from the wall-mounted fittings. The guard turned up the contrast to scan the dim shadows and confirm that nobody was lurking around outside. On one screen, he could pick out the shutter doors into the factory, which were better lit by an overhead incandescent light mounted within a cracked, white shade that swung each time a breeze drifted past, rocking the sphere of light on the ground back and forth. The wire mesh entrance gate was similarly lit, but the remaining views on his monitors consisted mostly of outlines. Brick walls of the two-storey main building were partly visible and also, lit by the one and only floodlight, was a car park, almost empty save for a couple of wrecks dumped in one corner that, it seemed to him, had always been there.

With nothing untoward to grab his attention, the guard returned to reading his newspaper and attempted to complete the Sunday crossword. This was not the most exciting job he had tackled, and the pay was not very good, but it was steady work, close to home and did not entail much effort or brainpower. He poured himself another cup of coffee from his flask and re-read the clues. In a few minutes time, Roy, the only other guard on duty that night, would arrive and, after a drink and a natter, they would swap tasks and it would be his turn to stretch his legs and walk the rounds, checking the offices. He looked forward to that part of the job, it gave him the chance to nose about and search other people's desks and benches. It was surprising, the things that some employees left lying about. He had even found a £10 note once, thrown with a handful of loose change and a bunch of keys on a desktop. The owner probably left in a hurry that Friday evening and forgot them. By Monday morning, he would have been unsure what he had left behind, and by then the guard had enjoyed a few extra pints in the local pub.

With his pencil poised above the newspaper, he was pondering about the answer to 27 across, when his thoughts were interrupted by the throaty roar of a 100-tonne low-loader disturbing the night air on its approach to the main gate. Headlights blazed through the wire link fencing, illuminating the entrance compound, turning night to day as the vehicle shuddered to a halt with the air brakes giving a long hiss as if to say, we are finally there. The guard looked up through the window, noticed the trailer was empty, except for a tarpaulin tied to it, and wondered what the driver wanted. He had not been informed of any equipment that was to be collected, and anyway, it was far too late and the foreman would have to be present to manage all the paperwork involved. He was probably at home, tucked safely in bed. The whole place, the guard knew, was empty, except for him and Roy. The driver was more likely to be looking for one of the other factories on this industrial estate in Crawley, and wanted directions. Usually, this happened because he had either taken a wrong turning and lost his way, or his vehicle had broken down and he was late, making it difficult for him to find his destination at night, with few or no people about to ask. It was always easier for a driver to stop at one of the factories and ask the night guard; it saved the bother of trundling around the estate looking for the premises he required.

The guard closed his newspaper and dropped the pencil on top of it. He rose wearily and slowly; it was approaching midnight on this Sunday evening and his twelve-hour shift was not yet half-way through. The chair screeched on the bare wooden floorboards as he pushed it away with the back of his legs and grabbed his flat-topped cap from a peg on the back of the door. Donning his headgear, he trudged down the three steps from the wooden security hut, banging the door behind him, and wandered along to meet the baseball-capped driver who was descending from his cab with a clipboard grasped firmly in his hand.

Questions and answers concerning directions to his destination were never given the opportunity to resound in the night air. Before a word could be spoken, the driver produced a gun from behind the clipboard, and bullets ripped into the guard's chest from a silenced weapon that puffed twice in quick succession, barely making a sound. With a look of incredulity, the guard sank to his knees, and by the time he hit the ground, five other baseball-capped members of the gang had appeared from the lorry, and with precision and silence they sprang into a well-rehearsed move.

Heavy duty cutters were produced, and sliced their way through the padlock with ease, opening the way for the low-loader to move into the compound. Connections to the cameras, videoing the entrance and loading bay, had their wires cut while the guard's place was taken by one of the gang after his uniform was removed and his body dragged behind the hut to hide it from any prying eyes, in case anyone should arrive.

The gang were well briefed on the layout, knew what they were after, where to go and what to expect. The main gate was closed, the padlock replaced, and the entrance door into the factory floor and loading bay was quickly breached. The object they were there to steal was big and heavy, contained a lot of electronic equipment, stood on hydraulic ram jacks and cost a small fortune to develop. This factory manufactured and sold aircraft and submarine simulators.

The new guard took his place in the hut, and placed his communicator on the desk, a valuable instrument with which he could talk to his boss in case of any problems. He opened the newspaper and stared blankly at the crossword in front of him. His eyes lit up at the sight of a cup of coffee on the desk. He touched the cup, felt it was still warm and drank it.

'Find the other guard and check that no one else is around,' instructed Ryall, to his trusted friend Alex, the tall, well-built driver of the lorry. 'He should be on his way here to change places with the one on the main gate. I want to make sure that we're not disturbed. Meanwhile, I want everyone else to keep quiet. Deliveries at this time of the night are not all that common, so I don't want the other guard getting jumpy and calling the police if he hears something unusual,' he demanded, throwing his baseball cap into the low-loader cab. His men sat quietly on the trailer and one of them, Taffy, rolled himself a cigarette.

Alex threw his cap down, allowing the mop of shoulder-length blond hair that crowned his head and flowed down the sides of his long, angular face, to drop into place. He ran his fingers through his hair, pulling it to the back of his head, before setting off to carry out the task with his usual ruthless efficiency. After all, killing was a job that he enjoyed, and he was good at it.

Ryall was himself no stranger to robbery, and more lately, murder. Nearly one-third of the 40-plus years of his life had been either spent in prison, or on the run from the authorities. In later years, he had become astute enough not to waste his time behind bars and used his enforced presence in Her Majesty's Prisons to stay fit, and learn skills that would help him once he had regained his freedom.

A muscular man, slightly under 6 feet tall, his craggy features, prominent cheek bones and full head of darkish blond hair, gave him a look that was a little on the hard side, but was not unattractive. His blue eyes helped to give him the appearance of being tough, yet gentle, a look which was at odds with his true nature. The only son of a poor family who struggled to make ends meet, he grew up with a chip on his shoulder. This was partly due to his parents separating when he was young, making life even more difficult. He was determined to better himself, even if it meant stealing to get what he wanted.

His dream was to pull off one really big job. He cultivated friendships that would be an advantage to him later on, contriving to get close to those who could teach him such talents that would enable him to achieve his aim of retiring very rich, and spending what was left of his life in modest luxury and comfort. This robbery was not the big job that he was waiting for, but it was the most daring one he had attempted so far – stealing a multi-million-pound aircraft simulator. The handsome pay-off would help him to live comfortably for a while, and give him the funds and breathing space he needed to seek out one last, very profitable heist.

Why on earth anyone should want such a piece of equipment he was not at all sure, but he could take an educated guess. Even so, he did not much care, though he had to admit to a certain amount of curiosity about what his client's ultimate aim was. His overriding concern at that moment, though, was to get safely away with all the parts, complete and in working order. The ram jacks had to be dismantled from the cabin and unbolted from the floor before the simulator could be loaded on to the trailer. His instructions were to deliver it to a warehouse somewhere along the south coast, where he would receive a not inconsiderable reward for his and his men's services. The exact location had been kept secret from him and would only be revealed when they were on their way with the goods, by the man his client had insisted on accompanying them during the robbery, the electronics expert, Mr Green.

Ryall's client was not interested in knowing any of the details about how the intended equipment would be acquired, or who might suffer because of the methods he used to obtain it; he simply wanted it delivered to his secret location, and in full working order.

Nearly ten minutes had elapsed before Alex returned from his search, wiping blood from the blade of his knife. 'There's no one to disturb us now,' he promised. 'I've had a good look around and they were, as we were told, the only ones here.'

'Good. Let's go,' Ryall said, clapping his hands. 'I want this thing loaded and ready to move in four hours absolute maximum. After that we could start to get visitors, and that's something none of us want.'

Taffy entered the factory by the side door and pressed the shutter button. Alex jumped into the cab and started the engine as light spilled into the compound from behind the massive grey shutters, slowly rising. They clanged upwards, allowing the lorry to be backed into the voluminous factory area, and such was the driver's speed and skill that the cab slid under the shutters with barely an inch to spare before it began its downward journey, thrusting the compound back into its peaceful gloom. By the time the shutters touched the ground and stopped, on this eventful Sunday night in May, the gang's main task had begun.

2

Coffee Break

At the simulator factory in Crawley, and with the closed shutters keeping out any prying eyes, and keeping in any noise they made, the men waited for their instructions. They stood patiently, watching their client's man search for the right piece of equipment. The large expanse of factory floor contained walkways and designated work areas, marked by painted white lines on the floor, in which several different types of simulators were sitting. It was important not to make a mistake and steal the wrong one, and they were eager to complete their job in record time and melt back into the darkness. Only then could they deliver the goods and receive their much-needed, handsome payment.

After checking several of the simulators, Mr Green announced, 'This is the one.'

'Right. Let's get it done,' yelled Ryall to his men, his voice echoing around the factory.

One man climbed the ladder to the overhead crane and it whirred into action, creating such a loud noise that it seemed as if anyone within a mile would hear, despite the closed shutters. The gantry rumbled along the runners, high above the floor, and was manoeuvred into position over the massive structure of the simulator they were to dismantle.

'It doesn't look much like an aeroplane; it's just a great big box on ram jacks! Are you sure this is the right one?' Ryall asked, scratching the two-day stubble on his chin, fearful of taking the wrong piece of equipment and not getting his payment.

'It's the right one,' Mr Green assured him. 'It doesn't have to look like an aeroplane on the outside. It's the cockpit layout and the electronics and visual display inside that make it unique to this particular model. The box is just a shell to hold it all.'

Ryall nodded. He disliked working with people that he did not know, especially those who were thrust upon him. But this bloke seemed okay and gave the impression that he knew what he was talking about, though he was a weedy-looking, boring type, academically good but with only a shallow character. Ryall liked people with a strong character, like Alex. He was a tall, ugly brute, but that did not stop him from attracting the women. They flocked to the animal instinct that he exuded and the muscles he displayed beneath intricate designs tattooed the length of his hairy arms.

Mr Green, on the other hand, had been fascinated by electronics all his life and had devoted many of his 43 years to working on prototype schemes on various projects, all for the same company. None had developed into anything anywhere near his expectations, let alone exceeded them, and few had been very successful. He had ended up as a small cog in a big machine, plodding aimlessly through life, producing a dismal state of affairs in his working career, which was mirrored in his personal life. There were however compensations, and he had become knowledgeable about electronics. The more his personal life, and especially his love life, suffered, the more he sank himself into his work. Now he worked for a new boss, Mr Black, who had recognised this turmoil in his life as an advantage that he could use, and recruited Mr Green with promises of great wealth, which would automatically bring many women flocking to his side. He would be able to have his pick of the lovely bunch with his new-found riches and select a different woman whenever it took his fancy. Mr Green dreamed of that day and worked enthusiastically for Mr Black in the expectation of his dreams coming true very soon.

Hoisting his wiry frame up the iron ladder, fitted to the side of the simulator, Mr Green walked along the gantry and entered the craft through a door at the rear. The men were manhandling lifting wires into position around the 25-feet-high structure, in readiness to hoist it on to the back of the trailer after the ram jacks and floor fixings had been removed.

'One of the electronic modules is missing,' declared Mr Green, emerging from the craft and leaning on the handrail, shouting to Ryall who was directing operations from below.

'Oh God! Bloody chinless wonder,' breathed Ryall. 'What do you mean?' he yelled, the tone of his voice showing anxiety and almost disbelief at the unexpected problem.

'There's an empty space in the electronic rack where one of the control modules should be fitted. It may have been taken out for repair or testing or something. We must find it. This contraption's just a heap of scrap metal unless it is properly reinstalled and working.'

'Oh, great! You two,' Ryall said, pointing to two of his men adjusting the lifting cable. 'Go with this bloke and find this bloody piece. And don't come back until you've got it.'

The men nodded, and left to search the offices with Mr Green.

'What are we looking for?' asked Taffy, a small man with a long experience of house breaking, but feeling a bit lost with this type of robbery.

'A rack unit, about 50 centimetres long and 20 centimetres high, with rows of indicator lights on the front of PCBs.'

'Centimetres? PCBs? What the hell are they? I only know feet and inches,' Taffy declared.

9

'About twenty inches long and eight inches high with PCBs – printed circuit boards,' huffed Mr Green, showing his displeasure at what he considered were two uneducated idiots.

Pushing open a door labelled 'Assembly Area', he flicked on the light switch. 'A green board like this one, with resistors and capacitors on it,' he said, lifting a PCB from a workbench.

The men looked bemused; high-technology was not one of their strong points. Jemmying open doors or windows and ransacking houses was nearer their mark. They searched the room and found nothing.

'Now what?' Mr Green was asked.

He scratched his head and thought for a moment. 'Test. We must find the test lab and look there. If they've done some modifications or updated any of the boards, they'll have to be tested before they go back into the module.'

The men barely knew what he was talking about. His technical jargon was like a language from another world. They looked at each other and shrugged. 'We'll follow you,' Taffy stated.

The trio moved into the main building and tramped down the long, dimly lit corridors where most of the rooms were offices and unlikely to contain what they were searching for. Descending a flight of stairs to an open area, Mr Green exclaimed, 'Ah! This looks more like it.'

Stepping into a room with 'Test' painted on the glass-topped door in red letters, Mr Green flipped down the light switch. The fluorescent tubes flickered on and off before illuminating the room. They were confronted with benches all along one wall, covered with tools, bits of wire, diodes, resistors and other components. A nearby wooden shelf held several modules, and a rack contained PCBs. A module, perched on its side on top of one of the benches, had components scattered around it next to a soldering iron, still plugged in, giving off the smell of molten solder that glistened from its hot tip.

'This looks like the one,' Mr Green stated, flicking through a manual lying open on the bench. He picked up a clipboard and ran his finger down the checklist pinned to it, then thumbed through the manual and peered at the part numbers on the PCBs which were still hooked into the test equipment. Ryall's men watched and waited.

Eventually, Mr Green announced, 'Good. Everything seems to be here. As I suspected, they are modifying the boards and testing them. We want all of these,' he said, indicating the module, boards and components that he required to be collected. He extracted the sheets from the clipboard and stuffed them into the manual, closing it with a thud.

'How about these things?' Taffy asked. 'Do we want any of them?' he said, pointing to the test equipment.

'No. I've got an oscilloscope and test meters, and this manual gives me all the information I need to complete the checks and reassemble the module,' he declared, shoving the book under his arm and turning towards the door.

The men collected all the parts and stuffed the smaller items into a cardboard box, which Taffy, being only small, quickly grabbed, leaving the heavier module for his mate to collect. They carried them back to the factory, following Mr Green.

He was Mr Black's ambassador on this venture, and was heavily impressed by him with the reliance for which he was responsible. It was Mr Green's duty to see that everything went as planned and he felt important, striding along the corridor with a swagger.

The group entered the loading bay, where Ryall was eagerly watching progress by the rest of his men. He was relieved to learn from Mr Green that all the pieces to get the simulator working had been retrieved, and Taffy and his mate placed them carefully in the lorry under the watchful eyes of the electronics man. The robbery was progressing on schedule with the massive structure in the process of being unbolted from the floor now that the crane was supporting its weight.

Ryall's communicator buzzed; he jammed it to his ear. 'Yeah, what is it Phil?' he asked his man guarding the main entrance.

'A police car's coming towards the gate. I'm going out to see what they want.'

'Okay. You know what to say. Give me a buzz when they've gone.'

'Right.'

Ryall waved at his men. 'Everybody stop what you're doing and don't make a noise. There's some coppers coming to the main gate.'

The men all stopped work. The factory fell into a hushed silence.

Phil wandered up to the two policemen now standing behind the wire mesh gate. 'Good evening officers. What can I do for you on this fine night?'

One of the policemen shone his torch in the guard's face. 'We're making our routine check of all the factories on the estate.'

'Oh! Right.'

'You're not the usual guard. Where's Roy?'

'He rang in sick, so they asked me to stand in for him tonight.'

'I see. Is everything okay?'

'Yeah. Quiet as a mouse,' replied Phil.

'Where's the other guard?'

'He's doing the rounds at the moment. I expect he'll be back for a chat and a cup of tea soon.'

'Yeah. Roy used to let us get a cup of coffee from the vending machine that's just inside the factory.'

'Oh! Right,' Phil replied, desperately trying to think of a way out of the problem that was threatening to engulf him. 'Why don't you have a seat in the hut and take a look at the paper while I get your drinks.'

'Well …' hesitated the policeman.

'There's a photo of a cracking bird on page three.'

The thought seemed to change their minds.

'Oh, okay. Mine's white with sugar and Brian's is white without.'

'Right. You make yourselves comfortable,' said Phil, unlocking the gate. 'I'll be back in a jiffy.'

The two policemen strolled into the hut and Phil marched to the factory, trying not to look in too much of a hurry. He entered through the side door. Ryall looked horrified at his arrival and dashed over to confront him.

'What the hell are you doing in here, and where are those coppers?'

'They're in the guard hut,' he declared.

'What!'

'They wanted to come in here to get a cup of coffee from the vending machine. Apparently the other guard usually lets them do that. I persuaded them to read the newspaper in the hut while I get their coffees for them.'

'Okay. Good thinking, Phil. Get the drinks and get back to them quickly. I don't want them wandering in here,' Ryall declared. 'And if it looks like it's getting a bit tricky and they become suspicious, kill them. We'll have to take a chance that no one else comes looking for them before we get finished.'

Phil nodded, went to the vending machine and put his hands in his pockets. 'You got any change?' he asked.

Ryall mouthed a few profanities and pulled out some change from his pocket. Phil took the money and purchased the two coffees. He trotted back to the hut with his fingers burning from the hot liquid and dropped them on the table, spilling some from one of the cups.

13

He licked his fingers. 'Sorry about that. They're a bit hot.'

The policemen picked up their coffees, blew into the cup and took a sip.

'You've not done this job here before, have you?' one asked.

'No. I'm just a sort of temporary odd job man with an agency. They found me this job when the other man went sick.'

'That seems a bit strange. They've usually got other guards that can cover anyone who's taken ill, because of the military stuff in this factory. Everyone needs clearance to work here.'

'That's why they picked me at the agency,' Phil bluffed. 'I've got military clearance 'cos I was in the RAF.'

'Oh, right,' the policeman said. 'She's got a nice figure,' he proclaimed, looking longingly at the scantily clad 17-year-old on page three.

'Yeah. It's hard to believe she's so young,' Phil agreed, admiring the picture.

The policemen slowly drank their coffees and glanced at the paper while Phil looked on anxiously. At last one of them downed his last drop of coffee. 'We'd better be off then,' he stated, looking at his mate, who swallowed the last of his drink and nodded.

Phil unlocked the gate and they opened their car doors and were about to leave when a clang emitted from the factory when Taffy dropped a spanner. They stopped and one of the policemen turned back.

'I thought I heard a noise from inside the factory?' he questioned.

'Yeah, err ... there's a few men working late on an urgent job,' Phil hurriedly replied, putting his hand in his pocket and feeling for his gun, in case he needed to use it.

'It's Sunday night and there was no mention of anyone working in there last night when we called.'

The guard hesitated, 'Err ... that's right. They told me that the parts they needed were only delivered earlier today. I believe that someone made a balls-up with something or other and they're rushing to put it right.'

'Typical!' said the policeman, turning to get into his car.

The guard waved to them, as they drove out of the factory entrance road, before returning to the hut. He grabbed the communicator, jabbed the button and pressed it to his face. Ryall answered.

'They've gone, but it was a bit tricky for a moment when they heard that noise.'

'Did you smooth it over okay?'

'Yeah. I told them that a few men were working on an urgent job. They seemed happy enough with that.'

'Good. Keep your eyes open,' Ryall demanded, then waved to his gang. 'You men get back to work, we've still got a lot to do.'

Over the next few hours, the hydraulic ram jacks were disconnected, freeing the cabin, held in mid-air by the support wires hanging from the lifting crane. When the last fixing was removed, the cabin swung violently, the weight causing it to roll to one side and slip round in its harness.

'Woah! Careful,' bellowed Ryall, watching the craft swing back and forth like a pendulum, before slowly coming to a halt. When it stabilised, the simulator was swung over the lorry, gently lowered and manoeuvred into a safe position by four of the gang.

The massive ram jacks were manhandled on to the trailer alongside the cabin, causing the vehicle's suspension to groan when the full weight was dropped on its back. The task of securing it all safely and covering it with a tarpaulin began.

Less than three-and-a-half hours after their arrival, Ryall and his men bundled into the lorry's cab. With their precious load strapped safely on the back, the vehicle roared once more into life. They motored out, leaving a big gap in the factory and scars on the floor where the simulator once stood. The night would soon begin to fade on this early Monday morning, with the first signs of dawn creeping ever closer to the horizon.

After picking up Phil from the guardhouse, they locked the gate, turned on to the main road heading out of the West Sussex industrial estate and left behind them the factory, with one missing simulator, two dead guards, and a soon to be highly embarrassed local police patrol unit.

3

Alert

After successfully absconding with the flight simulator, Alex, at the wheel of the low-loader, was directed to keep to A roads. This was to avoid the many security cameras found along motorway routes and junctions, although these days they were becoming a common site on many other main roads, especially on bridges. If there were no unforeseen problems, Ryall and his men could all be home by ten o'clock that morning and counting the proceeds of a good night's work. Mr Black, their employer, had provided Mr Green with a strict route that he was to ensure they followed, and he in turn insisted they kept to it. Ryall was anxious to comply with his quirky requests, and was not going to let a little thing like following a specific route ruin the chance of getting his hands on the big cash reward he had been promised. Not that there was any choice, as only Mr Green had the destination and the directions, and would undoubtedly report on any deviations from the route to his boss.

'How far is it to this secret hideout?' Ryall asked Mr Green, in a manner which showed that he though all this secrecy was unnecessary.

Mr Green gave him a sideways look. 'Not far, roughly sixty miles by road. It should only take us about an hour and a half, two at the most.'

'Good. The sooner we get this job finished, the happier I'll be.'

The thought had occurred to Ryall of keeping all the money for himself and Alex, by double-crossing his men. But, although the pay-off was good, it still was not enough to satisfy all his needs. He decided instead that they were a pretty good bunch of men and were loyal, and anyway, he may need them again when his big job came along; that would be the time to snatch all the money and disappear.

Ryall's craggy face forever looked suntanned, and he had not let middle-aged spread get to his figure too much. He still boasted a reasonably trim stomach and kept his body lean by exercising regularly. Lately though, he was finding this harder and harder to achieve, especially as he was partial to the more than the occasional pint of beer, a sure way to increase the size of your waistline in no time at all. In his youth he was the school bully and academically did not do very well. He hated school and was constantly in trouble with the police for petty offences, mainly pilfering from local shops. Much of this was blamed on the fact that his mother ran away from home with another man when he was only three years old. She left him to be brought up by his father, who was bitter over the incident and frequently spent most nights in the local pub, caring little for the son that he now saw as a burden to him.

When Ryall left school at the age of 15, he did not bother to look for a job, and instead took up with a local pickpocket and began his life of crime in earnest. Gradually, with more experience, he got more daring and the jobs got bigger. He graduated to stealing cars and housebreaking. His move from picking pockets to burglary was at a cost, and he spent time in prison. It did not cure him of his bad habits, and more robberies and more prison followed.

When, after trying to increase his takings by holding up a high street building society, he ran over an innocent bystander in his haste to elude the police, the die was cast. He was now responsible for someone's death and there was no turning back. If they caught him this time, he would be charged with manslaughter and put away for a very long stretch. He could not face that, and had become more ruthless in his crimes, being prepared to kill if the situation became serious enough. He teamed up with Alex Kirby, whom he met in prison, and whose ruthless approach to life was coupled with a willingness to kill at the slightest provocation. The association had taken Ryall deeper into worse crimes and now he was looking for one last, lucrative job to set him up for the rest of his life. It would enable him to escape abroad and sleep sounder at nights, without the worry of getting a wake-up call by a police raid at dawn. This anguish had forced Ryall to live a somewhat nomadic life, trying to keep one step ahead of the authorities by constantly moving from rented accommodation in one town to another, forever aware that someday his luck was sure to run out.

His clean-shaven, rugged, manly looks gave him an attractiveness that he used to satisfy his own ends, in both work and pleasure. He liked the company of women, but refused to let them dominate his life, and he tended to treat them with little respect. This fact had seen him drift from one female to another, with none caring to stay with him for any length of time. It had even caused him to be in trouble with the law on several occasions, and once ended in a prison sentence when he hit a woman who turned out to be the ex-wife of a magistrate. The prison psychiatrist blamed the loss of his mother at an early age as the overriding influence for his bad behaviour towards women, and his constant need to be accepted by his peers. This need was only satisfied when Ryall had a lot of money to flash around, and was the reason, the psychiatrist declared, that he was involved in so many robberies. Ryall himself thought that it was a load of bunkum. He stole because he wanted money so that he could live the good life. He was not capable of earning it – so he stole it. It was clear and simple to his way of thinking.

Being without one woman as a constant companion had not bothered him a great deal; at least it had not until lately. He had retained his good looks, which had even improved with maturity, but with middle age now fast approaching, thoughts of having someone to share his life were more prominent in his reckoning. Like many in his dubious profession, he was carried along by his dream of pulling off one master robbery, and with it, having enough to buy a plush mansion on the Costa del Sol or somewhere similar. There, he would spend his days lazing in the sun, with a drink in one hand and one or more good-looking, scantily clad females in reach of the other. He was sensible enough to know that it was a dream which most crooks had, but few achieved. However, it was something to aim for, and he was determined to achieve at least a part of his dream and retire to a warm climate. It would be a place where not only would he be free of constantly having to be on the lookout for the police, but he would also have a female companion who was good in bed. This job was a stepping stone to that goal.

The low-loader, with their stolen prize strapped safely on its back, had travelled only a few miles when, without warning, a police car caught them up. To their dismay, the blue flashing lights on the roof came to life and the siren let out a sharp wail for a few seconds.

'Shit!' exclaimed Ryall, eyeing the car in the rear-view mirror. 'What do they want? We seem to be attracting coppers like flies tonight.'

'Do you think the ones at the factory twigged that something was going on?' asked Phil.

'I doubt it, but we'll soon find out.'

Alex slowed the vehicle, pulled into the kerb and brought

it to a stop. Mr Green pulled some papers from his pocket and handed them to him.

'If they want to see your papers, give them this. It shows that we are transporting farming machinery to a company in the Portsmouth area from a warehouse in Birmingham,' he said, ducking quickly out of sight.

Alex grabbed the papers. 'Right. You think of everything, don't you?'

'We try to,' he replied, with a smug look on his face.

The police car pulled up behind them with the blue flashing lights still on, sending out a staccato beam that lit up the street in pulses.

'The rest of you men get down in the back, and no noise,' instructed Ryall, slipping off his seat to crouch on the floor next to Mr Green and pulling a gun from his shoulder holster. Alex pulled a curtain across to hide the men in the back.

Two policemen emerged from their vehicle and approached the low-loader. One walked around the vehicle to take a look, while the other came to the driver's door. Alex opened his window fully and leant his elbow on it.

'Good morning, sir. Would you turn the engine off, please,' the policeman began, looking up at the driver sitting behind the wheel. Alex nodded, switched off the engine and flipped the safety catch off his gun, which nestled in his lap.

'What can I do for you, officer?' he enquired.

'We noticed that one of your rear lights isn't working, sir,' he stated.

The men in the lorry all breathed a sigh of relief when they heard that it was only a broken light they were stopped for and not because of the robbery, or the fact that they were sitting in a stolen vehicle.

'I'm sorry about that, which side is it?'

'The off side, sir.'

'Okay. I'll get it fixed before we make the return journey.'

'We? Are you not alone?'

'Err ... yes, I am. I was referring to me and my lucky mascot, Rupert,' Alex hurriedly maintained, grabbing the fluffy teddy bear hanging from the rear-view mirror.

'Oh, I see,' said the slightly bemused policeman, joined by his colleague after his walk around the vehicle.

'Your load is a funny shape,' the colleague stated. 'What are you carrying?'

'Machinery parts.'

'Machinery parts? What sort of machinery parts?' he enquired.

'For farming equipment or something.'

'Farming equipment? It looks an odd shape for that,' the police driver persisted. 'What type of farming equipment?'

'I don't know, do I? I'm just a driver,' Alex replied, in a frustrated voice holding the manifest up. 'It simply says here – farm machinery.'

'Where are you taking it to?' asked the policeman, grabbing the manifest and squinting at it under the not too bright streetlights and a sky only just beginning to lighten.

'Portsmouth. They tell me to take a load from here to there and I do it, that's my job,' he insisted, his finger tightening on the trigger as his frustration at all the questioning got worse.

The two policemen looked at each other. One handed back the manifest and tapped on the door. 'Okay. Get going. And don't forget to get that light fixed.'

'I will,' promised Alex, firing up the lorry's engine.

The low-loader roared into life and juddered through the gears as it trundled down the road. Alex checked in the mirror, watching the police car get ever smaller in the distance until it finally disappeared.

'It's all clear. You can come out now,' he declared.

'Phew. That was a close thing,' Mr Green stated, wiping his brow.

Ryall and Alex looked at each other with quizzical looks on their faces that broke into smiles, which they hid from Mr Green. Both were thinking that if he thought such a minor encounter was a near thing, then he must have lived a rather sheltered life. He had probably led a boring existence which had not involved the authorities. They were right.

The low-loader continued its journey south towards the coast, before turning westwards along the coast road.

'Not much further now,' Mr Green told Alex, as he glanced at the map.

Turning off the A27, they headed towards the outskirts of Portsmouth where he checked the directions again. They motored on for a few miles while Mr Green reappraised his map.

'Keep your eyes open for a small, run-down industrial estate. The warehouse is around the back – out of sight from the main road,' he stated.

'Okay,' Alex nodded, scratching his long chin, covered with fast-growing stubble that had appeared since his shave the previous day. The morning was now just bright enough for him to turn the vehicle's lights off, which he did at the earliest moment to avoid a repetition of their problem with the police patrol car.

'It's just along here,' pointed Mr Green.

The dull, early morning sun picked out a broken sign, hanging by one corner. It read, 'Marlborough Industrial Estate'. The journey had taken less than two hours, despite their unwanted stop; they were ahead of schedule.

Alex dropped the lorry into bottom gear and turned it into the estate, chugging slowly up the overgrown, abandoned approach road.

'It's certainly well out of the way of any prying eyes. No wonder it's fallen into disuse,' commented Ryall, peering through the front window.

The vehicle swung into a dark, rectangular compound, fashioned from large concrete slabs, outlined with grass and weeds forcing their way between the cracks. The far end in front of them and the right-hand side were edged by derelict buildings with doors missing and large gaping holes in the mainly rusted, torn, corrugated iron factory modules. The left side, closest to the road, was covered with 3-feet-high grass and weeds, and was littered with rubbish. Beyond the last building was a gap where a curved roadway swung around the back of the factories, ending at the door of a much larger building, a warehouse.

Alex turned the low-loader on to the road and braked sharply when from out of the shadows stepped two guards. The lorry was only waved on when Mr Green signalled to them through the window. One guard spoke into his communicator as Alex jammed the lorry into gear and followed the sweeping road. On approaching the building, the main doors swung open, allowing the diffused lighting from within to illuminate the entrance area. Two men emerged from the warehouse and one beckoned them to drive the low-loader inside. Alex wound the steering wheel round, taking the vehicle in a wide arc to position it for a straight run into the voluminous old building.

Rows of fluorescent lights, mounted high up in the vast roof space, illuminated the interior of the warehouse with its iron girder roof supports and concrete floor. Apart from a bench covered with electronic equipment, a caravan parked in one corner and an overhead crane, essential for removing the simulator from the lorry, it was bare. Six more men, five of them armed with sub-machine guns, and two attractive women, stood by the bench and watched the vehicle shudder to a halt with a hiss of the air brakes. The warehouse doors were closed behind them, blocking out the start of a new day. A well-dressed man in his fifties stepped forward, brushing into place a few strands of hair on his almost bald head.

Ryall stepped down from the cab and nodded to the man who had hired him. He was followed by Alex, who picked up his sub-machine gun, and carefully positioned himself close to the lorry for protection, should it be needed. They were both acutely aware that the company they were keeping was made up of a group of ruthless men, and they were all armed.

Ryall was asked, 'Did everything go as planned?' in the positive tone of one who expected to be told that no problems were encountered. Problems were not what Mr Black wanted – he paid others to eliminate them.

'Sure,' Ryall replied, in a lazy way, conveying that he too knew how to take care of things and ensure there were no difficulties. 'Everything went like clockwork, Mr Black. There were no hitches.'

'Good. I am pleased to hear that Mr Ryall. Ah, Mr Green, I assume you concur with that assessment?' he asked, seeing his associate step down from the lorry.

'Yes, except that we were stopped by the police because a rear light on our vehicle was not working.'

'Where was that?' Mr Black anxiously asked, eager to keep the location of his hideout a secret.

'It was a few miles down the road from the factory and we watched carefully to make sure we weren't followed. I'm sure everything is okay and it was simply a routine stop because of the broken light,' Mr Green assured him.

'I hope you are right. That was careless of you, Mr Ryall, not checking to make sure there was no reason for the police to stop you,' Mr Black grumbled.

'I did check it,' Ryall lied. 'It must have blown on the way to the factory. In any case, snatching a 100-tonne articulated low-loader on a specific weekend and getting it to that factory was no easy task. Me and my men have done well,' he argued.

'Perhaps,' conceded Mr Black. 'But that is what you are

being paid handsomely for. Now, Mr Green, how soon can the simulator be assembled and the training begin?'

'Soon, but I do have some work to complete first. When I checked the simulator at the factory, one of the control modules was missing. We found it in the test department and I've brought it along with all the necessary components to reassemble and test it. It shouldn't take me more than a few hours. I anticipate that it will be completed by late this afternoon, by which time the simulator should be assembled and ready.'

'I hope so, Mr Green. I am counting on you, and time is short.'

Mr Green lowered his eyes and half smiled an acknowledgement that he needed to be both quick and accurate with his rebuilding of the module. Mr Black, he knew, would brook no delays.

Ryall, meanwhile, was ignoring all this chit-chat between Mr Black and Mr Green. His eyes had wandered to the two women standing behind them. Mr Black noticed Ryall's gaze.

'Do forgive me,' he said, with an exaggerated gesture. 'I have not introduced you to the female members of my little consortium. I would like you to meet my two lovely pilots, Miss Lilac and Miss Pink.'

'Miss Lilac and Miss Pink,' Ryall thought. 'Why does he insist on naming his people with stupid colours? Pilots, eh? They must be who this machine's for and something to do with the job he's planning.'

Miss Pink nodded courteously and looked disinterested. Both were attractive, but Miss Lilac smiled at him and Ryall returned the gesture. Eye contact was strong and lingered just long enough for him to think that if he made an approach it would not be rejected. He cast an eye over their lovely faces and shapely figures, especially Miss Lilac's. She had ample breasts that he would love to get his hands on, and the jumpsuit that she wore had the zip pulled down low enough to reveal glimpses of a red uplift bra that pressed her breasts together, giving a tantalising sight of bosom and cleavage. Though her face was undoubtedly attractive, she had a slightly hard look about her that hinted of someone who knew what she wanted, and how to get it.

'A woman to be careful of until you were sure of her loyalties,' he thought. Both would be in their mid-thirties he guessed. Miss Pink gave nothing away and was harder to judge. She kept her feelings well contained, and it was difficult to gauge what she was thinking.

'You've brought me a toy to play with,' Miss Lilac said, in a smooth, efficient voice, brushing a strand of her below-shoulder-length, red hair away from her bright red lips.

Ryall was about to answer when Mr Black interrupted. 'Mr Ryall's job is finished my dear, and he will be departing before long, after he and his men have received their money. That is so, is it not, Mr Ryall?' he maintained, with a crooked smile.

'Yes, of course,' he replied, slightly miffed that he had not been given the opportunity to probe further into the possibilities that he felt sure Miss Lilac's eyes had opened for him.

Trust was not something that Ryall had, when dealing with men like Mr Black. His gang of men stood around brandishing their guns, and he was aware of the need to be cautious. All Ryall's men were also armed, he saw to that, though most of them, apart from Alex and Phil, were strangers to weapons and would only use them when there was no other choice. Only Alex had so far ventured from the lorry; the others were instructed to remain in the vehicle until they were told that it was okay to leave. Taffy's eyes peered through the lorry window as he watched the proceedings.

Mr Black snapped his fingers and one of his men grabbed an attaché case and thrust it under Ryall's nose. He opened the lid to reveal its contents. It was stuffed full of crisp new notes, wrapped in £500 bundles.

'As promised, your reward for a job well done, Mr Ryall,' remarked Mr Black, his chubby cheeks quivering as he spoke. 'And all in small denominations – as agreed.'

Ryall quickly thumbed through a couple of the bundles to make sure they were all notes, not just those on the outside. He had almost fallen for that trick once before, and ended up having to kill the man and take back the goods, because he did not have the money and had no intention of paying.

Ryall nodded, the man closed the lid and handed him the attaché case. He took it and said nothing.

'And for the final part of our agreement, there's a limousine waiting outside for you and your men to return to London. My man is bringing it to the entrance now. It's stolen, so you'd better ditch it after you get back. I don't need to remind you that this location must be kept a strict secret. If I need you again I will ring,' he said, dismissing them.

Mr Black turned his slightly portly figure away, and strode over to the bench leaving Ryall standing there with his money. A hollow echo reverberated around the building when Mr Black's man stepped through a small door in the shutters, revealing the limousine parked outside with the engine running. Ryall nodded to his men, who were watching from the lorry windows, and they stepped down from the cabin one by one, keeping an eye on the armed men. Phil picked up Ryall's own attaché case from the vehicle and handed it to Alex.

The two groups watched each other carefully, as Ryall and his men backed out of the warehouse. Outside, Alex threw Ryall's case into the boot of the limousine and got into the driving seat as the men all bundled into the rear of the car. He jammed the vehicle into gear and motored away, glad to leave the place behind.

Pursing his lips, Alex breathed out with a huff. 'I thought that was going to be a bit tricky for a moment,' he said, spinning the wheel to take them out of the estate and on to the road leading home.

'Yeah, me too,' agreed Ryall. 'There's something evil about that man Black. I wouldn't like to be on the wrong side of him. Still, it's all over now, and we can relax and take things easy for a while,' he said, opening the attaché case to once again survey the proceeds of their crime.

'Too right, eh boys?' said Alex.

There were shouts of agreement from a bunch of smiling, happy faces crammed into the back of the car.

'With this money I can afford to put my kid through college,' Taffy remarked. 'Then perhaps he won't end up on the wrong side of the law like his old man.'

'Good for you,' praised Phil.

In the limousine, all the men were jubilant; each taking a swig from a can of beer that one of them had brought along.

'Did you see that female giving me the eye?' Ryall asked Alex. 'The one with the top of her tits poking out – Miss Lilac, as he calls her. I reckon I could score there … and I'm now getting interested to know what Black's plans are for that bloody great thing.'

'I'd leave well alone, if I were you,' Alex suggested. 'She's his associate, and looks a bit hard to me. And he might not take it too kindly if he found out that you were trying to make contact with her, especially if you started asking her a lot of questions about his plans. Anyway, she's a long way behind us now.'

'Perhaps. There's a small village just ahead. I noticed a car parked out in the road on our way in. I think I'll borrow it to take another look at that warehouse.'

'Look at the warehouse? It's the women you want to look at.'

'Maybe so,' smiled Ryall, taking two bundles of the money

and stuffing them in his pockets. 'Give the boys their cut and put the rest in the safe. I'll see you when I get back.'

'Okay,' Alex grinned. 'But you watch out for yourself,' he warned.

It was not unusual for him to see his boss chase after women at the slightest whim, but this was a different situation and one that could spell trouble.

'Drop me here,' Ryall said, patting Alex on the shoulder.

The limousine braked to a halt and he got out. Ryall dumped the attaché case on the passenger seat alongside Alex's sub-machine gun, slammed the car door shut and banged twice on the roof. The car quickly moved off and was soon out of sight. On the far side of the road, outside a couple of stone cottages, was parked an old, dark blue Vauxhall Cavalier. It was not even locked, and Ryall hot-wired the ignition and was soon making a return journey to the warehouse. Quite what he was going to do when he got there he had not yet figured out, but he would think of something, he always did.

4

Loose Ends

While Ryall's men journeyed home and he travelled back to the warehouse, inside his hideout, Mr Black stood at the bench and turned on a radar tracking scope. The circular screen lit up showing a green outline of the area with a white dot moving along the road. He flipped a switch, illuminating a red lamp.

'What are you doing?' asked Miss Lilac, she and Miss Pink stepping forward to watch, a look of consternation on their faces.

'Just tying up loose ends,' Mr Black replied. 'I don't trust them not to blab about their part in this job, and I don't want any outsiders knowing where this warehouse is. It's bad enough that the police stopped the lorry. Fortunately, that incident was dealt with, and no harmful consequences resulted. I intent to make sure that no other slip-ups put this location in jeopardy.'

Miss Lilac frowned. 'So what are you doing? You're not going to kill them, are you?'

'Of course! They have done their job and are now a liability. The car has a tracking device, so that I know exactly where they are, and the attaché case has a false bottom with explosives and a remote control detonator in it. When they are past the next village, they will come out on the hilltop road and I will eliminate that liability. The car will go over the edge and may not be found for some considerable time.'

'But if it is, the police may come snooping around here,' Miss Pink protested.

'I don't think so. It is far enough away from here for me not to have to worry about that. This is a deserted, run-down estate and no one comes here. If the police do arrive, we are ready to deal with that situation.'

'And what about all that cash? It's a terrible waste of a lot of money.'

'Counterfeit. Very good counterfeit, Miss Pink, but nevertheless, still counterfeit. The notes were quite expensive, but it is a sacrifice that I am willing to make in order to achieve my aims,' he said, eagerly watching the progress of the limousine on the screen.

'And it saves you having to part with a lot of real money,' Miss Pink sarcastically suggested.

'Quite so,' Mr Black agreed, ignoring her sarcasm.

'So, are we to expect the same treatment from you when our part is done?' complained Miss Lilac.

'No, of course not. You are partners in this project, they were merely hirelings, brought in to do a simple robbery. Not the same thing at all,' he said effusively, wishing to dampen down any misgivings they may have; at least until their part in the job was complete.

Mr Black beamed. He watched the screen with great anticipation at the feat he was about to perform.

'Not long now. I thought for a moment they were going to stop in the village, but they are almost at the high point.'

The dot on his screen travelled along the road and the car slowed to negotiate a bend at the top of a rise. The two women looked on intently, wishing there was something they could do to stop this horror, but knowing full well they were powerless to do so. Mr Black pressed the button and watched with delight as the dot split into a thousand pieces, showering in all directions like a firework in the night sky, before disappearing from the screen.

'There. That's taken care of that. Mr Ryall and his cronies won't be telling anyone about our plans or location.'

Miss Lilac looked at Miss Pink and frowned. All of a sudden this job had taken on a new dimension, and looked to have an entirely different set of dangers attached to it, that neither woman had realised before. The task they were to perform would itself be dangerous enough, but this episode had presented them with a new dilemma, one that neither yet knew how it would affect them, or how they would tackle it if it did.

'I'd like to get some rest,' Miss Pink informed Mr Black.

'Me too,' Miss Lilac agreed. 'After all, nothing will be ready for us until later today, or possibly even tomorrow, and we had to get up very early this morning in expectation of beginning our training soon.'

'Of course, my dears,' he replied, with a sickly smile. 'I will arrange for you to be taken back to the motel, though now the two of you have met, you can share a room this time. Mr Grey will go with you, and remain in the adjacent room to see that you are looked after.'

'That's very kind of you, but you needn't bother. It's really not necessary. I shan't be going out, and you can ring when you are ready for us to return,' stated Miss Pink.

'It's no bother. Mr Grey will be happy to watch out for you.'

Miss Pink threw a quick glance at Miss Lilac, realising that it was useless to argue. Mr Black, she could see, had already made up his mind to keep a close eye on them since they too now knew the location of his warehouse hideout, and had a fuller insight of his ruthlessness. At least they should be safe until after the job was done. Experienced pilots, willing to tackle this sort of assignment were few and far between. That, they hoped, was their security at the moment, but it would not last forever.

'Mr Grey, escort the ladies back to their lodgings and see they are made comfortable. I'll ring you when I want you to bring them back,' instructed Mr Black.

Mr Grey nodded curtly, his shock of blond hair falling over one eye. He jerked his head back, flicking the tangled mop into place, and waited patiently for the two women to collect their handbags and move towards the door.

Ryall had travelled no more than a few hundred yards in his stolen car, a short way past the last remote cottage in the village, when he heard the muffled explosion far in the distance behind him. At first he dismissed it, thinking nothing of the noise, but then it brought an awful notion to his mind. He braked hard, swung the car around and charged back through the village. Approaching the hilltop road, he tore round the sharp bend, and nearly slid off the edge of the road in his haste. Suddenly, an object caught his eye and he screeched the car to a halt. Backing up, Ryall looked hard at a broken and twisted section of steel barrier that was erected to protect cars from going over the edge. The break was clean and new.

Slamming the car door shut, he gingerly went to the edge and peered over. There, in a tangled mess, jammed into a tree, was the remains of the limousine, burning away. It had crashed through the barrier, demolishing a complete section, and plunged over the edge. Ryall scrambled down to the car and found Alex's body lying by the side of the wreck, along with one of the men. Alex had taken the full force of the blast to his side and was barely recognisable. The rest of his men were still in the back seat of the car, with flames licking their mutilated bodies. The smell of death and destruction filled the air and made him feel sick.

'That bastard Black! I'll have his guts for this,' Ryall screamed.

Now he was angry, very angry, and knew that he had to

calm down before doing anything rash. In the past he had been too headstrong, and it led to his downfall; the police had caught him. Age had brought with it some benefits, one of them being a maturity to recognise when he needed to stop for a minute and think more objectively about the action he was about to take. Ryall paced back and forth trying to sort out his thoughts and come to a sensible decision. The car boot had been torn open by the explosion. He looked inside, to where Alex had thrown his attaché case. It was not there. Taking a quick look around, Ryall saw it lying on the ground where the blast had flung it. The edges were scorched by the blast, but the case was intact. He grabbed it and checked the contents. They were okay.

He glanced at his men. 'I can't leave them like this,' he told himself.

Flipping open his mobile, Ryall pressed 999 then closed it again quickly. They would be able to trace the number. He searched Alex's pocket and found his mobile. He turned it on, it beeped and, miraculously still worked. He dialled again and when the emergency call was answered, he ignored the request for his name and telephone number, told them he wanted an ambulance and described where the accident had taken place, then rang off. He threw the mobile down, took a last look at his mangled, dead friend, then clambered back up to the road and jumped into the stolen car.

While motoring furiously back to the warehouse, Ryall muttered to himself, 'He's got a lot of men with guns, I've got to be careful – stay hidden – maybe try and pick them off one at a time. They think I'm dead – so that gives me an edge. They're not expecting any trouble of the kind I'm going to give them, and they've got to come out sometime. God, I wish Alex was still alive. He'd know how to handle it. He'd make them pay for what they've done.'

Entering the industrial estate, Ryall cut the engine of his

car and drifted it to a remote corner alongside the first factory module. Creeping to the rear of the building, he could see the warehouse entrance. He watched the guards lounging by one of the derelict buildings, chatting and having a smoke, and was checking his handgun when the warehouse door opened and Miss Lilac, Miss Pink and Mr Grey emerged. The man took Miss Lilac's elbow to lead her to the car, and Ryall noted that she pulled it away and gave him a look that said, 'I don't need your help'. Maybe she was angry with Mr Black as well. If so, she could be a useful ally.

The women were shown into the rear seat of a plush limousine and Mr Grey drove off. Ryall watched them leave, returned to his car, and followed. One of Black's men was on his own, and presented him with the ideal opportunity to start exacting his revenge for what they had done to Alex and his men. Maybe it would also give him a chance to talk to Miss Lilac and find out what Black's plans for that simulator were. It also held the possibility that he might discover whether she really was willing to explore furthering a relationship with him after their briefest of encounters.

5

Revenge

Witnessing the apparent death of Ryall and his men had shocked Miss Lilac and Miss Pink. They were now being driven in a limousine by their unwanted protector Mr Grey, acting as chauffeur and bodyguard, and were heading towards Portsmouth, a city renowned for its naval traditions and dockyards. Following at a safe distance behind them, with only light traffic on the roads at this early hour, was Ryall, still seething at Mr Black's double-cross, an act that had cost all of his men their lives.

Close to the outskirts of the city, Mr Grey's vehicle pulled into Morley's Motel, located on a high rise above Portsmouth. Being a little off the beaten track and on the fringes of the city was a major influence in it having become run-down and shabby looking. The motel needed a large injection of cash before it would attract more visitors. All this made it an ideal place to stay if seclusion was one of your requirements, and for Mr Black it was essential. The few customers who stayed there did so mainly because of its low tariffs. Most of them were unaware that they had only to cross the road outside and walk no more than 50 yards to enjoy a panoramic view of the surrounding area. Hidden behind a tree-lined expanse of grass lay Portsmouth, spread out below. In the early morning haze, twinkling lights were disappearing as the city was fast coming alive, encouraged by a dull sun forcing its rays through the rolling mist that drifted in from the sea.

Entering a courtyard, bound on two sides by 15 motel rooms and on the third by an open area that served as a car park, Mr Grey brought the limousine to a halt outside chalet number 5. A wooden walkway joined all the chalets and they each had a single lamp above a drab, peeling, off-white door. Mr Grey opened the limousine's rear door, allowing the women to step out. Ryall quietly coasted in and parked his car nearby, among the half dozen or so other vehicles situated there, several of them looking as if they had not moved in some time. He watched the trio enter the chalet, and saw the light switched on before Mr Grey pull curtains across the window to stop any prying eyes.

The two women wandered into the shabby room, which had a slightly damp odour lingering in the air. It contained two single beds, a dressing table of sorts and a bathroom with a toilet and shower. Rugs, either side of the beds, were the only cover masking the cold linoleum floor. They stared with amazement at Mr Grey unplugging the telephone and tipping out the contents of their handbags on the bed in order to collect their mobile phones.

'You won't need these,' he informed them. 'I'll let you know when it's time to go back and I'll be checking to see that both of you are okay every hour or two.'

He took the room key, slammed the door behind him and locked it.

Sitting in his car, Ryall watched and waited. Windows to each of the other rooms were in darkness, and little disturbed the still, early morning air. While he waited, Ryall saw Mr Grey shut and lock the door to the girls' chalet, before entering number 4, the adjacent chalet. The door slammed shut, the light came on and the curtains were pulled. Ryall lit a cigarette and pondered about what his next step should be.

'It's nice to be trusted,' Miss Pink mumbled to Miss Lilac in a sarcastic tone, while stretching herself out on the bed. 'My real name's Paula. We haven't had a chance to talk yet since we first met. I was kept in the next room where our jailer now is.'

Miss Lilac sat on her bed and they shook hands. 'I'm Tanya, and I'm a bit worried about what plans Mr Black has in store for us after seeing what he did to those blokes.'

'Yeah, me too. What on earth does he need two pilots for anyway?'

'I don't know. Maybe it's a two-seater plane or perhaps he wants a back-up in case one of us doesn't do very well on the simulator. He keeps his plans to himself. He told me that we were going to pull a heist, but nothing was said about killing a lot of people. Not that it particularly bothers me, as long as I'm not one of them.'

'Nor me. Have you got a partner?' Paula asked.

'Nah. Nothing regular anyway. There are plenty of blokes whose eyes light up and want to get their hands on my tits, including Mr Black, but usually that and a bit of sex is all they want. I might be able to use that to my advantage here and find out what's going on. How about you? Have you got a fella?'

'Yes, I have, and I'd like to see him.'

'You know Black told us that's not allowed. He said we weren't to have contact with anyone after we were selected to be a part of his elite little group.'

'I don't see why Mr Black, or anyone else for that matter, should tell me I can't see my fella.'

'I can't disagree with you there. Were you in the RAF? Is that where you got your pilot's training?' Tanya asked.

'Yes. I was one of just a few women fighter pilots they were training, and I was getting on really well until the fateful day my plane developed a fault at low altitude and I had to eject. That didn't do my back any favours, and because of my injuries they grounded me and wouldn't let me fly fighters any more. They said that I might be able to resume in a year or so if my back was okay and the doctor cleared me. Meantime, I was transferred to a desk job.'

'I bet that was a bit of a comedown after all that excitement?'

'Yes, it was. That's why I saw this as an opportunity to fly again, and make some real money at the same time.'

'Were you badly hurt?'

'No, not really. The Martin Baker ejection seat saved my life, but the force of the ejection does put the whole of your body under tremendous pressure. You're shot out of the cockpit by rockets and your spine is under a great strain. A lot of pilots who have to eject do get back problems afterwards.'

'Did you ever take part in a real conflict?'

'No, I never got that chance,' Paula conceded. 'I was still in training.'

'So, you've not killed anyone or shot another plane down?'

'Only in practice. What about you? Were you in the RAF?'

'Yes, I was, and I only left a short while ago.'

'Did they teach you to fly as well?'

'Yes. But I flew mainly transporters and the occasional light plane. A fighter's going to be a whole lot different.'

'Transport planes are big. You must be a good pilot to fly those.'

'Yes, I reckon so. Anyway, that's what I told Mr Black,' said Tanya.

'I'm fed up with working behind a desk, and if they won't let me fly any more, then I want to get out, that's why I took on this job. With the money I can buy my way out, and disappear into a saner world.'

'A saner world? You've got to be kidding. Especially with people like Mr Black around.'

'You could be right,' giggled Paula.

'It's a pity about that guy, Ryall. Did you see the way he looked at me?' Tanya asked.

'With that amount of cleavage showing I'm not surprised.'

'Yeah, it did catch his eye, didn't it? I rather fancied him myself. It's a shame they had to go and blow him up.'

'Yes. It definitely makes you wonder what he's got in store for us when this job's finished.'

'Hmm, that's quite a worry.'

'I'm going to see if I can sneak into one of the other rooms, and find a telephone to call my partner and let him know I'm okay. He wasn't very keen on me taking this job. Will you cover for me?' asked Paula.

'Sure. But how?'

'I'll turn the shower on. If that bozo from next door comes checking on us, you can tell him I'm freshening up.'

'Okay. But how are you going to get out? He locked the door and the windows don't open wide enough to squeeze through. Not for me, anyway.'

'Nor me. So watch.'

Opening her purse, Paula pulled out a lock pick, hidden behind a fold at the back. She inserted the thin wiry implement in the lock, and after a few deft movements they heard the lock click open.

'Where on earth did you learn to do that?' a surprised Tanya asked.

'When you're a fighter pilot, you're surrounded by macho men, and when you're a woman in a man's world, you have to learn a lot of useful tricks to stay one jump ahead of them.'

'I'll bet. I like the bit about being surrounded by macho men.'

'I'll be back soon,' Paula promised, opening the door, checking to make sure the coast was clear, and slipping out.

After turning the shower on, Tanya settled down on the bed to read, worried that events were looking even more dangerous now. There was something about Paula that did not seem right. Tanya had a nose for trouble, and Paula felt like trouble.

Outside, Ryall sat in his car and watched Paula lock the door and slip along to the end chalet, number 15, peer through the window, then after a hurried look around to see that she was not being watched, pick the lock. Once inside, a dim light showed through the curtains. Ryall was intrigued to know what was going on, but decided to bide his time.

Paula picked up the telephone and listened for a dialling tone. 'Thank goodness for that,' she remarked, pressing the buttons for Mike Randle's mobile.

Mike Randle and his partner Suzie Drake had met when they were both mercenaries in Africa, and formed a relationship that blossomed. After returning to England, they gave up their dangerous occupation, bought a house and became co-owners of a boat building company. But these days, despite their new, safer job, they found their old skills and talents were in demand for a variety of circumstances and, along with Paula, who was once Mike's partner, were persuaded to help when Mr Black's quest for two pilots became known to the authorities. He had eluded all their efforts to put him behind bars and they saw this as another opportunity to stop his crooked exploits.

This led to Paula Hardcastle and Suzie Drake, along with others who had applied, to be interviewed for the pilot's job. These interviews were conducted in an old converted Victorian house in the West Sussex seaside town of Worthing, and when Paula was chosen for the task she was instructed to return to the house.

From there, she was taken at night to Morley's Motel in Mr Black's MPV, fitted with darkened windows to prevent her seeing the location she was driven to. Mike was trailing her, but found it difficult to keep the vehicle in sight at night without being seen. The MPV driver took an evasive route to ensure they were not followed, and Mike frustratingly lost them approaching Southsea in Hampshire. He and Suzie booked into a local bed and breakfast, hoping that Paula would get the chance to telephone them; a call which arrived at 6.30 a.m. on this Monday morning. Mike picked up his mobile.

'Mike, it's Paula.'

'Paula, I'm glad you could ring. Where are you?' he asked, sitting up in bed. Suzie stirred and propped herself up on one elbow.

'I'm at Morley's Motel, somewhere near the outskirts of Portsmouth. I'm not exactly sure where, but it's near the top of a hill. How quickly do you think you can get here?'

'Morley's Motel in Portsmouth,' repeated Mike, waving his finger at the telephone directory. Suzie grabbed it and started to search for the motel's address. 'We're quite close, so I should be able to get there within about half an hour.'

'Good. I've sneaked out and am hiding in chalet 15 at the moment, but we were locked in chalet 5 by a chaperone who's staying next door in number 4. If I'm discovered, he'll put me back in chalet 5 with the other female pilot.'

'Okay.'

'Our chaperone looks mean and he's armed, so watch out.'

'Right. I'll get there as quickly as I can.'

Mike turned off his mobile and stared lovingly at Suzie, sitting on the bed stark naked, thumbing through a telephone directory. 'It's a good job I'm in a hurry Miss Drake or I'd be sorely tempted to give you a seeing to.'

Suzie looked up and smiled. 'You can do that when you get back, Randy. If anything crops up, ring me on my mobile. The motels here,' she said, pointing to a place on the map.

'Okay, I've got that. Gotta go,' Mike said, pulling on his clothes and grabbing his car keys.

Nearly half an hour later, Mike's car pulled quietly into the motel car park and drifted to a halt. He glanced furtively around before gently closing the car door and entering chalet 15.

A few moments later, Paula came out of the room and wandered back to chalet 5 to speak with Tanya. When she entered, Tanya noticed that her blouse was unbuttoned from top to bottom, and she was not wearing a bra.

'My partner Mike has arrived, and we're going to spend an hour or so together while we can. Are you okay with that?'

'Sure,' Tanya replied. 'It looks as if you've already started having fun.'

Paula pulled the blouse together and looked coy, as if she was slightly embarrassed about it. 'He's a great lover, but no finesse.'

'I'll see you in about an hour,' Tanya said, waving her away.

Paula left. Tanya threw her magazine on the bed and opened the bathroom door. 'At least I can take a shower in peace,' she said, stepping into the bathroom and twisting the chrome shower knob to adjust the temperature.

While the shower was running, Tanya undressed in the bedroom and put on a towelling bathrobe. Before stepping back into the bathroom she heard a key in the lock and Mr Grey entered.

'Don't you bother to knock before coming into a room?' Tanya curtly asked, pulling the lapels of her bathrobe together. 'I might have still been in the shower.'

Her question remained unanswered. 'I'm checking to make sure that you're both okay. Where's Miss Pink?'

'She's taking her turn in the shower. Any more questions?'

'If you've showered, then why isn't your hair wet?' Mr Grey demanded.

'I … er … didn't wash it because there's no shampoo in the bathroom,' she hurriedly stated.

'Oh, right.'

He seemed satisfied and, after a glance around the room, left, locking the door.

Tanya sat on the end of the bed and let her pulse slowly return to normal. The door lock rattled again and Mr Grey entered. She sat motionless, wondering if he had guessed what was happening, and waited for him to get angry and start demanding answers from her. Instead, he produced a bottle of shampoo, threw it on to the bed and, after taking a lingering look at her cleavage, locked the door behind him. Tanya breathed a sigh of relief.

Outside, Ryall had seen Paula slip back to chalet 5 before returning to the room where the man was. He then saw Mr Grey step in and out of chalet 5 a couple of times before he too returned to his room. With the activity now at least at a temporary stop, Ryall pulled his gun from its shoulder holster, deciding that it was time for him to make a move and get some answers.

'This is a good chance to get one of Black's men on his own,' he told himself, screwing the silencer into the barrel of his gun. 'I can't waste the opportunity. It looked like Miss Lilac wasn't too keen on having a guard, and he's locked her in. Maybe she'll tell me what Mr Black's plans are, and also what Miss Pink is up to with that other bloke.'

After checking the clip and slamming it home with the heel of his hand, Ryall threw his half-smoked cigarette away, checked the coast was clear and sneaked up to chalet number 4. He lifted his head above the window ledge and peered through a tiny gap in the curtains. Mr Grey was lounging on the bed reading a magazine. His jacket was slung over a nearby chair, revealing that he also wore a gun in a shoulder holster slung under his left arm. Was the door locked? That was the question. There was no handle, only a mortise lock, so it almost certainly was.

Suddenly, Mr Grey rose from the bed and came towards

the window. Ryall pulled back, with his gun at the ready, and flattened himself against the wall. He heard the curtain yanked aside and saw the window opened a couple of inches to let some fresh air in. Mr Grey was not enamoured of the damp smell the rooms exuded.

This was a golden opportunity.

Grabbing the window, Ryall stood and jerked it open as far as it would go. A look of shock came over Mr Grey's face, when he saw a man he thought was dead, and he went for his gun. He was not quick enough and Ryall's weapon spat once, the bullet hitting his target squarely in the chest, propelling him back towards the bed. Mr Grey slumped to the floor, his shock of fair hair falling over one eye and the front of his once clean, light-blue shirt turning crimson with his blood.

'That's the first one for Alex and the boys, and there'll be others to pay for their deaths,' Ryall announced to himself, satisfied at the start he had made.

He reached in through the window and twisted the door key. Once inside he checked Mr Grey; he was dead. Slung in an ashtray, on a bedside table, was a chalet key. Ryall picked up the key with a large number 5 on the circular copper label, and wondered how Miss Pink had managed to unlock her door. Now was his opportunity to find out, and to turn his attention to Miss Lilac. He was intrigued to discover whether or not he had correctly read the signals from her eyes.

Leaving the window open, Ryall pulled the door shut and tiptoed along to the next room. Slipping the key in the lock, he twisted it gently and pushed the door open, slowly. Stepping inside, he was immediately aware that the room was empty. Splashing noises, coming from the shower room, drifted to his ears. Miss Lilac's jumpsuit, along with her red bra and panties, were lying where she had tossed them on the bed. He picked up the soft, silky underwear and rubbed the garments against his prickly cheek.

'Hmm. They're still warm.'

The bathroom door swung open and Miss Lilac stepped into the bedroom wearing a bathrobe, with a towel twisted around her wet hair. She stopped suddenly at the sight of Ryall perched on the end of her bed, holding her knickers.

'You gave me a fright,' she complained, hand on heart. 'What the hell are you doing here? I though you were dead,' she remarked, pulling the lapels of her robe together.

'So you knew what Mr Black had in store for us?'

'No, I didn't. At least, not until after you'd all left. Then he told us what he was about to do. I protested, but there was nothing I could do to stop him,' she said, snatching her underwear from his grasp.

'You protested?' echoed Ryall, in a voice that suggested disbelief in her statement.

'Yes, I did,' she retorted, with eyes opening wider to emphasise that she did not care for his insinuation that she had lied. 'I took this job on to fly a plane, not watch a bunch of unsuspecting crooks get massacred. How come you're still alive anyway?'

'I got out of the car for a pee,' he lied.

'Lucky you.'

'Yes, lucky me. That's more than you can say for the rest of my men. They were either blown to bits or burnt to a cinder.'

'How horrible,' Miss Lilac gasped, screwing up her face.

'And what about Miss Pink? Did she also protest? And what is she up to?'

'Yes, she did, but it didn't do any good. Mr Black is the boss and does what he wants. He's told Mr Grey to keep an eye on us, and wouldn't like it if he knew that she's rung up her fella so he could come over and have some nooky.'

'That's nice for him. He's just arrived. How about you, have you got a fella?' Ryall probed.

'No, not at the moment. It's probably just as well with this job hanging over me. This whole thing's looking a lot more dangerous than I was led to believe.'

'Why don't you get out then?'

'I'm in too deep to back out now, even though I hadn't realised that I stood a chance of getting blown to bits. But, in any case, we're virtually prisoners here, so I couldn't, even if I wanted to. Mr Black insisted that we have an escort and he's going to check on us every hour or so. I haven't got a car, so I wouldn't get far before he'd find out that I'd left. And anyway, Happy Henry next door has locked … us in,' she finished hesitatingly. 'How did you manage to get in here? Can you open locked doors as well?'

'I can with this,' he replied, holding up the door key. 'Mr Grey, or Happy Henry as you so charmingly called him, is now in the happy hunting ground for ex-gunmen.'

Tanya's eyes opened wide. 'You've killed him?' she asked with astonishment, sitting down on the bed.

'Yes. I killed him for what he and the others did to my men.'

Ryall inhaled the clean, sweet, fragrant smell that surrounded Tanya, masking the bad odour of the room. He liked the bouquet, and it gave him a strong urge to see the body that it exuded from.

'In that case, perhaps there is nothing to stop me from getting out of this mess right now.'

'Nothing, except the rich reward it could provide us. I suspect that Mr Black doesn't do things by halves, so he must be after a large pay-off. What do you know about his plans?'

'I noticed you said "us". There is no us, and I don't know what his plans are. All I know is that he wants two pilots to fly a plane and do a job for him; stealing something, I think.'

'So what's the simulator for?'

'He wanted pilots who had flown military planes, preferably fighters. I've flown, but only transport aircraft. So then he asked if I could learn to fly a fighter plane from a simulator. I said yes, of course. The money he was offering was very good, and I need it, so I was anxious to get the job.'

Ryall moved in closer. 'He must be setting up a very big job to go to all this trouble. With you on the inside, and me waiting to snatch the goods when he gets them, we could share a fortune. What do you say?'

'I don't know. What's he gonna do when he finds out that Happy Henry's dead?'

'I'll take care of that. I'll sort something out.'

'It's sounds a bit risky to me.'

'Life is full of risks. You said yourself that you were now wondering what plans he has in store for you. Well, he thinks I'm dead. I can be your invisible guard and stop him from harming you, Miss Lilac.'

'Tanya,' she replied, thinking deeply about his offer. 'If I go along with this, what's to prevent you from killing me and taking everything for yourself?'

'I don't kill women. And anyway, it's Mr Black and his gun-toting cronies that I want, for double-crossing me and my men. And if I can put a spoke in their wheels and get rich, all at the same time, then so much the better.'

'And what about Paula and her partner?'

'Who?'

'Paula, she's Miss Pink, the one that's having nooky.'

'Oh, right. Well, I had a look in that simulator when we snatched it – and there's only one pilot's seat. No co-pilot.'

'That's not unusual for fighter planes, but it's something that I've been wondering about. My guess is that he only needs one pilot, and the other is a back-up, which he won't need when the job gets going.'

'Then you've got to make sure that you're the one he chooses, or you're dead,' declared Ryall, seeking to put pressure on the woman that he wanted as a partner – for more than simply business.

'Paula has flown fighter planes before. She's a lot more qualified to do the job than I am.'

'Then perhaps we should try and do something to change that,' he suggested.

'How much money do you think Mr Black is after?' Tanya asked, warming to the idea of suddenly becoming very rich.

'I don't know. It could be millions.'

'He offered to pay me fifty thousand pounds for my part in the deal.'

'What! That's the same price he paid me and all my men, and he was willing to blow it to bits, just to get rid of us.'

'That's because it's counterfeit money. He told us.'

'Counterfeit!' yelled Ryall, pulling one of the bundles from his pocket. He scrutinised the notes carefully. 'You're right. They're fakes. Very good fakes. I'm looking forward to killing that bastard.'

'If I agree to do this with you, then we split everything fifty-fifty?'

'Fifty-fifty. That's fine with me. Is it a deal?'

'I guess so,' Tanya answered, a smile playing on her lips.

This man was very assured, and quite good-looking, she thought. And if he was able to get his hands on Black's fortune and share it with her, then it was worth sticking with him, for the moment. He could also be useful if she looked to be in any danger – Black was an unpredictable man, and she would feel safer knowing Ryall was nearby.

'When is your friend due back?' he asked.

'Not for a while yet.'

Ryall took hold of the sash tying Tanya's bathrobe together and slowly pulled. 'Then maybe we ought to cement our alliance with a more positive union. Don't you think?'

Tanya lay back on the bed, answering his question with action instead of words, and felt the sash gently slip from beneath her. The bathrobe fell away, revealing glimpses of her silky smooth, fragrant skin. Ryall grabbed the lapels and briskly pulled the robe wide apart, eager to feast his eyes on her naked body.

She was delicately curved, with large aureolas around her nipples, one of which he covered with his mouth and gently sucked, holding her ample breast with both hands. She began to squirm with the pleasure that it gave her, and moaned in satisfaction as he repeated the movement with her other breast. Their lips met for a fleeting moment before he pulled back, briefly kissing both her nipples and releasing the belt on his trousers.

He purposely disrobed slowly, letting her watch him undo all the buttons on his shirt before he dropped it to the floor. His trousers and underwear fell to his ankles and he stepped out of them. His body was in good shape, not exactly a muscle man, but he clearly took care of himself. She saw that he was ready and eager for her, the anticipation making him bold and hard. He moved towards her, she grabbed his arm and pulled him on to the bed and rolled over on top of him, kissing him so hard that it made his lips sting. Pulling away from his grasp, she slipped down his body, grabbed his member and thrust it into her mouth. Now it was his turn to utter moans of satisfaction as she massaged him with hand and lips, watching his twisting and groaning with excitement. He basked in the pleasure of it all until he could stand it no longer, and knew that he would come soon if he did not stop her.

He tried to pull her away but she resisted him, instead increasing the speed of her massage. It was more than he could stand, and the ecstasy brought him quickly to a climax, with Tanya kissing his throbbing erection. At the release he cried aloud with the pleasure his ejaculation brought him. Now the moment was over, he relaxed, and the excitement wound down in him.

Ryall felt drained after the energy-sapping experience, but

knew that he would soon recover and want more. It had been a long time since such a euphoric sensation had embraced him when making love; this alliance could have more benefits to it than were apparent at first, and it pleased him that he had read her signals correctly. The years may be passing, and faster than he would like, but he fancied that he still had what it took to pull a good-looking woman.

His ardour subsided and Tanya moved to his side and lay next to him.

'That was obviously very good for me, but how about you?' he asked.

'I enjoyed it, but I crave much more satisfaction than that. In a few minutes we will make love, and this time it will be my turn to receive much pleasure. You should be able to stay active for quite a while, now that your carnal urge to have sex with me has been gratified once already, and I will bask in the enjoyment that you will provide for me. It will be a much longer love session for us to look forward to, instead of the wham-bam, thirty-second quickie that would have happened otherwise.'

'That would only be due to the excitement of a first encounter with a new, and very lovely, woman,' Ryall gushed, wishing to counter any criticism that Tanya would only have otherwise got a quickie.

They kissed passionately and Ryall could already feel the urges rising within him. This was a clever female who manipulated situations to her advantage, even when making love. She would need to be watched carefully. An alliance between them may now exist, but trust was still a long way off.

While their extended lovemaking was shaking the bed and giving Tanya the prolonged satisfaction that she would not have otherwise received, Paula and Mike were also busy.

Mike had served many years in the Army before becoming a mercenary, and fought in the battle for The Falkland

Islands. In the Army he had trained hard, had the muscles to show for it and kept himself in trim. At six feet tall, with a square jaw and aquiline nose, his good looks attracted the attention of women, a factor he found hard to suppress until Suzie reminded him she was his partner. He and Suzie, on several occasions, found themselves persuaded to work for Sir Joseph Sterling, a troubleshooter for the government on police and intelligence matters. Mike and Paula's time was spent mainly in talking about the events of that morning.

'I don't know where the simulator was stolen from, but there can't be that many companies that make them,' Paula suggested.

'No, I agree. Sir Joseph will be able to find that out soon enough. It may have been reported to him already if the robbery's been discovered, but I can't ring him until nine p.m. tonight.'

'Nine p.m. tonight? Why not? Surely this is urgent?'

'It is. But he's worried about security and the possibility that the phone call might be overheard or intercepted. It seems that Black can get hold of information that is not intended for his ears. He's doing this to protect us.'

'Right. I'm sorry that I can't be more helpful,' Paula retorted.

'Not at all. This information is vital. And you say that Mr Black killed all the men who stole the simulator, in order to keep his warehouse location a secret?'

'Yes. He's ruthless. He paid them in counterfeit notes so that it wouldn't cost him too much. The quicker I find out what his plans are and get out, the better I'll like it.'

'Me too. Do you have to go back? We could let Sir Joseph know what we've discovered so far and let him raid the warehouse,' suggested Mike.

The option sounded good to Paula, though it fell far short of what she had hoped to achieve. She thought about it and also thought about flying again. If she could prove to the

RAF top men that she had not lost her nerve and was still capable of flying a jet fighter, even if it was only on a simulator, maybe they would relent and put her back in the programme.

She finally made a decision. 'No, I can't do that. I must go back and find out what he's up to. Sir Joseph said he's slipped past him before and we need to catch him red-handed. That's the only way we can stop him for good.'

'Can't we get him for murdering all those men?' asked Mike.

'How are you going to prove that he personally planted a remote control bomb in their car, then detonated it? I don't imagine there's much left to identify, anyway.'

'You and the other woman are both witnesses.'

'I don't know if Tanya would testify, and in any case, he would have a dozen men say differently.'

'True. Okay, in that case I'll follow you back to the warehouse and wait outside, until you can get out with the information.'

'Be careful, Mike. He's got guards outside and he'll have no qualms about killing you if you're seen by any of his men.'

'The same goes for you if he finds out that you're a plant engineered by Sir Joseph. Black knows that he's been after him for quite a while.'

Paula nodded. 'We've got a little while before I have to go back to my room,' she said, glancing at her wristwatch. Moving closer to Mike, where they sat on the bed, she let her already unbuttoned blouse flap open, making her intentions clear.

'You're still a very attractive woman ...' began Mike.

'And you're still an attractive man, and I told Tanya that we'd be spending our time making passionate love,' Paula said, running her fingers through his hair. 'You wouldn't want to make a liar out of me, now would you?'

Mike hesitated, 'Well ...'

'It's okay, I won't tell, Suzie. After all, it should be part of our cover, just in case Tanya or the guard decide to drop in on us for one reason or another.'

Mike smiled, 'True. In that case, I wouldn't dream of making you a liar.'

They embraced and kissed. Paula unbuckled his belt and they fell to the floor and made love. It was as if they had turned back the clock a few years. Memories of each other's desires, and the good times enjoyed by them together in the past, came flooding back. The heightened tension of the dangers of their job, and the knowledge that this was something they would want to keep a secret, added extra passion to their ardour.

Back in chalet 5, almost an hour of lovemaking left Ryall feeling shattered and sleepy, though Tanya still looked fresh and awake.

'I thought most people wanted to sleep after having sex, especially after they've had a marathon love-in,' he stated.

'You call that a marathon love-in?'

'Well, I can only think of a few occasions when I've had sex that's gone on for quite so long,' lied Ryall. He did not wish her to think of him as that wham-bam lover who indulged in sex that was over in a few minutes and then turned over and went to sleep, though this was a lot closer to the truth.

'Perhaps you've not had the right encouragement,' she suggested.

'Perhaps,' he agreed, thinking that she certainly did not need any encouragement with the sexual appetite that she has. 'We ought to be planning what we are going to do about Mr Black and his cronies, and your rival, before she returns. She could be back any minute,' he suggested, looking at his watch and turning his mind to money matters, now that his sexual desires had been fully satisfied for the time being.

'Yes. What do you suggest?'

'I have an idea that might work. When you get back to the warehouse ...'

After Mike and Paula had finished their lovemaking she remarked, 'I'd better get back before Tanya wonders what's happened to me. It's been more than an hour already, and our guard said he'd look in on us every once in a while.'

'Okay. Don't forget, I'll follow you to the warehouse when you leave.'

Paula nodded, slipped her bra on, fastened the bottom button on her blouse and gave Mike one last kiss before they slipped outside.

Ryall had barely closed his car door before he saw Mike return to his vehicle and Paula creep back to chalet 5. Tanya was lying on the bed.

'I'm sorry I was a bit longer than I said. I was enjoying myself too much,' explained Paula, doing up the rest of the buttons on her blouse.

'That's okay. I'm glad you had a good time,' remarked Tanya, swinging the belt on her bathrobe and smiling inwardly to herself. 'I had the shower that you were supposed to be taking.'

'It's a good job that Mr Grey didn't come in then,' stated Paula, slightly concerned that Tanya had not covered for her as she had asked.

'He did, and I told him you were in the shower. He believed me then left, so I though it was unlikely that he'd bother us again for a while.'

'Good. Thanks. I'll take a shower now. So, you've not heard any more from our jailer?'

'Nah,' said Tanya. 'Apart from a thud from next door shortly after he left, everything's been quiet.'

'A thud? What sort of a thud?'

'I expect Happy Henry fell out of bed after ogling my cleavage,' Tanya joked.

'Maybe we'd better take a look.'

'We're supposed to be locked in, so we'd better be careful.'

'Yeah,' agreed Paula.

They crept along to the next chalet and peered through a gap in the curtains. Paula drew back with a sharp intake of breath at the sight before them. Mr Grey was lying in a pool of blood with his eyes wide open. The door was slightly ajar and they cautiously opened it further.

'Oh, God! What's happened to him?' Tanya asked, holding grimly on to Paula's arm as they stood in the doorway.

'Somebody's obviously shot him,' she exclaimed, stepping up to him and feeling the side of his neck for a pulse. 'He's cold, so I reckon he's been dead a little while. I must tell Mike before he leaves,' she said, making for the door.

'Mike. Why do you want to tell him?'

'I told him what happened to Ryall and his men. He's an ex-soldier and carries a gun, and he's a bit worried about me.'

'Well, this'll make him even more worried,' Tanya maintained.

'Maybe,' Paula agreed. 'But I think I should tell him anyway. He'll know what to do.'

Paula hurried across to Mike, sitting in his car. She quickly explained about the dead guard and they returned to the chalet.

'This is my partner, Mike,' Paula said, introducing him to Tanya.

Tanya smiled at this clean-cut handsome man standing before her, and breathed in hard, expanding her chest. Mike smiled back, and could hardly take his eyes off her ample bosom, most of which was now made visible by Tanya thrusting her hands deep into the pockets of her robe.

Tearing his eyes away, Mike searched Mr Grey's pockets. 'I can't find a wallet. I guess he was mugged, and perhaps shot by the intruder when they saw he had a gun,' he said, checking the pistol in his shoulder holster. 'It seems a bit strange though, his car keys are still here.'

'Yes,' agreed Paula. 'The problem is, what are we going to do now?'

'We'll have to go back to Mr Black and tell him he was mugged. It's not our fault,' insisted Tanya.

'I guess so,' Paula reluctantly agreed. 'Though I'm a bit worried about what he might say or do. He's a volatile man and doesn't like problems.'

'We'll be okay,' suggested Tanya. 'He needs us to fly his ruddy plane.'

'I suppose you're right.'

'I don't like it, but I guess the only other option is to get out now,' suggested Mike.

'I'd like to, but I need the money he's paying me for this caper,' Tanya stated.

'Then I'll tag along behind you and keep watch outside the warehouse, in case you need me,' Mike informed them.

'You don't have to do that. It could be dangerous for you,' Tanya insisted.

'I agree, Mike. We should go back alone. I'll contact you when I can,' Paula stated.

'Don't be silly. I know how to take care of myself and I couldn't sleep at night if I let something bad happen to one of you lovely ladies. No, I'll tag along behind you and wait nearby.'

'Would you really?' purred Tanya, moving towards Mike. 'I'd be ever so grateful.'

'We'd both be grateful,' stated Paula, eyeing this vamp with her bosoms close to pushing their way out of her bathrobe.

She gave Mike a coy, little-girl look with head dipped and fluttering eyelashes. One he found difficult to ignore.

'I want both of you ladies to be safe in the knowledge that

help is only a scream away.' He eyed Paula, aware that they both knew he was getting the come-on from Tanya. 'I'll leave you two to get ready. When you return to the warehouse, I'll be right behind you,' he stated, checking the ammunition clip in his gun.

'The hideout is on a run-down industrial estate,' stated Paula, pretending that she had not said anything to Mike about the location. 'And there are armed guards outside.'

'Right. I'll wait nearby when you turn into the place, and check to see if the guards are making sure you've not been followed. If it's all clear, I'll drive in slowly a few minutes later.'

Mike went back to his vehicle, unaware that Ryall was hiding in his car nearby, watching him. After a short while the two women emerged from their room.

'We'd better close the window and lock both chalets, and take the keys,' Paula stated. 'We don't want someone walking in on a dead body.'

'Oh, okay. I guess you're right,' Tanya reluctantly agreed.

They collected their mobile phones, returned to Mr Grey's limousine and Tanya drove them out of the motel, heading towards Mr Black's hideout. Ryall ducked low in his vehicle and heard them drive off, followed by Mike.

He sat up and smiled to himself. 'Things are going well for a change. First I get the opportunity to kill one of Black's men, then I enjoy a marathon love session with a big-busted sexpot, and now I could be on the verge of pulling off that big job I've always dreamt of. And, they're bound to send someone back here to collect the body and verify the ladies' story. That could give me another chance to get at one of them.'

Paula and Tanya motored back to the warehouse, followed at a distance by Mike. They were unsure of what Mr Black would make of the morning's events, and even more uncertain of what he was likely to say or do about it. This was a nervous and dangerous time for them both.

6

Return

The door crashed open, echoing around the warehouse, and the guard stepped inside with Tanya and Paula, each grasped firmly by the arm. He marched them towards Mr Black who was huddled over the bench with Mr Green, discussing the progress he was making with reassembling the simulator's missing module.

Looking up, Mr Black angrily demanded, 'What the hell are you two doing here? And where's Mr Grey?'

'He's dead. An intruder killed him,' Paula growled back. The trio halted before him.

'Dead? How did this happen?' he asked.

Yanking her arm free, Paula insisted, 'We don't know. We heard a thud and went into his room to investigate and saw he'd been shot.'

'Shot! You found him shot?'

'Yes, we did. We think he was mugged,' Paula suggested. 'His wallet is missing.'

'How did you get out? You were supposed to be locked in,' Mr Black questioned.

Paula had to think fast. 'It's an old, rundown place and the doors don't fit very well. We were able to pull ours open. Mr Grey's door was already open.'

'I see.'

'That's what she wants you to believe,' Tanya interjected,

stepping forward. 'But what really happened was that she opened the door and telephoned her lover and partner in crime, Mike, to come over, and they killed him. They were trying to find out when and what you're planning to rob, then steal it from you. He wouldn't, or couldn't tell them. They had an argument and her boyfriend ended up shooting him.'

Paula looked amazed. She could hardly believe what she was hearing.

Mr Black turned towards Paula, with eyes wide in anger. His men pointed their guns at her, and he moved in closer, confronting her.

'And what do you have to say about that?'

'It's not true. We found him dead in the next room. I did sneak out for a while to be with Mike, but only so we could make love before it was impossible to see him again until after this job was over. She must have killed him, and now she wants to put the blame on us.'

'She was out with her man all right, they were planning it together. If you want any more proof, you should know that he's followed us here and will show up outside any minute now, and of course, he's got a gun,' insisted Tanya, realising that there were a lot more people in the warehouse now.

Mr Black had been busy during the few short hours they had been away. Many men had been eagerly beavering away at assembling the hydraulic ram jacks to the cabin and bolting them to the floor. Now, they all stopped to listen.

Mr Black bellowed out an order. 'Mr Blue, take some of your men and wait for this man. If he turns up, I want him either captured or dead. He is not to escape, is that understood?'

'Yes, sir,' he nodded, waving to four of his men who were all brandishing sub-machine guns, and hurrying from the building.

'You can't,' Paula demanded. 'He's done nothing to hurt

you. All this shit from her is a lie. Mike's only followed us here because he's worried about my safety after I told him what you did to those men who stole the simulator, that's all. He's got no intentions of trying to rob you.'

'That doesn't matter. He knows too much and the location of my hideout has been compromised. He is to be neutralised. And Mr White, take a man with you to check the motel and remove Mr Grey's body and dispose of it. I don't want any of our men to be investigated by the police at this late juncture in the proceedings. Where are the keys?' he asked the women.

'She's got them,' Tanya stated, pointing to Paula.

Paula took both keys from her pocket. Mr Black snatched them away and handed Mr White the key to chalet 4.

'Tell me, Miss Lilac, how is it that you know all this?'

Tanya lowered her eyes in a coy look and confessed, 'I heard shouting in the next room and took a look. Miss Pink's man and Mr Grey were fighting. I was on my way to his car to see if he had a mobile phone to ring you, when I heard a shot. Her man came out holding a gun, so I knew he was armed and had shot him.'

'You're a liar!' shouted Paula. 'It's not true, you bitch!' She made a grab for Tanya and snatched a length of her hair and yanked it sharply. Tanya screamed and took a punch at Paula, which missed, as the guards intervened to drag them apart.

'They planned to rob you after you've pulled the job and thought they'd persuaded me to join them for a cut of the proceeds. I went along with them because, if I didn't, they would have killed me too,' Tanya said, glancing up at Mr Black with her big blue eyes.

She was hard to ignore, but the expression on Mr Black's face remained stoic, giving no hint of what was going through his devious mind, nor indicating whether he believed her or not.

Outside, a car glided into the industrial estate and silently rolled past the abandoned buildings with Mike at the wheel. When he reached the curved road to the warehouse, Mr Blue and his men jumped out behind him brandishing their weapons. Taken by surprise, Mike ducked and accelerated along the road. They began a continuous wave of sub-machine gun fire at his vehicle, shattering the rear window. With only the single track to the warehouse in front of him, no other exit in sight and only long grass surrounding him, Mike was trapped. He braked hard, slewed the car round in a 180-degree handbrake turn and charged back toward the men, keeping low and driving blind, hoping to dodge the bullets. Holes riddled his vehicle before the gunmen had to jump out of the way into the rough grass.

He motored past them, screeched around the derelict corner factory module and crunched over the concrete slabs as he charged towards the road. But, with the exit to the industrial estate only a few yards away, a car pulled across his path, blocking the route. The driver crouched behind his vehicle and began firing. Mike yanked the handbrake on and performed another skidding U-turn, with all four wheels locking up and smoke pouring from the screeching tyres. The wheels spun furiously round with the car making little headway until the tyres gripped, shooting the car forwards, back towards the onrushing men. They scattered in all directions, with guns still blazing, and two tyres on Mike's car were hit and burst, shaking the vehicle into an uncontrollable sideways skid. His car ploughed through a stack of rusting oil drums and smashed headlong into the front of a corrugated iron module, demolishing the bottom section.

His vehicle finally ground to a halt, with the front half of the car buried in the building, leaving only the rear end poking out. Seconds later, with Mr Blue and his men dashing towards the stricken vehicle, it burst into flames. The men stopped and stared; seeing the danger they turned and ran.

At that same instant, the flames licked the petrol tank and it exploded with a deafening roar, sending the men scurrying for cover as debris blasted into the air.

Inside the warehouse, Paula listened to the shooting with alarm, but was held by two of Mr Black's men and could do nothing about it. Mr Black noticed the rest of the men had stopped work to listen to the firing.

'Come, come now,' he urged, clapping his hands. 'Continue your tasks and ignore the commotion outside, in the same way that I am.'

The exploding car rattled the corrugated walls, and even Mr Black instinctively ducked, wondering what had happened. He stopped for a second to turn and look in the direction of the noise. Paula, too, worried about the explosion. What had happened? Was Mike okay? She was soon to find out.

The noise outside abated, and a few moments later the shutter door swung back and Mr Blue entered the building, followed by his men. 'The driver refused to stop and we had no choice but to fire on him. His car crashed into one of the abandoned buildings and exploded. He's dead. There's no way he could've survived that.'

Paula drew a sharp breath, and looked at Tanya with hate in her tearful eyes and contempt in her voice. 'You'd better pray that I never get my hands on you, bitch, because if I do, you'll also be dead.'

Tanya tried to look unconcerned, but a flush coloured her face. Shrugging her shoulders, she turned away, nonchalantly flicking her long red hair over her shoulder.

'Do not worry Miss Lilac, you are safe here with me,' assured Mr Black. 'Good work, Mr Blue. Ask your men to resume guarding the warehouse. I want no more unauthorised visitors, especially after all that commotion. Is that clear?'

'Of course, Mr Black. Consider it done,' he said.

'After that, I want you to take this woman back to the motel,' he said, staring at Paula. 'Mr White should still be there, so you can leave her in the room that Mr Grey had, and make it look as if it was her that was attacked and killed. How you achieve that I will leave up to you. Also, make sure that the other room is empty of anything that could link it to us. Do you understand?' he asked, tossing him the key to chalet 5.

'Perfectly, Mr Black,' he said, tying Paula's hands behind her back and marching her to the door. 'You come with me, Terry,' he said, to one of the guards.

'I'll get you, you lying bitch,' screamed Paula, as she was dragged to the car.

Turning to Miss Lilac, Mr Black smiled his sickly sweet grin and stated, 'That seems to be the end of that. There are no more problems to get in the way now, are there?'

'None that I know of,' she replied, wondering why he needed to ask.

Perhaps he still did not trust her, and suspected something. No matter, that was all over now, and her rival who, nice as she was, had got in the way of her greedy plans and was now out of the picture. However, until an opportunity to discover Mr Black's plan revealed itself, Tanya would have to continue her efforts to gain favour with him.

'If it's all right with you, I'd still like to get some rest. It's been a difficult morning and there's nothing I can do here for the moment. I'll not be any good to you if I'm half-asleep.'

'Certainly. Mr Brown,' he called. 'Show Miss Lilac to my caravan at the back of the warehouse, and leave a man outside to guard her. She is very valuable to me, and I don't want a repeat of the troubles she's had to contend with,' he stated, wishing to impress his concern about the limited choice of pilots he now had.

Mr Brown, a thin man who wore rimless glasses and looked more like a banker than a thief, nodded.

Turning to Miss Lilac, Mr Black pronounced, 'There's a double bedroom that you can use. It's not as roomy as the motel, but it's safe and I'm sure you'll be comfortable there.'

This was not what Miss Lilac was expecting; she smiled and followed Mr Brown to the caravan.

Paula was bundled into the back seat of a car and it roared off towards the motel. She turned to stare at the burnt-out wreck of Mike's smouldering car, jutting out from beneath twisted corrugated panels that were once the front of a thriving business. She muttered under her breath, 'Bitch'.

While these events were going on, back at the motel Ryall knelt by the door to chalet 4 and swore. He had asked Tanya to leave the door unlocked if she could, but to his dismay he found that it was shut fast. He checked the window, but that was also locked. Trying desperately to pick the lock, he hoped that no one would come past and see him. Picking locks was an art that he had never bothered to learn, because his usual method was simply to prize the door open with a jemmy to gain entry. This was something he would do now, if only he had his jemmy with him. He did not, so instead he struggled to open the door, and in desperation even tried forcing it open with his shoulder. Eventually he gave up and decided on a different approach.

Stepping towards the motel office, he cautiously peered through the window at the reception desk. The office was as run-down and seedy-looking as most of the rooms. Behind the counter was a rack, fitted to the wall, with the room keys, each one dangling from a hook. The manager was sitting at the desk reading a newspaper. Ryall could hear the man's television blaring away through the open door to his nearby private room. He eyed the spare key which he desperately needed, hanging on a hook marked chalet 4, and tried to think of a way to get his hands on it. He placed a hand on his gun and considered killing the man in order to get the key.

On the television, a tuneless jingle announced the start of a daily, 10.15 a.m., half-hour quiz show, *Guess My Crime*. The manager threw his newspaper on the desk and strolled into his room to watch the programme, leaving the door ajar.

Ryall gently pushed open the office door, tiptoed past the manager's room and quietly lifted the key to chalet 4 from the hook. A sudden burst of laughter erupted from both the television and the manager. Ryall stood motionless until the noise died down and he would be able to hear any movement, then he quietly tiptoed back out.

Once outside he almost ran to the chalet. It had been over half an hour since the women had left, and one of Mr Black's men could return any moment now.

Entering chalet 4, Ryall took Mr Grey's wallet from his pocket and was about to return it when he heard a car approaching, its tyres crunching up the twisty gravel entrance way. He barely had time to replace the wallet and leave the chalet, shutting the door behind him, before the car stopped outside. Ryall hid behind a nearby vehicle and returned to his own car after Mr White and his friend had gained entry to the room.

Again, Ryall sat in his car and waited, while the room was cleared of all the evidence of Mr Grey's visit, then finally, surreptitiously, the two men carried out a rolled-up rug and dumped it in the boot of their car.

'That's one way to hide a body, I guess,' muttered Ryall, slipping the safety-catch off his gun.

His hand was on the car door handle and he was about to make his move when the second car, carrying Paula, arrived and parked next to Mr White's vehicle. Ryall sank back into his seat and watched. The two drivers exchanged a few words before Mr White handed over the key to chalet 4.

Mr White and his friend then left to dispose of the body. After dumping it in nearby woods, they returned to the warehouse with a report for their boss.

'What did you find there?' Mr White was asked.

'Mr Grey had a single bullet wound to the body. His gun was still in its holster and his room was not very tidy. Also, he still had his wallet, but it was not placed properly in his pocket. It looked as if it had been returned there in a hurry,' he suggested.

'Hmm. Miss Pink said that his wallet was missing. Why should she lie when she knows that it's so easy for me to check?'

'Perhaps she didn't expect us to return there and collect the body?'

'Possibly. Even so, that doesn't prove anything, but it all seems a bit suspicious. I want a close watch kept on Miss Lilac. There's something about her story that doesn't ring true. Mr Grey was quite a careful man. I find it hard to believe that he would let a stranger into his room without drawing his gun first.'

'I'll see to it myself,' Mr White assured.

'Mr Brown, I'd like a word with you,' he called, to his man returning from the caravan after seeing that Miss Lilac was comfortably settled in.

'Certainly, Mr Black.'

'I recall that you finally talked to three possible candidates for the job of pilot?'

'That is correct, all three were women. Miss Lilac was a definite because she'd flown fighter aircraft, and there were two others who both had flying experience. After lengthy consideration we chose Miss Pink.'

'Was the other woman suitable for the job?'

'Perfectly. It was difficult to choose between them, but a decision had to be made. Miss Pink had RAF training, so I made the recommendation to choose her, and you agreed with that decision,' he defended, not wanting to take sole responsibility for picking a candidate who had a question mark against her and they were now less sure of.

'I presume you can get in touch with the third woman?'

'Yes. I took a contact number in case there were any problems with either of the other two candidates.'

'Good. Ring her, and get her to agree to be a replacement for Miss Pink.'

'Of course. She was a Miss Drake, if I remember rightly. I'll arrange a meeting with her to discuss it. I have her mobile phone number.'

'She will be Miss Ochre,' Mr Black decided.

A few miles away at the motel, Mr Blue and his mate Terry took a furtive look about them to make sure the coast was clear, then shoved a bound Paula back into chalet 4. The two men slammed the door shut and slung her handbag on the floor.

'This job is one I'm going to enjoy,' Mr Blue assured Terry, ripping Paula's blouse open and shoving her on to the bed ...

7

Morley's Motel

In an abandoned factory module on the Marlborough Industrial Estate, an aching, battered figure awoke on the floor, and peered into the gloom. Mike, bruised and bleeding, but alive, slowly got to his feet and staggered towards the wreck of his car.

Light spilled in, where his vehicle had jammed into the corrugated sheeting of the front wall, illuminating patches of the dim interior. His car had left a large, jagged hole in its travels, big enough for Mike to squeeze through.

When the vehicle had skidded and burst through the corrugated shell, and caught fire, during his attempts to evade the hail of murderous gunfire, Mike had thrown open the door and sprinted towards cover for all he was worth. Seconds later, the explosion ripped through the vehicle, sending fragments of metal and glass showering in all directions. The force of the blast catapulted him into a pile of rubbish stacked in a corner, where he lay unconscious until now. He had no idea how long he had been there, but guessed that it was quite a time because the car had almost burnt itself out, and was now only a smouldering wreck with the doors and boot gaping wide, blown open by the blast.

Outside, two guards now wandered up and down in front of the abandoned factories, following Mr Black's orders to prevent any further intrusion. Dressed in suits, with their guns hidden in shoulder holsters, they looked more like businessman than the hired gunmen they really were, ready to challenge anyone who was unfortunate enough to wander on to the estate. Mike tiptoed to the hole and trod on something plastic that crunched beneath his foot. He picked it up and was dismayed to see that it was his mobile telephone, flung during the crash from the car dashboard where it usually resided.

'It was probably broken already,' he muttered to console himself, slinging the pieces away.

He peered at the guards through the hole. What he would not give for his trusty commando knife right now. With it, he would have no bother in taking care of these two. He cursed at not having the foresight to bring it with him. He would now have to improvise.

'I'm going around the back for a leak,' announced one guard to the other.

'Okay,' his companion nodded, watching him disappear around the far side of the building.

The opportunity that Mike needed beckoned him and he took advantage of it straight away. He tapped lightly on the shell of the car, making a hollow, echoey dong, like an out of tune bell. The guard turned and frowned, curious to know where the noise had come from. He approached the wreck, took out his pistol, released the safety-catch and stared into the gloomy factory. Nothing. He must be hearing things; there was nothing there, only a gentle breeze that was not strong enough to disturb anything. The guard turned, and by the time he had taken one step, Mike had ducked through the hole and was upon him. With an arm clasped around the man's neck, Mike grabbed his forehead and wrenched it round. The crack confirmed that his neck had been broken, and he slumped into Mike's arms.

Dragging him through the opening into the abandoned factory, Mike spotted the first guard turning the corner while zipping up his trousers, and pulled his victim's legs through the hole with barely a moment to spare. The guard searched in all directions for his mate. He slipped his gun from its holster and checked the clip.

'Pete? Are you there, Pete?' he shouted.

'By the car,' came a muffled reply. 'Look what I've found!'

Mike was unsure whether he would fall for it, but it was worth taking the chance. The only alternative was to shoot him, but gunfire would warn the others. Unbuttoning the dead guard's coat, Mike took his shoulder holster and strapped it on. From the gloom of the factory he watched the first guard cautiously close in on the car. Dragging the body out of sight, he picked up a short length of abandoned scaffold pipe and waited by the opening.

'Where are you?' the first man asked. 'I can't see you.'

'Inside,' was the short, sharp reply.

The guard approached the hole, ducked and foolishly stuck his head through the gap. He never saw the makeshift weapon that slammed into the side of his head, breaking his neck and killing him instantly.

After hiding both bodies under a pile of rubbish in a far, dark corner, Mike emerged from the gloom. He darted across to the end factory, where the road to the warehouse began, and hid, where he could survey the area without being seen. The only cover between him and the building, was the high, rubbish-strewn grass that littered most of the run-down estate. Standing alone, was the large, dark, isolated warehouse at the end of the road, with all the windows boarded up and no other guards keeping watch outside. Mike kept low and made his way through the long grass, then scouted around the building, looking for a safe entrance. He had no way of knowing whether Paula was still inside or not, but it was clear to him from the ambush that he had been expected, and he was eager to find out if she too had been discovered.

At the back of the warehouse, among more long, wet grass, was a rear entrance. The corrugated covered door, on a broken, rotting wooden frame, was stuck fast. The top of the door submitted to Mike's leverage with a lump of discarded wood that he picked up nearby, but not the bottom. It would not budge, held back by tufts of grass that had been allowed to grow wild since the estate was abandoned. Mike wrenched the top open, carefully bending the corrugated metal back, anxious not to make a noise. He vaulted in through the gap. The door sprang back into shape and Mike jabbed out a hand, catching it inches away from closing with a bang. Immediately facing him was the light blue paintwork of the side of a rusting caravan. He dropped to the floor, scrambling underneath the van to the far side and peered at the men still beavering away to get the simulator working, now anchored to the floor behind the low-loader.

'It looks as if they've more or less completed assembling the monster,' he said to himself. 'There's no sign of Paula though.'

Slipping back underneath, he crawled to the far end of the caravan, in the dirt and gloom near a corner of the warehouse. Through a partly open window, Mike could hear voices from inside the caravan. A man and a woman were talking about plans for the job. She was asking a lot of questions, and the voice was familiar to him, but it was not Paula's – it was the dulcet tones of Tanya's voice that drifted to his ears. A picture of her ample cleavage came to mind, along with an intriguing wonderment of how much of it she was showing at that moment.

'So, the robbery could be worth millions of pounds, you reckon?' asked Miss Lilac, sitting up in bed, smoking a cigarette.

'Yes, I'm sure it will,' replied Mr Black, caressing Miss Lilac's voluptuous breasts. He was prepared to divulge some small snippets of information about the job to her, in return for the pleasure of having sex with this ambitious female. A middle-aged, pot-bellied man like himself would not normally be able to attract such a gorgeous, young woman as her. But he had something that she wanted, information, and the power to be able to give her a job whereby she could earn a lot of money. He took full advantage of the situation, while remaining cautious about how much he allowed her to know.

'Perhaps I should get a bigger bonus, now that you're solely relying on me to pilot the plane?' she suggested.

'I might consider that,' he agreed, knowing that he had to be careful not to lose his only pilot until he was sure of getting a replacement for Miss Pink. Searching for another pilot would delay things, and he did not have time for even a short delay.

Hearing that comment confirmed Mike's fears that Paula had certainly been discovered. The question he now asked himself was, what had they done about it?

'Do you think Miss Pink was a policewoman?' asked Miss Lilac.

'No, I don't think so, but it doesn't matter anyway. When the boys have finished having their fun with her at the motel, they'll take care of things. Neither she nor her boyfriend will be telling the police anything.'

While Tanya felt slightly guilty about Paula's demise, though not showing it and dismissing the thought from her mind, Mike's ears pricked up at the mention of the motel. The discovery of where they had taken Paula and what they were planning to do, had at first pleased, but then quickly alarmed him. He now knew that he had to get there fast. Sneaking back out of the warehouse, anxious to hurry, the torn corrugated door sprang back and caught his arm, ripping the sleeve of his shirt and gouging a chunk out of him.

'Shit!' he exclaimed, grasping the wound to stem the blood, seeping through his denim shirtsleeve.

He needed a car, and his best hope of getting one was if one of the dead guards had a car, and the keys were still on him. Ducking back into the abandoned factory, Mike searched the dead guards' pockets and found a key ring with car keys and a remote locking blip on one of them. He crept among the group of vehicles parked outside the front of the warehouse pressing the blip's locking button. A Land Rover flashed its indicator lights in recognition, and unlocked its doors. Mike jumped into the vehicle and within a few seconds was silently slipping away, hoping the noise of constructing the simulator had masked the sound of the car's engine.

'I pray that I'm not too late,' he mumbled to himself, 'or that the missing guards aren't discovered before I get to the motel. I haven't got time to worry about that.'

If Mr Black discovered that he was still alive, Mike was likely to find his henchmen waiting at the motel for him. He was desperate to get there in time to save Paula from the clutches of this evil man, and he put his foot to the floor, racing back towards an uncertain reception at Morley's Motel on the outskirts of Portsmouth.

8

Rescue

At Morley's Motel, Mr Blue and his accomplice Terry closed in on Paula, lying on the bed where they had thrown her. With her hands tied behind her back and looking unable to prevent them from carrying out anything they wished, the two men were anticipating the pleasure they were about to enjoy. Intent on raping her, before carrying out Mr Black's instructions to kill her, they drew near.

Paula lashed out with her foot, catching Terry with a hefty kick to the crotch. He doubled up in pain and sank to his knees. Seeing this, and anxious to avoid the same thing happening to him, Mr Blue lashed out at Paula with his gun and caught her with a blow to the head.

A gash appeared on her forehead and blood trickled down the side of her face. Paula's eyes rolled, she sank back on to the bed and became distantly aware of the bare light on the ceiling, spinning round and round.

Mr Blue turned to his mate. 'Are you okay, Terry?'

'Just about,' he reflected, rising to his feet, clutching himself. 'Christ that hurt!' he exclaimed, tears welling up in his eyes.

'It serves you right for being so eager. We've got plenty of time, so take it easy. We might as well enjoy ourselves.'

Paula opened her eyes and blinked repeatedly. 'So, you thought this was going to be easy, did you?'

'It makes no difference to us, lady. You can have it easy, or you can make it difficult. If you make it easy, I'll kill you quickly afterwards. If you want to make it difficult, I'll beat it out of you, still get what I want, and leave you to die slowly. The choice is yours.'

'You call that a choice! Either way I get raped and die. That's no choice. How about making a deal?' Paula asked, desperate to delay them while she worked on the bonds behind her back.

'What sort of deal?' Mr Blue asked.

'I've got friends who will pay you a lot of money for my release. You'll both get a nice bonus and then I'll disappear. Mr Black need never know what happened. You can tell him I'm dead and you've got rid of my body.'

'A nice bonus? You must be kidding, lady. Mr Black told us to leave your body here. He wouldn't think twice about killing us if we double-crossed him, and anyway, your friends might see things differently. They could bring guns instead of money and try to persuade us to let you go. And we wouldn't get the pleasure of having you, any way that we want. No, you'll simply have to be raped and killed, however difficult you try to make it. Grab her legs, Terry.'

Terry had not learned much; he made a half-hearted grab for Paula's legs, and got a kick in the face for his troubles. Paula was determined not to give in without a fight.

'Bitch!' yelled Mr Blue, jumping on top of Paula to smother her actions, and prevent her from lashing out any further.

He smashed a fist into her face, almost knocking her out, then grabbed her bra and ripped it off. 'Let's see how much fight you have left after I've dealt with you,' he spat.

Without warning, a hole ripped through his chest and blood spattered Paula as Mr Blue suddenly fell on top of her with all his weight, and remained still. Terry, nursing his bruised nose, heard the muffled report and turned to stare, horrified, at the sight of Ryall standing in the doorway, gun in hand, and a wisp of smoke drifting from the silencer. He opened his mouth to speak, but before he could say anything, the gun spat once more and, wide-eyed, he crashed back into the bedside cabinet and slumped to the floor, with blood oozing from a hole in his chest.

Paula, in her dazed state, was aware that something was happening, but could see nothing with Mr Blue slumped on top of her. She wriggled on to her side, shoving the body off. It crashed to the floor beside Terry, and only then did she comprehend what was going on.

'Ryall!' she blurted, surprised at this ghost standing before her. 'I thought you were dead.'

'No. Fortunately for you, I'm not.' He gazed at her naked top. 'You have a nice figure, Miss Pink. I'm glad that those bastards didn't get the chance to enjoy themselves with you,' he remarked, unscrewing the silencer from his gun.

'Not half as much as I am,' asserted Paula, turning her back to show him her tied hands.

'Oh, sorry,' he remarked, slipping the silencer in his pocket and the gun back into its holster. He sat on the bed beside her and untied the knot.

'My name's Paula, not that stupid name of Miss Pink.'

'Paula, that's a much nicer name,' Ryall claimed, turning on the charm.

Paula grabbed a tissue from a box on the bedside cabinet and wiped the blood from her face and body. She pulled her blouse together, but only one, middle button remained with which to fasten it.

'I thought that you and all your men were dead. Black put a bomb in your attaché case along with the fake money.'

'So I found out. I was luckier than they were. I stopped for a pee in the bushes, just before the bomb went off,' he said, taking the tissue and wiping some blood from her face. His touch felt soft and gentle after the rough treatment she had endured from her captors.

'Why are you here?' Paula asked.

'I went back to the warehouse, bent on revenge, and saw these two leaving with you and followed them here,' he lied. 'It gave me a chance to get even by killing a couple of Black's murderers.'

'They're not the only ones to die in this room today. One of Black's men brought us here earlier and ended up with a bullet in him. You don't happen to know anything about that do you?' she asked, with suspicion in her voice.

'No. Nothing to do with me. But I can't say that I'm unhappy about his man getting killed.'

It sounded a little dubious to Paula, though she wanted to believe him after his intervention to save her from the clutches of her tormentors.

'And what about me? I was working for Black as well.'

'After what I've seen here, I'd guess that you're not working for him now, are you?'

'No.'

'And anyway, I don't kill women. You're quite safe with me. It's Black that I want to get.'

'He killed Mike,' choked Paula, the horror of his death overtaking her subsiding fears and the realisation hitting her for the first time.

'Who's Mike?' asked Ryall.

'He was a close friend, once.'

'Once?'

'We split up a long time ago.'

'But you still care for him?'

'Yes, of course. Black's men killed him.'

Ryall put an arm around Paula's shoulder, and she buried her face in his chest as tears ran down her cheeks. He kissed the top of her head and rocked gently back and forth, like a mother comforting her child.

'It will pass,' he reassured her. 'It will take time, but it will pass.'

'It was that bitch Tanya that lied to Black about us. Why would she do such a thing?'

'Who's Tanya? The other female with the cleavage?'

'That's the one.'

'Jealousy? Perhaps to get in good favour with Black? Who knows?'

'I know one thing – she's dead if I ever see her again,' Paula hissed, pulling away from Ryall and looking him in the eyes.

He caressed her face, wiping away a tear with his thumb. Cupping her face, he moved to give her a kiss. She pulled back, and then relented. Ryall kissed her, but there was little response from Paula. His fingers went to the button on her blouse.

'No, not now,' she said, touching his hand. 'I'm grateful for what you did, but ...'

'I understand. It's too soon after your friend's death.'

'Yes, some other time – perhaps. In the meantime, I have something that I must do.'

Paula stood, took a pace towards the door and stopped suddenly as a figure entered the doorway.

Her face lit up. 'Mike! You're alive? How?' She rushed to him and threw her arms around his neck. 'They told me you were killed when your car blew up outside the warehouse.' She kissed him. 'You don't know how good it is to see you,' she enthused, running her fingers through his hair and squeezing him tightly.

Mike had his arms around her, while keeping his gun pointed in the direction of the man sitting on the bed watching them. 'I managed to jump clear at the last moment. Are you okay? I was afraid I wouldn't get here in time,' he said, looking at the wound on her head and the bruise, fast turning a dark mauve, on her chin.

She fingered the bruise on her face. 'Yes, I'm fine. What about you? There's a lot of blood here,' she remarked, peeling back the sleeve of his shirt. 'That's a nasty gash.'

'It'll be okay. Who's he, and who are these dead men?' Mike asked.

Ryall stood to face them.

Paula turned to look at him. 'He's the man who stole the simulator, and just saved my life. He stopped two of Black's bastards from raping and killing me. This is Ryall.'

'Ryall? I thought you said he was dead.'

'I did, but it turns out that he wasn't in the car when it exploded. His men weren't so lucky.'

Mike holstered his gun and extended his hand. 'I'm sorry about your men. I owe you a great deal of thanks,' he said, shaking hands with Ryall while keeping his other arm around Paula's shoulder.

'Think nothing of it. I'm glad to have stopped two of Black's cronies from carrying out his dirty work.'

Mike turned to Paula. 'Now that I know you're safe, I ought to get back to the warehouse. I want to keep an eye on Mr Black and his hoods. It won't take him long to realise that his two guards are missing.'

Paula raised her eyebrows asking the question.

'I killed them both and stole their car,' answered Mike.

A gentle smile crossed Ryall's face when he heard Mike mention that two more of Black's men were eliminated. That made five men that he had now lost; he must be getting worried.

'I have to find out what he's up to,' declared Mike.

'Me too, and I want to get my hands on that rat, Tanya. She's the one that grassed on us,' Paula said.

'I wondered why they were waiting for me. I understand your anger, but let me take care of it; it's too dangerous for you now.'

'No more than for you,' Paula insisted.

'Yes, it is. They know your face, but they're unlikely to recognise me. It would be much better if you went back to see Sir Joseph and reported to him what's happened.'

'Okay. If you insist,' Paula reluctantly agreed, collecting her handbag from the floor. 'But let's check out the warehouse first, so that I can give him the latest information.'

'All right. Are you coming with us?' Mike asked Ryall.

He hesitated; he did not want Mr Black to find out that he was still alive, and he did not want Mike or Paula to interfere with Tanya's efforts to obtain details of Mr Black's robbery and mess up their plans to double-cross him. Playing both sides called for a delicate balancing act, and knowing what these two were up to might help him to maintain that fine line.

'Umm, yes, okay, I'll tag along in my car, but remember, I don't want to get too close because he'll recognise me as well.'

The two cars sped back to the warehouse. It was nearly noon on a sunny, Hampshire day and there was now more traffic about on this bright Monday morning. Ryall glanced anxiously around him as they drove through the village where he stole the car. His luck held, and there was no one outside to see them passing through, but he noted the presence of a police car outside the cottage where he had stolen the vehicle. He made a mental note to ditch the car at his first opportunity, and steal something new.

Mike drove into the industrial estate and was immediately aware of something amiss. 'The cars are all gone,' he told Paula.

He motored along the back road to the warehouse.

'Be careful, Mike. If there's anyone here they'll see us.'

'I don't think so. I reckon they've all scarpered.'

'They can't possibly have moved that lot already, surely?'

With a squeal of the brakes, Mike's car skidded to a halt. He drew his gun and, bending low, hurried to the small corrugated door and gingerly opened it. Stepping through the opening, he was immediately aware of an eerie silence.

The warehouse was bare.

'Damn!' he exclaimed. 'How the hell are we going to find them now?'

Paula joined him as Ryall drew up in his car. They searched the warehouse for clues, but found nothing; everything had been removed, even their rubbish.

'He certainly moves fast when he has to,' Paula remarked, standing with hands on hips in the centre of a large empty space. It was as if no one had entered since the building was closed. Only a few holes and scratch marks on the floor told differently.

Mike checked the factory where he had left the bodies of the two guards. They were gone, but the burnt out wreck of his car was still there, smouldering gently. Soon it would be no more than a lump of rusting metal.

'They must have found the bodies and decided to move everything to a different location. They barely had time to take the thing apart, let alone load it on to a lorry and scarper. When I saw it, the assembly was almost complete. I reckon he must be moving it with the ram jacks still fitted. Our Mr Black certainly plans things carefully; he must have already organised backup premises somewhere else.'

'So, what's next?' Paula asked.

'Start looking for them, I guess. It would be useful if we could get the police to help in our search, but that's not possible at the moment, not until I can contact Sir Joseph anyway. What about you, Ryall? Are you going to look for them?'

'I don't know,' he replied, realising there was more to this pair than he had at first thought. 'It was Black and his murderers that I was after for killing my men, and five of them are already dead.'

'I'm sorry about what happened to your men,' remarked Mike.

'They weren't a bad bunch of guys. Petty thieves mostly.

They were all on the wrong side of the law, but didn't deserve to be blown to hell at the whim of a bastard like Black. I aim to get him for that.'

'Perhaps you should team up?' suggested Paula.

'How about it?' Mike asked Ryall. 'We could help each other.'

'I'm not sure. What's your interest in all this?

Mike and Paula looked at each other. They guessed what the other was thinking; should they tell him the truth about why they were there, or not?

Paula shrugged, 'Why not? Two heads are better than one, and he does have a legitimate interest.'

'Okay,' agreed Mike. 'The police have been trying to catch Mr Black for quite a while, without any success, as I'm sure you are aware. He was once an inspector in the Metropolitan Police Force, before he turned to a life of crime, and he still knows a lot of men in the force. Many of them, it seems, remain loyal to him because they feel that he got a raw deal. They still refuse to believe that he's turned sour. That's why he's able to get information on what the police are doing. Every time they get close to him, he finds out about it and slips through their fingers. It's thought that he even murdered another policeman who managed to con his way into becoming a gang member. I'm an ordinary citizen, an ex-mercenary, and Paula's in the RAF. Neither of us has any connections with the police force. We were asked to try and infiltrate his organisation, after the police had discovered that he'd put out a request for a pilot to join his consortium.'

'By who? Who asked you? The police?' enquired Ryall, a frown on his forehead, evidently concerned about what he was hearing.

'Sir Joseph Sterling,' added Paula. 'He's a sort of trouble-shooter for the government, watching over difficult situations that crop up with political figures, the police or with Special Branch, for instance.'

The names of those police establishments sent shivers up Ryall's spine. 'I'm a crook. Not a particularly good or clever one, but nevertheless a crook, and I've done time in jail. I don't think it would be a good idea for me to get mixed up in this with you. I'm still wanted for a few minor offences, and of course I stole the simulator.'

'I'm sure that Sir Joseph would overlook a few minor offences if you were able to help us. Especially when I tell him that you saved my life,' Paula stated, glancing at Mike for confirmation, which she got.

Ryall scratched the back of his head. 'I don't think so. It goes against the grain to work for the police, and besides, I want to see that my men get a decent burial first. Explaining things to their wives and girlfriends will be difficult, but I feel a duty to my men to do it. Black will wait. I've got plenty of time to search for him.'

Mike and Paula were a little puzzled by his remark, and sensed that there was more to it than he was telling. Perhaps he wanted to get Mr Black himself?

'Okay, if that's the way you feel. So be it,' agreed Mike. He looked at Paula. 'There's an airport near here at Eastleigh. Can you fly a light plane if I hire one?'

'I sure can. Thanks to the good old RAF. Have you changed your mind about letting me search with you?'

'Just for the moment. It'll be a lot easier searching the ground for their vehicles if somebody else is piloting.'

'Okay.'

'What about your licence and logbook? We'll need those before they'll let you fly.'

Paula searched in her handbag. 'They're still here, and so's my mobile, thank goodness.'

'Great. With luck we should be able to hire something and start the search. They can't be very far away, and a large lorry like that, along with a convoy of cars and a caravan, should be easy enough to spot from the air so long as we start looking in the right direction before they get too far away.'

Paula nodded. 'I'll drive. I know how to get to the airport. I was born in Southsea, not far from here. Are you sure you won't join us?' she asked Ryall.

'Maybe, later.'

Mike shook Ryall's hand again. 'Good luck, and thanks once again.'

Paula gave him a kiss on the cheek. 'Look after yourself, and many thanks. You never know, we might meet up again sometime.'

He nodded, and left.

They watched him drive out of the site. 'Strange,' remarked Mike. 'I though he'd be only too willing to help us track down this mob.'

'Mmm, me too. Especially with all the threats he made to kill Black after what he did to his men.'

'I'd better ring Suzie and let her know what's happening,' said Mike.

He rang Suzie on Paula's mobile and gave her a quick account of their progress. She agreed to return to her flat and wait to hear from Mike what his next move would be.

'Let's get going. Black's getting further away all the time,' Mike stated.

He and Paula jumped into their car. As they motored out of the industrial estate, on their way to Eastleigh Airport, a pair of eyes watched them from a car, hidden behind long grass and bushes. When they were out of sight, Ryall pulled a tracking device from his pocket and turned it on. He listened to the beep-beep and watched a row of indicator lights. He scanned the device back and forth, noting which direction illuminated the maximum lights. That was the direction the transmitting device was sending out its signal. He smiled, slapped his hand down on the gearstick, put the car in gear and drove off.

9

Investigate

Sir Joseph Sterling sat at the solid oak desk in his plush, Victorian, Whitehall office, and thumbed his way through a pile of papers, his rimless glasses perched on the end of his nose. He had experienced a busy weekend sorting out some problems which had brought him both good and bad news, though this had not prevented him from taking his regular Saturday and Sunday afternoon walks with his dog. This was a ritual that he felt both he and his dog needed, though for very different reasons.

It was mid-morning on a slightly overcast Monday in London, and his secretary, Miss Wilson, had just received the weekend reports. Minutes later, even before she had sorted and brought them through for his attention, the intercom, a relic of a bygone age that Sir Joseph was reluctant to do away with, buzzed and he pressed the button. Miss Wilson informed him that Detective Inspector Brooke was on the line.

Brooke was both a friend and a work colleague. A muscular man of over six feet tall, he had a cleft chin that had a constant look of stubble on it, though he shaved once and often twice a day. His friendship with Sir Joseph Sterling went back several years, to the time when he was a police sergeant eager for advancement and through his tenacity was instrumental in solving a difficult case in which the Whitehall troubleshooter had become involved. The association with Sir Joseph remained, and their personal friendship had grown over the following years.

'Put him through, would you please, Miss Wilson,' instructed Sir Joseph. His telephone rang. 'Good morning, Colin. How are you?'

'Very well, thank you, Sir Joseph, and yourself?'

'Fine; though I've had a busy weekend sorting through a pile of papers. And what is worse is the unmistakable fact that I still have not been able to persuade my bosses to let me retire to my country cottage yet.'

'You're too hard to replace, that's your trouble. Perhaps you should make a few gaffs and let them think you're over the hill, then they might let you go.'

Sir Joseph smiled at the suggestion. 'I doubt it. But anyway, it's not in my nature – I couldn't do it. Not deliberately.'

'No. I have to say that doesn't surprise me. How are Jim and Jenny?'

'My son and his wife are doing well, especially since they went into partnership with Mike and Suzie in their boat building business. That, and his marriage, has given him a little more purpose in life, and he seems to be enjoying the challenge of both. But I'm sure a senior officer in Special Branch didn't telephone me simply to talk about them.'

'No,' replied Brooke, in a more serious tone. 'The main purpose of my call is to acquaint you with a rather nasty robbery that has come to my attention this morning. One that I'm sure you will want to know more about.'

'Oh, what happened?' Sir Joseph asked.

'An aircraft simulator was stolen from a factory in Crawley, West Sussex, over the weekend.'

'Was anyone hurt?'

'Yes. Two guards were killed. One was shot and the other had his throat cut.'

'It sounds nasty, but I don't understand why you think I should be interested.'

'When you hear which aeroplane the simulator is for, you … may change your mind.'

'You have intrigued me, Colin. Which aircraft is it?'

'It's an RAF Harrier Jump Jet.'

'A Harrier! Now why would anyone want to steal a simulator for that?' asked Sir Joseph, his sharp mind running through all the possible answers in a flash.

'Why indeed. Several unsavoury possibilities come to mind, which I'm sure you've also thought of.'

There was a pause. Sir Joseph tapped his teeth with a pencil, while he calculated the various consequences of what the theft might bring.

'Er, yes. You were right to let me know,' he said, running his fingers through his thick, greying hair. 'I must get in touch with the Chief of the Air Staff and warn him to tighten security in all the airfields where Harriers are based.'

'I thought you'd probably want to do that,' Brooke stated.

'Yes. In the first instance, we must assume they've stolen the thing in order to train someone to steal a real aeroplane. The reason behind that will have to wait until later. What are you planning to do first?'

'I'm taking a team to the factory to investigate the robbery. We'll be leaving quite soon. I'll give you another ring after I've done a preliminary check and formed a better idea of what happened.'

'Okay, Colin. I'll speak to you again later,' promised Sir Joseph, returning the telephone to its cradle and pressing the call button on his intercom. 'Miss Wilson, get me the CAS, will you please.'

A team headed by DI Brooke drove the 30-mile journey to Crawley in order to begin their investigation. The security cameras at the factory were linked to a recorder and caught the start of the robbery with the brutal slaying of the guard. That was where Brooke and his team began.

After he had viewed the recording and talked to the manager of the plant, Brooke listened to the information that his men had gathered in their interviews with the factory and office section leaders. All the rest of the staff had been sent home and would have to be questioned at a later date if it was thought necessary.

Sitting in his car with the door open, Brooke telephoned Sir Joseph. 'We've got little to go on, apart from a description of the lorry used, and some rather general details of the men involved. It looks as if about seven men took part in the robbery. The local police patrol unit was able to give us a better description of a bogus guard. They called at the factory and spoke to him, but left after thinking that everything was okay. The camera didn't get a clear view of any of the intruders' features before the wires were cut, because they all masked their faces with baseball caps pulled low. The dim lighting in the area didn't help and allowed them to stay in shadows most of the time.'

'It sounds as if they knew what to expect,' said Sir Joseph.

'Yes. The thieves searched the offices for a module that was missing from the simulator and took it with them, along with a manual showing how to reassemble it. Whoever took it must have some electronic know-how to fix and reinstall it. From the way this robbery was planned, I'd say they probably had some inside information about the layout and security system,' Brooke concluded.

'Hmm. How many people work there?'

'Several hundred. It's quite a big place.'

'That'll make it difficult to find an inside man. Colin, I think we should have a chat about this. Can you come to my office this afternoon?'

'Yes, sir. It'll take me about two hours to get there, depending on how heavy the London traffic is. I should be able to make it by—' he looked at his watch, 'say, four-fifteen to four-thirty.'

'Good. I'll see you about half past four then.'

Brooke slung his mobile on the passenger seat, and slammed the car door shut. He had a brief word with his sergeant before motoring off and heading back towards London.

10

The Search Begins

Following Mr Black's hurried departure from his warehouse, Mike and Paula drove to Eastleigh Airport to hire a plane and search for him. The Cessna 152, piloted by Paula, swept in a wide circle over the main roads leading from the Portsmouth area, but the search for Mr Black's convoy proved fruitless.

The small flying club at Eastleigh was adamant that Paula's flying ability was checked before they allowed her to take out a plane. They insisted that an instructor fly with her for a short test as she was not a member of their club. The Cessna was a plane that she had not piloted for many years, and despite her experience, they were anxious to take all precautions to ensure flight safety. Mike suffered the frustration of knowing that Mr Black was gaining valuable time to escape, and his protestations regarding the urgency of their flight fell on deaf ears. After Paula's test, they at last got airborne, and searched for almost an hour for Mr Black's low-loader and the group of cars in which his thugs and workers would almost certainly be following.

Buzzing over main roads heavy with traffic, and minor roads skirted by green fields, trees and hedges, they were nearing the limit of their search area when Mike noticed a PSV. It was towing a caravan along a single-carriageway minor road, almost a mile behind a canvas-covered lorry, both heading west.

'I saw a PSV similar to that outside the warehouse,' he relayed to Paula over the headset. 'And there was a caravan inside the warehouse, so that could be them.'

'Maybe. But they don't look to be travelling with a lorry, and there are a lot of those types of vehicles on the roads these days.'

'Still, we could check it out.'

Paula banked the Cessna over and they dropped down in height to fly over the PSV and continue above the road. Further along the road was a low-loader with a tarpaulin cover over the freight on its back.

'That caravan had something sticking out of the back window. Did you see it?' asked Mike.

'No. I can't fly the bloody plane at treetop height and examine the vehicles as well. That's your job.'

They approached the lorry.

'That could be it. Get in closer, I want to take a better look at that load,' said Mike.

'We've got to be careful, Mike. The airport called on the radio and said we are in controlled air space and we must move away immediately.'

'Don't worry about that. We can move away when we've taken a good look at that lorry. You saw it when it arrived at the factory. Does it look the same?'

'I didn't really take that much notice. It was just a lorry, and I certainly couldn't tell from this height.'

At that moment a police helicopter swooped into view and travelled along side them. The pilot called them on the radio and repeated the warning that they were flying in controlled air space. To avoid a long explanation, and having in mind that Mr Black may be tuning in to their frequency, Mike said they were checking the area with a view to buying land for a development.

'You can't go buzzing around the countryside willy-nilly in controlled air space without permission,' informed the policeman. 'I'd like a word with you. Please follow me back to Eastleigh Airport.'

'But …'

'No buts sir, or I may be obliged to see to it that your pilot's licence is revoked.'

'I haven't even got a pilot's licence,' muttered Mike, softly.

'We'd better do as they say,' suggested Paula. 'I have, and I don't want to lose it.'

'Yeah, I guess you're right. It's a pity, though – I'd like to have taken a better look at that lorry, just in case.'

They broke away from the roadway and followed the police helicopter back to Eastleigh Airport where, after touching down, Mike carried on his protestations that they were only looking for a suitable building site. They were given a ticking off, as if they were naughty schoolchildren, and let off with a warning, after Mike had concocted an elaborate story to explain his torn and blood-spattered shirt. When they were finally allowed to leave, Mike and Paula jumped into their borrowed Land Rover and headed back towards London.

'It's a good job they didn't want to check our vehicle papers as well,' moaned Mike, 'or we could have been in real trouble.'

'Never mind. We tried our best and couldn't have searched for much longer anyway. At least my licence is still intact.'

'Yes, that's true. It's a pity we were delayed with so many damn questions, otherwise I'd like to have gone back and taken another look for that lorry we spotted.'

'Well, it's too late now. It will be long gone.'

'You're right. Let's get going. We'll need to stop at my flat for a few minutes while I change my clothes. It was bad enough explaining to this lot about the blood, I don't want to visit Sir Joseph wearing a torn shirt like this. It won't take me a moment,' he promised.

'That's okay, we've no need to rush. A few more minutes aren't going to make any difference,' Paula insisted, putting a friendly hand on Mike's leg.

He was flattered by all the attention she was giving him. They had been partners for more than three years before they broke up, and had lost touch until Sir Joseph brought them back together again for this job. Though saying nothing, when she heard that Paula was to be involved in the project, Suzie was a little unsure about Mike working with an old flame. She recognised that he was a bit of a flirt and, although she knew in her heart that the relationship was over and Paula was unlikely to come between them, she was also aware that Mike was not above sleeping with her if he thought he could get away with it. Mike enjoyed playing the irresistible lover, though he wondered if Paula was a bit jealous of his relationship with Suzie and was trying to put a spanner in the works. She had always been a little on the jealous side and it had occurred to him, at the motel, that she may be toying with his affections in order to get even with him for ending their relationship. She blamed him for the parting but, if the truth were known, it was more her anger and jealousy that had driven a wedge between them. When Mike came out of the Army and joined a band of mercenaries who were about to leave on a dangerous mission to Africa, their split became permanent.

'I'll ring Sir Joseph when we get to the flat and arrange a meeting with him. Perhaps he'll be able to find out where Black and his cronies have disappeared to,' said Mike.

The Land Rover slowed to a halt outside number 20, where Mike had a flat in a converted Victorian house in the London suburb of Surbiton. He and Paula clattered up the concrete steps and across the wooden floorboards to the front door of flat number 4. Once inside, Mike shoved the car keys in his pocket, entered the living room and stepped towards the telephone to make his call. A red light on the answerphone was flashing, letting him know that a message had been left. He pressed the button to listen to the call and heard Suzie's voice.

'Mike, I've tried ringing you on your mobile phone, but I can't get a reply. Mr Brown, the man who interviewed me for the pilot's job, telephoned to ask me if I was still interested in it. I said yes, of course, and he wants me to meet him to talk about it and has asked me to bring clean clothes with me, so he must be expecting to take me somewhere straight away. I delayed the time of our meeting for as long as I could, hoping to get in touch with you so that you could follow us. If you get this message in time, I'm to meet him at the entrance gate to the old Portsmouth Docks where all the exhibitions are now held. I'm seeing him at five-thirty. I hope you can make it. If not, I'll try to contact you when I can. Love you. 'Bye.'

'What's the time?' he asked Paula.

'Nearly half past three.'

'Damn. There's barely about enough time for me to get there. I lost my bloody mobile in that burnt-out car. I should be there to follow them. We need to know where Black has moved to and I don't want Suzie left out on a limb on her own. I must get going straight away or I'll never get there in time.'

'Do you know your way around Portsmouth?' Paula asked.

'No, not very well. I'll follow the signs.'

'Well, I do. I'll go instead. You telephone Sir Joseph and arrange to meet him as we agreed. He'll want to know the latest details. If I get to the meeting place in time, I'll follow the pair of them and give you a ring on my mobile with the location of their hideout.'

'Okay. I suppose that's a better idea. You get going now, and be careful, Black's a ruthless man and he knows your face.'

'I'll be okay. Like Ryall said, he thinks I'm dead, so he won't be expecting me.'

'He may not be so ready to believe that when his guards fail to return.'

'True. Anyway, I'll be careful,' insisted Paula, giving Mike a kiss on the cheek. 'I'll need the car keys.'

'Oh, yes.'

He pulled them from his pocket; Paula took them and smiled a goodbye as she stepped through the doorway.

'I guess it's the train for me,' Mike said to himself, lifting the receiver to telephone Sir Joseph and make his appointment. 'Or maybe I could borrow a hire car from the garage down the road. The owner owes me a favour. That's a good idea. I think I'll ring him first.'

11

Whitehall Boss

Leaving his sergeant to continue the investigation of the simulator robbery in Crawley, DI Brooke drove to London. The Whitehall offices that he was heading for in the heart of the capital had their own underground car parking spaces. Brooke was thankful they did, as he slowly cut his way through the dense central London traffic and headed down the ramp, after showing his ID card to the armed man on guard who scrutinised it carefully, despite Brooke's frequent use of the car park. Things looked casual enough at the entrance, but this only disguised the hidden depths of security that existed, ever since an attempt to blow up the building had been detected and foiled. The bomb was found more by luck than because of any vigilance, and additional security cameras and armed guards were deployed following the discovery, to counter any further attempts.

Brooke arrived at Sir Joseph's Victorian office a little after 4.30 p.m., composed himself, and was shown into the room by his portly and slightly frumpy secretary, Miss Wilson.

'Come in, Colin. Do sit down. Would you like a cup of coffee?' asked Sir Joseph, rising from behind his well-polished antique desk and laying his glasses on top of the large blotting pad.

'Yes, please. I'd love one.'

'Two coffees please, Miss Wilson, if you would be so kind.'

Miss Wilson smiled her consent, and Sir Joseph closed the door behind her.

Brooke sat on the vacant chair, ever present in front of Sir Joseph's desk, and inhaled the glorious smell of polished wood. It gave the room a distinctive aroma, one that brought the office to mind whenever he encountered it. Sir Joseph returned to his seat.

'I asked you to come here because … well, I've a slight confession to make.'

A surprised look came over Brooke's face. 'I can't imagine what it can be. Nothing serious, I trust?'

'No, nothing too serious. But I have gone out on a bit of a limb, with the best of intentions of course.'

'Of course. So it's not serious enough to get you dismissed then?' Brooke said, tongue in cheek.

'Oh no, nothing like that. Just an eagerness to get results.' Sir Joseph paused for a moment and took a deep breath. 'Do you recall the sad case of the death of Inspector Tom Williams?'

'Ah, yes. Williams was a friend of mine. In the early days we were on the beat together. He was trying to infiltrate the gang of that rogue ex-Metropolitan police officer, Robert Black, when he was found with two bullets in his back.'

'That's right. We naturally suspected that Mr Black had a hand in it, and assumed that he'd found out about Inspector Williams because he still had some contacts in the force somewhere. But we never managed to establish where the leak came from, and we were never able to prove anything against him.'

'No, we weren't. However, there was a lot of circumstantial evidence which suggested that it was him. I'm still hoping that we'll get Black for that one day.'

'You may yet get your chance, and soon,' Sir Joseph intimated.

Brooke rose visibly in his seat at the remark. 'Just tell me how, and give me that chance.'

'Well, recently I got a tip-off about our Mr Black. I was informed that one of his known associates was scouting around for a couple of pilots, presumably for a job that he, or someone he's working with, has in mind.'

'A couple of pilots!' Brooke exclaimed. 'It must be something very big that he's planning. It sounds like he wants to either smuggle something in or out of the country, and I would imagine that he's not likely to find too much trouble in getting someone to do that for him,' he suggested.

'Ordinarily, I would agree with you. His difficulty, though, was that he was looking for two combat pilots.'

'Combat pilots? Now that does change things, and it can't be a simple smuggling operation either. It sounds much more sinister to me. It also makes his search a lot more difficult, even impossible. Combat pilots don't usually turn to a life of crime when they leave the services. Most of them want a job where they can keep flying, or at least still be around aeroplanes.'

'Yes, I agree. That's partly why I asked Mike, Suzie and Paula to get involved in this investigation.'

'Mike Randle and Suzie Drake? The ex-mercenaries who now run a boat building business with your son and his wife?'

'The same. Suzie is very talented, and knows how to fly an assortment of aeroplanes. I considered that if Mr Black couldn't get a combat pilot, he may think it worthwhile recruiting a good all-round pilot and taking a chance with them.'

'I'm beginning to follow you. Who's Paula?'

'Paula Hardcastle. She's an old friend of Mike Randle's, or perhaps I should say she's an old flame. They met when Mike was in the Army and she was in the RAF. They were quite close for a few years. After a while they drifted apart, and when he became a mercenary and went abroad, they split up. Then, of course, Mike met Suzie and they've been together ever since.'

'So why Paula? Isn't it a bit risky bringing her and Mike together again?'

'Yes, it may be. But I needed her expertise as well. I wanted to try and make absolutely certain that I got at least one person accepted into Mr Black's gang. I met Paula Hardcastle through an old friend of mine who's a Group Captain in the Royal Air Force. Paula's an intelligent woman who has a passion for flying. She'd mastered most light planes, gliders, and even some helicopters, and was still looking for more. Because of her flying skills and her eagerness to get on in life, she got herself selected for the training course on fighter aeroplanes. That's quite a feat for a woman. She flew them until quite recently and seemed an ideal candidate, so I asked if I could borrow her – if she agreed to the idea.'

'I presume she did?'

'Yes, though she did ask for some additional favours. I was happy to use what influence I have to help her get back into flying afterwards, but less keen on giving her the extra money she asked for.'

'Money before country, eh? Did you agree to that?'

'Yes. She was, as she so forcefully pointed out, risking her life for something that she did not volunteer for, so I acceded to her request for danger money.'

'She wasn't forced to do the job for you.'

'No, but I made it clear that I was desperate to get her on board. Even so, she was happy to get away from her desk job, and jumped at the chance when she learned that Mike Randle was also involved.'

'A desk job?'

'Yes, she was forced to eject when her plane developed a fault, and they grounded her temporarily.'

'I see. Does Suzie Drake know about her involvement?'

'Oh, yes, of course. I wouldn't dream of letting her face that situation without first telling her and giving her the opportunity to reject it, if she was too unhappy about it.

She is very professional, and she trusts her instincts about Mike.'

'So you have your team, but did Black accept either of them?'

'Both women were seen by his man, a Mr Brown, but unfortunately there were other pilots to consider and he rejected Suzie, but did accept Paula, probably because of her fighter training.'

'Could he discover the real reason why she's there?'

'I hope not – for her sake. The beauty about all of these people, is that none of them are connected to the police force in any way, so are not likely to be known by Mr Black. I've kept the whole thing unofficial, so that news of what they are doing for me cannot leak out and put them in danger. I don't want a repetition of the problem that Inspector Williams unfortunately had.'

'I understand that. So what is all this is leading to? The assumption that the simulator robbery is a part of Black's plans?'

'That's right. You've just come from a company that's had a Harrier Jump Jet simulator stolen. A highly sophisticated combat fighter aeroplane.'

'I get your drift. So, he's going to use it to train a couple of pilots, and then what? Steal a plane to sell it, or perhaps to use it for a robbery?'

There was a gentle tap on the door and Miss Wilson entered with a tray carrying a plate of biscuits and two cups of coffee, which she handed to each of them, laying the plate on the desk. Sir Joseph quickly grabbed the plain chocolate digestive. Not that Brooke would have taken it, knowing that it was his favourite biscuit.

'Thank you, Miss Wilson,' said Sir Joseph, waiting for the door to be closed before continuing. 'Yes, for a robbery I suspect. Mr Black's not into revolutionary things. But, having said that, he's greedy and wants riches and the power that it brings, so it is possible that he may try stealing a Harrier simply to sell it to some unsavoury person, or country.'

'Even without any logistical back-up or spares?'

'It's surprising what you can buy on the black market these days,' stated Sir Joseph, sipping his coffee.

'I see. So, do you have any more information about what Black's up to or where he's located?' Brooke asked.

'No, not yet. I'm hoping to receive those details very soon. Mike Randle is keeping an eye on the situation for me. He telephoned a short while ago to say that he's coming in to see me. Paula was with him, but she is going off somewhere for some reason or other. He'll explain it all when he gets here.'

'Paula? If she was with him do you think that means Black didn't want her after all?'

'Possibly. We'll find out when he arrives. He didn't give me any details, because I told him not to ring me unless it was important, and even then under no circumstances to say anything about the job over the telephone, in case it was overheard.'

'Is that possible, here in Whitehall?' Brooke asked, somewhat incredulous.

'It is possible. There's a lot of sophisticated electronic eavesdropping equipment available on the market these days and, after the unfortunate death of Inspector Williams, I don't want to take *any* chances. I would like you to stay and sit in on this one, Colin. I need someone who I can trust to handle the police work on this job, and keep me informed of what's happening.'

'Of course. I'm happy to do anything I can to catch that turncoat Black.'

Mike Randle arrived a little over half an hour later and was shown into the office. He and DI Brooke had met in the past and knew one another through Sir Joseph. After accepting a welcome cup of coffee, he related the hazardous events that he and Paula had been through. He told them about the other pilot, Tanya, and related how Ryall, the man who stole the simulator, had saved Paula's life at the motel. After adding his moan that Mr Black and his entourage had disappeared, presumably after finding his dead guards, he explained that they had searched the area by plane, but had obtained no results before they were challenged by the police and were instructed to return to the airfield.

'If Ryall's been to prison then we should have a file on him. What do you know about this other woman, Tanya?' asked Sir Joseph.

'Not a lot. Mainly what Paula told me. That she used to fly transport planes for the RAF. She's about thirty-five, attractive, has an outstanding figure and red hair.'

'In that case she shouldn't be too difficult to trace. I'll make enquiries with my RAF contact later,' decided Sir Joseph, lifting his telephone and asking Miss Wilson to arrange for the file on Ryall to be sent over from Records straight away.

'What you've said ties in with a report that I got first thing this morning,' stated Brooke. 'It seems there was an anonymous telephone call to the emergency services informing them about a car that had gone off the clifftop road near Southsea. When the police got there, all they found was a burnt-out car, a lot of bodies and counterfeit bank notes scattered everywhere. Forensics are looking into the possibility that it was a bomb that caused the accident. That must have been the car with Ryall's gang in it that you spoke of.'

'At least that part appears to check out. Do go on,' Sir Joseph insisted.

Mike then gave more details about Paula's close shave with Mr Black's men, and said how grateful she was that Ryall had intervened to save her life.

'We decided to explain to Ryall what we were doing, in the hope that he would help us search for Black. But he wanted to see that his men got a decent burial, so he declined to join us,' Mike told them. 'We were sorry that he felt unable to team up with us. He said it was because of an outstanding record for petty crime that the law wants him for, and he was unhappy about getting involved with the police.'

'I'm sure that we could have turned a blind eye to any petty crimes considering the seriousness of this investigation and the possible dire consequences if Mr Black were to succeed. However ...'

'We told him that,' interrupted Mike, 'but he was still reluctant to join in with us.'

There was a tap on the door and Miss Wilson entered clasping a red folder. Sir Joseph took it and smiled a thank-you at her, then opened it, slipped on his glasses and began to scan the details.

'Well, as I was about to say, I'm sorry to disappoint you, but Mr Ryall is not quite what he said he was,' Sir Joseph stated.

'What do you mean?' asked Mike, a frown crossing his brow.

'You said that he is the one who organised the stealing of the simulator from the factory in Crawley,' said Brooke. 'I've just come from that factory; two guards were killed in the robbery.'

'And according to this file, he is also suspected of several other murders and has a hit-and-run manslaughter charge hanging over him.'

Mike looked shocked. 'He told Paula that no one was hurt in the robbery.'

'He lied. I wonder how many more lies he told you,' said Sir Joseph, peering over the top of his glasses.

'He still saved her life,' Mike maintained.

Brooke spoke up. 'That may well have been solely to avenge the death of his men. I'm sure that we're all very grateful to him for saving Paula's life, but it doesn't excuse the other atrocities that he's carried out.'

'No, of course not. It's just that it's such a disappointment to find out that he's not the man I thought he was.'

'I understand,' said Sir Joseph. 'He must be apprehended for his part in this crime, but our first priority is to find Mr Black and stop him from whatever evil deed it is that he is embarking on. Do you have any idea what that may be?'

'No, but we might still get an opportunity to find out,' stated Mike. 'Paula and I dropped into my flat on the way here. Suzie tried to ring me and left a message on my answerphone. It seems that the man who interviewed her for the original job, a Mr Brown, rang her back this morning and asked if she was still interested in it. She told him she was, and is due to meet him sometime around now. Paula has dashed down to Portsmouth to see if she can get there when they meet, in order to follow them.'

'That means they must want her as Paula's replacement. What a stroke of luck,' said Sir Joseph.

'She said they'd arranged to meet near the old docks in Portsmouth. If I hadn't lost my mobile in the car explosion, I could've been there to keep an eye on them.'

'Never mind. Paula's on their trail and we've still got Suzie close to them.'

'I just hope that Paula gets there in time. She didn't have long, and it's cutting things a bit fine,' Mike declared.

'Yes. Unless we can locate Mr Black, Suzie is going to be in the same position that Paula was, out on her own, and unprotected,' Sir Joseph stated.

'And the traitorous female pilot, Tanya, is there. It seems that she'll do anything to eliminate any rivals.'

The intercom buzzed. Miss Wilson informed Sir Joseph there was a telephone call for him. It was Paula on the line, using her mobile.

'Is Mike with you?' she asked.

'Yes, he's here.'

'Will you kindly give him the message that I was too late

to meet our old friend? She had already left on her venture.'

'Thank you, Paula. I'll tell him. I think you should return home now, for a much-deserved rest after your exertions. I'll contact you in a day or two. Goodbye.'

Sir Joseph returned the receiver to its cradle and tapped his teeth with a pencil.

'Bad news?' asked Mike.

'Yes. Paula was unable to get to the meeting place in time to follow Suzie.'

'Damn. Now Suzie really is out on a limb and with all the problems that Black has encountered today, he is unlikely to allow her any freedom to make a call.'

'Yes. I'm sure you are right, but Suzie is resourceful. I'm certain she'll find some way of contacting us.'

'I hope so.'

'I'll get some men to check that warehouse and the motel,' stated Brooke. 'It might give us a clue. And I'll see if the traffic control boys can get a lead on where that low-loader is heading and put out a general call for the boys in blue to be on the lookout as well.'

'Thank you, Colin,' said Sir Joseph, rising from his seat to shake his hand. 'Report anything directly to me. Don't use the telephone to pass on any critical information, unless I indicate to you that it's all right to talk.'

Brooke understood. 'Due to the difficulties in passing on any information, perhaps we should meet again in a couple of days to review our progress?'

'A good idea, Colin. We'll meet here in my office. Ring me during the afternoon to confirm what time I'll be available.'

'Okay,' agreed Brooke, smiling a goodbye to Mike before leaving.

'I'd better get searching too,' Mike announced.

'I'll arrange for an army helicopter to be at your disposal. You should be able to cover a wider area in it without any problems of straying into controlled air space. Do you have any idea which direction they are likely to take?' Sir Joseph asked.

'No, not really, though I think it's unlikely they would come back towards London after hijacking the plane and making for the Southwest. I spotted an MPV from the air that looked similar to one I saw in the warehouse car park, and there was a lorry not too far in front of it. Unfortunately, that's when we were interrupted by the police helicopter patrol, before we were able to check it out. They insisted that we returned to the airport with them.'

'That's a pity.'

'Yes. I could have done with your assistance then, but knew it was too risky contacting you on an open line. So I'll start in that locality and move in a westerly direction. I've got a hunch that it's where he's heading for.'

'Good. I agree,' stated Sir Joseph, extending his hand. 'Keep me posted on even the smallest development, but be careful what you say over the telephone. I don't want Mr Black slipping through my fingers this time, or letting him find out about Suzie's involvement.'

They shook hands and Mike left to continue his search. The big difference now was that it was a crucial search for the one woman in his life who really meant something to him, Suzie. He knew it was like searching for a needle in a haystack, but he had to keep trying. Her life may depend on him.

Later that evening, Suzie arrived at Mr Black's new hideout, an old barn, set in the corner of a large field and hidden from the road by a small copse. Mr Brown had met her in Portsmouth and taken Suzie to a nearby restaurant where he had wined and dined her. During the meal he explained about the riches that she could quickly earn, before asking her to join their 'consortium', as he put it. He said that things had not worked out with one of the previous candidates, and they had had to let her go, paying her off with a handsome bonus. Suzie knew that Paula was one of the two pilots who was chosen to join them and wondered if it was her they had paid off, and how they had paid her off. She was astute enough to realise that Mr Black was not the sort of person to take chances.

Suzie had met Paula only once, at the start of their mission to infiltrate Mr Black's group. The only previous knowledge that she had of her was from what Mike had said, some of which was critical of her attitude, though he remained fond of her. Even so, Suzie feared for what they might have done to her.

With agreement reached about what was expected of her, and how much she would earn for her skills, Suzie was driven by Mr Brown on a 100-mile journey to the hideout on the outskirts of Honiton in Devon. By the time they reached the barn it was late, and Mr Black and Miss Lilac were already occupying the double bedroom in the caravan.

The barn itself was big – very big. It was large enough not only to house the simulator and the caravan, but also the low-loader and a mobile lifting crane, tucked away in one corner.

Suzie was shown into the caravan, but slept in a cramped single bedroom, wondering if Mike had got her message in time and was able to follow them. She was also curious to know whether it was Paula in the next room with Mr Black. The following morning would bring the answer to her question.

12

The Task

In the barn, on the outskirts of Honiton, Tanya emerged from the caravan bathroom and muttered to herself about wanting a proper shower, and not simply having to make do with a strip-down wash. Suzie, from her bedroom, listened to her moans and could understand her sentiments, though she had encountered much worse conditions in the jungle when she was a mercenary. Much of this annoyance had begun the previous evening when Mr Black mentioned to Tanya that another female pilot would be joining them. The presence of another women would interfere with Tanya's plans to squeeze more money and information out of Mr Black, and she did not care for that. Gone was the lever that she was the only pilot, and he would have to take special care of her, giving her a better opportunity to find out more about the robbery that he was planning.

It was 8 a.m. on Tuesday. The early morning sun, beginning to filter through the haze, was already heating up the barn, which in turn heated up the caravan. Tanya had skipped outside for a smoke, watched by Suzie from her window. She was now aware that Paula was the one she was replacing, and being by nature careful, knew that she needed to find out how close this female bed-partner was to Mr Black before taking the risk of confiding in her, if she was ever to do that at all.

Suzie had a wash and dressed in a canary yellow blouse and matching shorts. She wandered down the corridor into the kitchen area, and looked through the cupboards. The choice for breakfast was very limited. It was either cereal or toast; at least there was some milk in the refrigerator. Suzie sat at the pull-down table in the dining room and ate a bowlful of cereal and had a cup of coffee.

To the casual onlooker, she was idly glancing around while eating her breakfast. In reality, Suzie was closely observing things and noticed that the caravan rear window, table, floor and many of the fittings had recent damage to them. Chunks had been gouged out of the woodwork and the window frame was severely dented. She was aware that Mr Black's hideout had previously been in the Portsmouth area and wondered if this damage had anything to do with his sudden move.

Tanya came in and jammed two slices of bread in the toaster, which disappeared when she shoved the lever down. She made herself a cup of coffee and did not try to disguise the fact that she was unhappy about something.

'I'm Suzie,' said the new arrival, extending her hand. 'Though it seems that I'm to be called Miss Ochre for some strange reason.'

'Miss Lilac,' replied Tanya, ignoring the offer to shake hands, instead lighting another cigarette now that Mr Black, who complained about the smell, was outside checking on the progress his men were making. 'All Mr Black's employees are known by a colour.'

'Oh, why's that?'

'It means that if the law catches any of them, they can't give too much away, including anyone's identity.'

'That seems a little odd, but I guess it's a sensible precaution. What happened to the woman that I'm replacing?' asked Suzie, finishing her cereal.

'She left,' was the terse reply.

111

Suzie wanted to ease herself into place slowly and not cause any ripples. Miss Lilac was clearly annoyed by something, so she dropped that line of approach.

'Have you flown fighters before?' Suzie enquired in a gentle tone, trying not to aggravate the situation by verbally retaliating, and wanting to be seen only as friendly.

'No. Only transporters. Not that it's any business of yours,' Tanya said, biting an aggressive chunk out of her toast.

She was making it clear that she was not interested in talking, so Suzie picked up her bowl, strolled to the sink and rinsed it. After putting it in the rack she went to the bathroom to brush her teeth, with the brand new toothbrush that Mr Brown had provided for her, in the right colour of course.

'Even the toothbrush is ochre,' she mused. 'Colour co-ordination of everything.'

Stubbing her cigarette out, Tanya stood in the caravan doorway and Suzie, emerging from the bathroom, stood behind her. Mr Black approached. Tanya wondered how long it would be before the job took place, and how often she would have to try keeping him sweet on her while at the same time avoiding him taking advantage of her at every opportunity. Worse still, was he likely to try the same thing with the attractive new arrival? She thought that it was highly likely, and if the new woman found more favour with Mr Black than she did, that would put a severe dent in her plans and totally nullify her effort in getting rid of the previous candidate.

'Ah, Miss Lilac, it's good to see you looking refreshed once again, after your difficult experience and the delay,' Mr Black enthused, rather more than was necessary she thought. He glanced over her shoulder. 'And Miss Ochre. Welcome to our consortium. I am Mr Black, your new employer,' he said.

'Thank you, Mr Black.' Suzie smiled, ingratiatingly, knowing that Tanya could not afford to keep ignoring her if she looked like becoming a rival to reckon with.

'The barn is very cosy, but it smells,' Miss Lilac complained.

'I'm sure you'll get used to it. We'll only be here for a few days and it's the best alternative to the warehouse. At least you still have the comfort of the caravan. The rest of my men have to make do with sleeping bags on the hard floor,' Mr Black chided.

Miss Lilac shrugged her shoulders slightly, with a look of resignation at the slight rebuttal she was obliged to endure in front of the new arrival. Mr Black offered her a hand as she descended the three steps from the caravan, which she declined to his slight annoyance, but Suzie did not, wishing to create an early good impression.

'The caravan seems to have been damaged recently,' Suzie probed.

'Ah, yes. Well, unfortunately we were forced to move in rather a hurry and didn't have time to fully dismantle the simulator ram jacks. The quickest way to transport them was to load them into the caravan via the rear window,' said Mr Black, slipping comfortably back into the method of explanation that he had learnt in the police force. 'It was a bit of a tight squeeze to get them in and some damage resulted. It shouldn't spoil your stay there.'

'No, I'm sure it won't,' agreed Suzie.

'Mr Green has completed his work on the modules, or whatever it was that needed doing, and we're ready for the two of you to begin. As there is only room for one of you at a time in the simulator and you can absorb only so much information in one go, you will take turns in using it, while the other one watches. You should endeavour to learn from each other.'

Suzie cast a sideways look at Tanya, thinking, 'That might not be as easy as it sounds unless she lightens up. I wonder what the problem is. Ten to one it's because she sees me as a rival for the job. If I remember rightly, there's only one pilot's seat in a Harrier and it almost certainly means that when it comes to the real flying, he'll only need one of us, so I'll have to make sure he chooses me.'

'I hope that thing is safe. It's a long way up there,' Tanya insisted, staring up at the simulator cabin mounted on top of the four massive ram jacks.

'Mr Green has assured me that everything is working properly, and he has run through all the test procedures without any problem.'

'Yes, I know. The noise of those jack things going up and down kept me awake last night,' she grumbled.

'You must be a very light sleeper, my dear. I didn't hear a thing and slept like a log.'

The two women climbed the steps leading to the rear entrance of the simulator. At the top, Suzie stopped and turned to face Mr Black.

'What exactly is it that you want us to do with this aircraft?'

'All in good time, Miss Ochre. For the moment, all I want the pair of you to do, is learn to fly the Harrier so expertly that you could do it in your sleep. Is that clear?'

'Perfectly,' she replied, 'but it would help us to know how long we've got, to become experts.'

'All in good time.'

He was not going to give anything away before he needed to, she realised. Not that it was any great surprise to Tanya. She had already discovered that Mr Black liked to keep control of everything himself.

'Still, he did say we'd only be here for a few more days. That must mean the date for the job is close,' Tanya thought. The comment had not gone unnoticed by Suzie either, despite Mr Black's reluctance to confirm exact details.

Outside the barn, the first day of June brought with it a clear sky and sunshine, blessing people with their first real

114

taste of a hot summer's day. Inside the barn, under a timber and thatched roof, the cool temperature gradually rose and climbed even higher in the enclosed cockpit of the simulator cabin, with the electronic modules only adding to the heat. Both women had removed their outer garments and donned anti-gravity flying suits. Mr Green showed them how to buckle up in the seat, set the dial for their weight, and plug in their radio and air connectors. Their training then began, with Tanya insisting that she be the first to get behind the controls. It was not long before beads of sweat glistened on her face, made her hands sticky and ran down between her breasts, irritating her.

While the women were in the simulator, under the watchful eyes of Mr Green controlling things from his electronics console, Mr Black and Mr Brown left on a journey. They were cautious, and wanted to check out the premises where they were to conclude the deal after perpetrating their crime. The move to the barn had been very inconvenient, but brought with it one distinct advantage; the location of their final transaction was now much closer. The barn location was even considered as a possible site for the whole operation at one time, but was rejected for its lack of seclusion compared to the warehouse.

With their journey now a shorter distance, Mr Black and Mr Brown returned within three hours to the barn, where Tanya and Suzie were taking a lunch break. Suzie noticed that Mr Black looked sternly at the pair of them as he entered, and wondered whether he expected them to continue right through the day without a break.

'Tough luck if he did,' she thought. 'My brain needs a rest every once in a while; it can't take new commands continuously. I'm really thankful that I've such a wide experience of a variety of planes, or it would be an almost impossible task to absorb so much new information. Tanya must be struggling to grasp it all.'

Following their short break, the women returned to the simulator where Tanya's annoyance at Suzie's presence kept her from concentrating properly. She became frustrated with mistakes that she continually made, and her inability to remember the instructions passed to her by Mr Green over the headphones.

'Oh fuck!' she yelled, after having crashed the plane for the fourth time in a row.

Leaning over her shoulder, Suzie put both hands on top of hers. 'Gently, Miss Lilac. This isn't a big lumbering plane like the ones you've been used to. It needs coaxing slowly.'

With Tanya's hands beneath hers, Suzie manipulated the controls with dexterity, lifting the Harrier from the ground in a successful vertical take-off.

'How on earth did you manage to learn that so quickly?' Tanya asked, in amazement.

'I've flown quite a number of different planes, including a variety of helicopters. You need patience, and a similar light touch to lift some of them off the ground slowly and keep the aircraft on an even keel. It's all a question of balance.'

'Oh, right. Thanks.'

'That's okay. We should try to help each other. It looks as if we've only got a few days, and that's not nearly enough time to learn how to fly a sophisticated plane like this properly, even if we are experienced pilots.'

'Yes, you're right,' said Tanya, warming to Suzie now that her anger had subsided.

Light streamed into the cabin as Mr Black entered. 'That was a good lift-off Miss Lilac. I watched it on the screen outside. You are definitely getting the hang of it.'

'Yes, she's doing well, isn't she?' commented Suzie, eager to get into Tanya's good books to better her chances of having an ally and coaxing information from her.

'I am improving,' she declared. 'But how the hell do you

116

expect me to fly this very difficult plane when I'm sweating like a pig?' she asked.

'You could remove your anti-g flying suits. That should cool you down quite a bit,' he suggested.

'We have to know how to fly this contraption with a full kit on. It's the only way we'll get a true feeling of what it's like piloting the real aircraft. Unless, when it comes to the job, you are expecting us to fly the plane practically naked.'

'No, of course not, my dears. But you could learn to master the controls first, and then try it with full flying equipment on afterwards.'

That made sense. 'Okay, but we don't want all your blokes coming in here to gawk at us.'

Suzie nodded in agreement.

'I shall see to it personally. Only Mr Green and I will enter the simulator while you are in here.'

Tanya squeezed out of the cockpit, and divested herself of the flying suit, which left her dressed only in bright red underwear. Mr Black gazed at her glistening figure and ample cleavage, with desire written all over his face. Suzie slipped out of her suit under the roving eye of Mr Black, admiring her slim, athletic figure. Two lovely females, but with differing qualities. What a lucky man he was, to have such an agreeable choice, but now was not the right time, he knew. His cheeks expanded as he puffed the air out of his lungs, licked his lips and turned to exit the cabin. Tanya smiled after the door had closed, once more cutting out the bright sunshine of the day.

'It's obvious that he fancies you,' stated Suzie.

'I know,' Tanya replied. 'He likes slobbering over my big tits.' She knew what was on his mind, and knew that it was the one weakness in his armour she was able to exploit; though so far she had been able to extract few details about the job and none of what his plans were.

'It's a bit of a problem,' she conceded. 'I badly need the

money from this job, so I don't want to upset him, but I'm not happy with him thinking he can have me any time he wants to. You'd better watch out too, I saw the way he looked you over. I'm sure he'll try to get into your knickers as well. It wouldn't do for both of us to let him have his way,' she warned, making it clear that she did not want Suzie to rival her in attempting to gain an advantage from Mr Black.

'Well, I need this job and the money too. I'll have to deal with that problem if and when it arises.'

'I'm sorry I was a bit off with you earlier,' Tanya said, trying the friendly approach.

'That's okay. It's always difficult when someone new comes in at the last minute.'

'My name's Tanya,' she said, extending her hand.

They shook hands, with Suzie happy that they had broken the ice between them at last.

'Paula, the woman you replaced, didn't leave. Not of her own accord, anyway,' Tanya stated.

'What do you mean?' she was asked.

Tanya told Suzie the same story that she gave to Mr Black about Mike and Paula. Suzie knew that Mike would not have been so stupid as to threaten Mr Grey with a gun and then shoot him, and concluded that Tanya's story was a lie. For what reason, she was unsure, but after experiencing Tanya's attitude towards her, and knowing how much importance she seemed to place on the job, she could make a likely guess and not be far wrong.

'So what happened to them?' asked Suzie.

'Paula was taken away. I don't know if they let her go or got rid of her,' she lied, 'and her boyfriend's car caught fire and blew up after they shot at it. They said he was killed.'

Suzie had to suppress her shock at the news as best she could. Even so, she was unable to hide it completely.

'Are you okay?' asked Tanya.

Suzie had to think quickly. 'Yes, thanks. Though it gives

you quite a fright to know that Mr Black kills people who work for him when he's finished with them. It makes you wonder what he's got in mind for us after the job's all over.'

'Yes. That's my worry too, especially as he also got rid of all the men who stole the simulator for him.'

'He sounds ruthless. Perhaps that's why Mr Brown insisted that I gave him my mobile, to stop me telling anyone where I am?'

'Quite likely. He's taken mine as well. Mr Black's very paranoid about keeping the location of his hideout a secret. That's why we had to move in such a hurry.'

'I'm still a bit hot,' said Suzie. 'I think I'll go for a short walk outside to get some fresh air.'

'Good idea. I'll join you in moment for a smoke.'

Suzie slipped into her blouse and shorts, and stepped outside the barn. There, she thought about Mike and all they had been through. Tears welled up in her eyes and she wanted to cry, but knew she could not. The guard, roaming up and down, would see that something was wrong. Suzie wiped away a tear that rolled down her cheek, and quietly resolved to avenge his death. And if Tanya had grassed on him as she suspected, then she too would have something to answer for. Meanwhile, Suzie knew that she must gain her confidence if she was to learn more. She took in deep gulps of air to compose herself before Tanya joined her. They chatted for a few minutes while she smoked her cigarette, after which they returned to the simulator, watched intently by Mr Black and Mr Green.

By late afternoon, both women had made progress and needed a short rest. Mr Black allowed Tanya to wander outside to have a smoke. After putting on an overall, she grabbed her handbag, slung it over her shoulders and stepped from the simulator. Outside in the bright sunshine, Tanya lit her cigarette and puffed away as the large orange ball in the sky threw out its warm shimmering rays on its inexorable drop towards the horizon. While Tanya smoked her cigarette, Suzie made a cup of coffee in the caravan for the two of them.

Stubbing out her cigarette butt, Tanya wandered among the cars and scanned the distant fields and woods for Ryall, while attempting to look disinterested in her surroundings.

The guard wandered up and down with his sub-machine gun slung over his shoulder. When he had reached the far end of the barn, and was at the farthest distance away from Tanya, she was suddenly hit by the sun's reflection. It was directed at her from among the trees, and flashed at her a couple of times. It was a signal from Ryall; it had to be. He had used the tracking device and found her. They were back in touch again and could now continue with their plan. Tanya dipped into her handbag, pulled out her lipstick and compact, and pretended to freshen her lips. She turned the tracking device off, hidden in the bottom of her lipstick holder, in the way that Ryall had shown her when he gave it to her at the motel.

The mugs of coffee smelled good when Suzie brought them out, and the pair chatted while they drank and Tanya lit another cigarette, now much happier that Ryall had made contact.

'How was it that the previous location wasn't kept a secret?' Suzie casually asked.

'Well, they discovered that two guards were missing and Mr Black ordered the move straight away. I've never seen so many people shift so quickly. They had everything packed and ready to go in less than an hour. They practically forced the ram jacks into the caravan through the back window.'

'I saw the damage. So, did they find the guards? What happened to them?'

'Yes, they were dead, and they didn't waste time once they were discovered. Everybody was ordered to help get the move under way. They didn't even bother to bury the blokes.

They simply bundled them into the boot of a car and presumably got rid of them after we arrived here. Why do you ask?'

'Just curious,' said Suzie. 'Mr Brown told me they'd decided to move when we were talking in the restaurant, but didn't say why. That's the reason we had to come such a long way, he said.'

'Oh, I see.'

'And it again shows how little they think of the people who work for them.'

'Yes. That's a bit frightening.'

'Did they say who they thought was responsible for the dead guards?'

'No. No one mentioned anything about it. They quickly packed and left. You seem very interested in everything that's going on.'

'I'm trying to get a full picture of what this crowd is like, and what my chances of survival are,' insisted Suzie, 'and I'm not very happy with what you've told me.'

'I can believe that.'

Tanya seemed satisfied with the explanation and Suzie decided not to push her luck with any more questions. She was curious about the deaths of the two guards. It was the sort of handiwork that Mike was capable of. Could he still be alive? From what Tanya had told her it seemed doubtful, but Mike was a versatile man. It gave Suzie a faint hope to cling on to.

Her cigarette finished, Tanya stubbed it out with her heel and they returned to the barn. She felt much less isolated than she had on her way out. It gave her a lift to know that Ryall was nearby and knew where she was. Mr Green was still fiddling with his electronic gadgets and making sure the simulator was working properly when they entered the building. He gave them a quick glance and smiled, then busied himself compiling programs to test their ability to handle the Harrier in the event of a problem arising. He enjoyed putting them to the test and was able to arrange for the aircraft to have any number of faults occur during the flight, from a fire on board, to an engine failure, or both at the same time.

By eight o'clock that evening the women could not absorb any more. After a day's intensive training they were tired, and their brains refused to accept further instructions. Mr Black was happy with their progress, and agreed to let them finish for the day. While Tanya went outside for another smoke, in the still bright but fading sun, Suzie went into the caravan to see what was available to counter her hunger. She was closely followed by her employer. He sat on the long seat in the diner and patted the place next to him. Suzie heeded his request and sat beside him.

'I wanted to have a little chat with you, without Miss Lilac being present,' he began.

'Hello, here it comes,' thought Suzie. 'He's going to try out his charms on me, to gain himself a choice of females. The trouble is, he knows he's in a strong position and neither of us can afford to say no. This could be tricky.'

'Miss Lilac is beginning to worry me a little,' he stated, in a quiet, homely voice.

'Oh, why?'

'I noticed that her progress was much slower than yours.'

'No, not really,' defended Suzie. 'I'm only a little better at flying the plane than she is. I'm fortunate enough to have flown a variety of planes and that has helped. There's still plenty of time for Miss Lilac to improve,' she insisted, wishing to promote herself, but not to the extent that would cause Mr Black to get rid of Tanya. She may need her as an ally.

'Perhaps you don't realise it, but when she is in the cockpit with the headset on, it is possible to hear you giving her guidance and instructions. I doubt if she would be anywhere near as advanced if you had not helped her.'

'Well, you did say that we should endeavour to learn from each other.'

'True, though it seems to be all one way at the moment.'

Suzie did not respond.

'I'm sure you are wondering why I am training two pilots in a single-seater jet simulator. Well, let me tell you. I like to have a back-up in everything that I do. If all goes to plan, then the time may come when I shall need only one of you. I am sure that you would want it to be you, and so do I. You are much more competent, and I am willing to pay the pilot, who eventually does the job for me, a lot of money.'

'I obviously want that to be me,' purred Suzie, guessing what his next move would be.

Mr Black put a hand on her knee. 'You are a very attractive woman, as well as being clever, and I could be persuaded to see that you are the one who is chosen to fly the Harrier during the robbery.'

'So it is definitely a robbery,' thought Suzie. 'When he gets excited about making a conquest he lets things slip. I'd like to tell Tanya about this weasel, but I don't trust her enough, and I must stay close to him until I find out more about this robbery he's planning.'

'If I'm better than Miss Lilac then you'll probably choose me anyway.'

'True. Except that the important word you used there is "probably". If I am persuaded that you are the one, then "probably" can be turned into "definitely".'

'Then I'm sure I can persuade you, if Tanya is not there to spoil things,' Suzie declared.

'You let me worry about her,' Mr Black stated, undoing the buttons on Suzie's blouse. 'You keep our little arrangement a secret, and I'll see to it that you get your reward.'

Suzie offered no resistance as he undid her blouse and removed her bra. It was too important that she found out what his plans were, and she was able to shut off her

123

feelings from the performance that her body was about to play.

Mr Black removed her shorts and knickers then undid the zip on his trousers. Suzie was now naked as he pressed her down on the seat and lay on top of her. The seat was narrow and he had to be careful not to move too close to the edge. He penetrated her immediately, not bothering with any fore-play, eager to satisfy the lust he felt for this attractive woman, his latest sexual conquest.

'I hate to think what Mike would have thought of me doing this with his murderer, or perhaps attempted murderer,' Suzie thought, as she submitted to Mr Black's wishes. 'This will make my revenge on him that much sweeter. Why is it that men always want to prove how good they are with women, even when they're old, fat and way past their prime? It must be an ego thing with them.'

During Mr Black's gratification of his sexual desires, Suzie played along with him, making noises of enjoyment and caressing him. He slobbered all over her, grabbing her breasts and harshly fondling them in his eagerness to extract as much pleasure from the union as he could. He thrust into her with some difficulty, his portly figure and the restricted space on the seat adding to his inelegant movements.

Suddenly, Miss Lilac entered the caravan, saw what they were engaged in, and departed quickly with a furious look on her face, slamming the door as she left. Mr Black enjoyed his seduction, though it was soon over, much to Suzie's thankfulness, and he moaned with pleasure at his finishing stroke and discharge. She faked a climax, and was sure that he could not tell if it was real or not. He probably guessed that she was exaggerating the excitement he had provided for her, but did not care as long as he was satisfied with his sexual conquest. He left, with a smile on his face, soon after they had finished, and Miss Lilac came storming back into the caravan as Suzie was strapping on her bra.

'What the hell do you think you're playing at, undoing all my hard work in getting him to trust me?' Tanya snapped.

Fastening the last of her blouse buttons, Suzie replied, 'I had no choice. You of all people must realise that. And I'm not trying to get him to trust me more than you,' she protested. 'I don't imagine that he trusts either of us that much. But, I need this job, and if it means letting him have me occasionally, then so be it. After all, you're doing exactly the same thing, and you don't think I really enjoyed it, do you?'

'No, perhaps not,' conceded Tanya, suddenly realising that she was being hypocritical. 'But I don't want you queering my pitch.'

Now Tanya was worried. If Mr Black preferred Suzie to her, she may not be able to find out about the robbery in time, if at all. Something had to be done. She had to speak to Ryall again; he would know how to handle it.

The tasks undertaken that day by the women were reviewed by Mr Green, who charted their progress. The initial difficulties with vertical take-off were well on the way to being mastered by the two would-be fighter pilots, he maintained. Following this upbeat assessment of their progress, they retired for the night, creating a situation that Suzie thought of as ridiculous when Mr Black stepped into the bedroom to sleep with Tanya.

'I wonder what deceitful excuses and arrangements he is offering her, in case things don't work out with me,' she thought. 'I'm sure he's playing us off against each other, and offering sweeteners to satisfy his sexual appetite for younger women. When the crunch comes, he'll have no qualms about killing either of us, I'm sure of that. I can't trust Tanya, because she is so desperate to do the job and get her reward. I just hope that neither of us suffers the same fate that looks to have befallen poor Mike and Paula.'

Alone in her bedroom, Suzie had time to think about

Mike and tears flooded from her eyes as she thought about all the good and bad times they had been through. Since the day they first met three years before, when they found that their skills complemented each other, a bond of trust emerged between them. From then on they had always worked as a team and had been there for each other, watching one another's backs. Now it looked as though he may have fallen at the hands of an evil crackpot, desperate for money and the power it would bring him. If so, she swore to avenge his death and make sure that the evil Mr Black knew exactly why he was about to die.

Eventually, Suzie cried herself to sleep.

13

Discovery

Detective Inspector Brooke telephoned Sir Joseph Sterling's office at around 4 p.m. on Wednesday, to confirm the time of their meeting that evening.

His secretary, Miss Wilson, told him, 'Sir Joseph was requested to attend a Foreign Office function this afternoon to greet a visiting dignitary, and it is certain to extend well into this evening.'

'I see. Do you know what time he expects this function to end?'

'It is unlikely that he'll be back until quite late, probably not before ten o'clock,' she stated. 'He would like to know if you wish to postpone the meeting until tomorrow evening.'

Brooke though for a moment and glanced at his watch. 'No. I'll have a bite to eat and come back to the office around ten o'clock. I'll wait for about half an hour in the lobby. If he hasn't shown up by then I'll go home and ring him again tomorrow for another appointment.'

'Very well. Sir Joseph is due to telephone me a little later on, so I'll inform him of your decision,' she said with stark efficiency, ending the conversation.

That evening, Brooke went to one of his favourite eating establishments near Soho. Tho's Vietnamese Restaurant was on his patch when he patrolled the streets of London ten years earlier. The restaurant had only been open for business a few days when the owner was beaten up by a local gang of racketeers, to encourage him to pay for protection. Tho Huyn, who had endured a troublesome journey to England as one of the Vietnamese boat people, was a slightly built man of only 5 feet in height. He refused to be intimidated like so many others in the area, and stood firm. This resulted in his restaurant suffering severe damage when the gang returned to teach him a lesson and smash the place up.

That was when Brooke became involved, and with his persuasion, Tho allowed the police to stake out his restaurant. When the gang came back for their money, a big fight broke out. During the mêlée, the gang leader tried to shoot Tho, and Brooke intervened to save his life. The protection racket was smashed and the gang members were rounded up. With Brooke and Tho's evidence, they were all convicted and sent to prison for a long time. Many other restaurateurs and shop owners in the district breathed a sigh of relief at the gang's sentences, and slept much better after they were all put away.

PC Brooke was commended for his part in bringing the criminals to justice and so began his rise up the police ladder towards the rank of Detective Inspector, which he now held. Tho and Brooke had remained friends since that fractious time. Brooke was always made very welcome whenever he called into Tho's restaurant for a meal, and he was usually persuaded not to pay. This was especially true if he was on his own, as he was that evening.

Big Ben was ringing out its constant message to Londoners, informing everyone that the time was now ten o'clock, as Brooke smiled at the security guard, flashed his ID card and entered the quiet, empty lobby to wait for Sir Joseph. His footsteps echoed on the cold marble floor as he stepped over to the visitors' waiting chairs and made himself comfortable. He looked at his watch, even though the chimes of Big Ben had barely finished ringing in his ears. It was late, he was tired, he had eaten too much and felt bloated, and wanted to get home to lay his weary body down on his soft, comfortable bed. Wondering how long he would have to wait, his question was answered almost immediately by Sir Joseph, smartly dressed in his evening suit and bow tie, emerging through the front entrance.

'Thank you for waiting, Colin. I realise that it's a bit late, but it would be good to review our progress. It shouldn't take too long.'

Brooke acknowledged the fact with a slight nod of his head, and they proceeded to climb the red-carpeted wooden stairway to the first floor.

Sir Joseph took a bunch of keys from his pocket as they approached the room, grabbed the door handle, and was about to insert his key in the lock when he realised the door was open. Miss Wilson and he were both very careful to ensure the door was locked when they were absent, because classified information was held in his office filing cabinets.

'This door is supposed to be locked, and checked that it is by a guard every half an hour,' Sir Joseph informed Brooke. 'Do you have a gun?'

Brooke slipped his Glock Model 19 from its shoulder holster and released the safety-catch. Despite the public's perception that policemen do not carry guns except on special duty, Brooke was becoming accustomed to carrying a firearm more and more, especially when he was in London or one of the other major cities.

Quietly pushing the door wide, they stepped inside Miss Wilson's office, saw a torchlight beam flickering, and heard filing cabinet drawers in Sir Joseph's office sliding open. The door to his office was ajar, and Brooke crept over to it, quickly shoved it open wide, turned the main light on and moved into the room with his gun ready to shoot.

An almost bald, elderly man in a uniform, startled at the intrusion, was searching through papers from the cabinet. His face went red with embarrassment.

Sir Joseph stepped forward. 'Hello, Harry. You're a long way from the Records department. What brings you snooping around my office, and how did you get in here and get the cabinet unlocked?'

The man looked shocked, mouthed a few words, but could think of nothing adequate to say. Sir Joseph took the papers that he was holding and looked at them. It was his personal file on Mr Black and his activities, with all the details about Paula, Suzie and Mike's involvement in the present case.

'Now why should you want to look at this file?' Sir Joseph asked, then turned to Brooke. 'I think that after all this time we've actually discovered Mr Black's informant, Colin. Please call Security.'

Brooke holstered his gun and picked up the telephone. Sir Joseph approached the man.

'Why, Harry? Why? Sensitive information passed on to someone that you know has no right to see it.'

The man looked crestfallen, his eyes lowered. 'You know that Lucy had cancer and needed a lot of expensive treatment some years ago. Well, a job in Records doesn't pay much and I was desperate to get her seen by a specialist, or she would have died. The consultant was very expensive and Inspector Bob Black lent me the money. The operation saved Lucy's life. I couldn't repay the loan very easily, and Lucy still needed a lot of care. That cost more money – money that I didn't have. The Inspector said that I was not to worry about it, he would pay the bills, but he asked for small bits of information from Records that he hadn't got clearance for. He said that the paperwork was held up with a lot of red tape; but of course, the clearance for it never did arrive.'

'I can guess the rest, Harry.'

'Yes. Once I'd given him some sensitive information I was trapped, and he wanted more and more classified stuff. I

130

was in a hopeless situation,' he mumbled, tears of sadness filling his eyes.

'Why didn't you come and see me? I thought we were friends, Harry. We could have worked something out,' said Sir Joseph.

Two security guards entered the room.

He glanced at them and replied, 'I'm almost at retirement age and I need my pension to keep me and Lucy going. I was afraid that I might lose my job and the pension with it.'

Sir Joseph gave a resigned sigh. 'You may have lost a lot more than that now, Harry. What information have you given to Mr Black recently?'

'None,' he quickly replied, desperate to minimise his deceit. 'He hasn't asked for anything for some months, until today. My face is well known to the guards, so I can get into the building at any time with no bother. I waited until late this evening, when things are normally quiet, before making a search of your room.'

'And the keys?'

'I found out where Miss Wilson keeps her keys when I came in late one evening as she was packing up to leave. She didn't suspect anything. I've known her for years, and it didn't occur to her that I was watching where she put things. I was able to make a copy of the keys to your office and her desk one evening when she was powdering her nose before going home.'

'I see. What did Mr Black ask you to get?'

'Nothing specific. He simply wanted any information you'd collected about him in the last couple of months.'

'Hmm,' pondered Sir Joseph. 'At least no damage has been done this time,' he suggested.

'And how do you get the information to him?' asked Brooke, looking for a way to locate Mr Black and his gang.

'He rings me at work. If I've got something for him, he

sends a motorcycle courier to my home that evening to collect it.'

Brooke looked at Sir Joseph. 'If he thinks there's a package to collect, we might be able to set something up and follow the courier.'

'Good. Take care of it, will you please, Colin?'

'We'll need a couple of motorcycle policemen to track him. I'll get that organised first thing in the morning,' he said.

Sir Joseph nodded to the two guards who took the man by the arm and led him away, his head bowed. He closed the door behind them and stood thinking for a few moments while Brooke waited.

'This is serious, Colin. Why did Mr Black ask him to get the information now? He must suspect something, and he must think that I am involved,' he said, moving to his desk and sitting down.

'Maybe he's trying to play safe, and wants to be sure that you know nothing before he makes his bid to steal a plane,' offered Brooke, sitting in the vacant chair on the opposite side of the desk.

'Perhaps. I hope that's all it is and he's not aware of Suzie Drake's connection with me. If he is, she could be in a lot of trouble, especially as we don't know her whereabouts at the moment.'

'I'm sure that he is simply being cautious. And as for getting the information from you, you're an obvious choice. He caused you a lot of problems after he left, not the least of them being the disappearance and murder of Inspector Williams. You've been chasing him ever since for that, and he knows it.'

'I hope you're right. It's such a shame that he had to drag a nice, but vulnerable man like Harry Mortimer into his evil web. I hope that he had nothing to do with Inspector Williams getting caught by Mr Black. If so, things will be very difficult for him, and us. Security should have got suspicious about him, during one of their sweeps, long before this.'

'What do you think will happen to him?'

'If he cooperates, and I'm sure that he now will, I'll suggest they give him early retirement, as long as he's not implicated in Inspector Williams's death. He's too old to go to prison. It would kill him and his wife. He'll lose some of his pension of course, but I'll remind them of his lengthy service and see what I can do.'

'Good. He looked frail and harmless enough and if, as he said, he was virtually blackmailed into it, they should take that into account.'

'Yes. Meanwhile we've still got to locate Mr Black and Suzie Drake and while I'm thinking of it, Major Blood tells me that the other woman pilot is Tanya Gibson. She was a co-pilot on transport planes and was involved in a mid-air near miss with a fighter plane that shook her up a bit. It seems that after the incident she was reluctant to take the controls again and was a bit nervous of flying, so they released her from the RAF.'

'Perhaps she wanted to use the simulator to regain her confidence before trying out the real thing.'

'Possibly. Anyway, it's of no consequence to us at the moment, Mr Black is. What new information do you have for me?'

14

Weight Lift

The barn had become a virtual prison for the two women, who practised in the simulator under the watchful eyes of Mr Black and Mr Green.

The next two days went quickly for both Tanya and Suzie, with much to learn and master. For the first time they were instructed on how to use the Harrier's two 25 mm cannon and the underwing Sidewinder missiles. This increased their realisation of how dangerous the job might be, and they were forced to accept that killing someone could be a part of it. Mr Black assured them both that learning to handle the Harrier's weapons was merely a precaution in case of a problem arising, and would probably only be needed to give a demonstration in a show of strength.

The evenings were worst for the women. Mr Black shared the bedroom with Tanya and wanted to take advantage of his hold on her and have sex each night. He was not short of lustful desire, despite not being a young man, and displayed a voraciousness for sex that belied his age and looks. Feigning tiredness had worked for Tanya on one occasion, but then Mr Black went straight into Suzie's bedroom for an hour, so Tanya reluctantly submitted to him on the remaining night, wanting to keep in favour with him and afraid that he might prefer Suzie. She knew by now that he was not going to tell her about his plans, and that she would have to bide her time and wait to find out what they were. Suzie was no more fortunate, though she at least spent the nights on her own as there was not enough room in the cramped single bed for him to stay the whole time.

Despite taking frequent stops to go outside and have a smoke, Tanya had not heard from Ryall again, a fact which, because she desperately wanted to speak to him, aggravated her. Meanwhile, both women continued to learn, even though the atmosphere between them was a little frosty because of Tanya's annoyance at being unable to get her own way.

Mr Green, on the other hand, was enjoying himself, letting them think that everything was going smoothly, before introducing a catastrophic failure of one sort or another to shake them up. Suzie was coping with the emergencies better than Tanya, who realised this, adding to her problems. It made her more worried that she would not be picked to fly during the robbery, no matter what assurances Mr Black had given to her and how ever many times she consented to let him have his way with her.

Storming out of the simulator, Tanya yelled over the balcony to Mr Green below, fiddling with his electronics, 'How the hell am I supposed to learn how to fly this bloody thing when you keep pissing everything up.'

'It's good practise for you, and should help you get to know the aircraft thoroughly,' he smiled, pleased that he had managed to rattle her while unable to take his eyes from her cleavage as she bent over the railings dressed only in her underwear. Women had largely ignored him most of his life, and this was a golden opportunity to get his own back on at least two of them. He was determined to make the most of it.

Suzie emerged from the cabin, donned an overall, and stood behind Tanya thinking, 'While she keeps getting upset like this, my chances of staying in favour must be good.'

'How are you doing, my dears?' Mr Black intervened,

calming the situation and staring up at Tanya with pleasure, as she stood in her underwear, showing an exciting amount of bare flesh.

Tanya breathed in heavily through her nostrils. 'As long as the aircraft doesn't have a total engine failure, catch fire, have a wing fall off unexpectedly or get hit by a bloody missile, I can fly it without too many problems,' she asserted, with more than a slight hint of sarcasm in her voice.

'Good. I'm pleased to hear that. Could the pair of you manage to fly the aircraft, without crashing it, if it had to lift something that is quite heavy?'

A bemused look crossed the women's faces as they stared enquiringly at one another.

'Quite heavy? How heavy? And lifted how?' asked Suzie.

'Quite heavy,' Mr Black repeated, looking at Mr Green.

'Several tonnes, in fact,' added Mr Green. 'Lifted by chain, from a hook located beneath the central fuselage.'

'Several tonnes?' the women echoed in unison.

'Exactly how many tonnes?' asked Suzie. 'It could be critical.'

'About four tonnes,' conceded Mr Green.

'Four tonnes? That's a hell of a lot of weight.'

Suzie wandered down the steps, considering the matter, deliberately allowing her unbuttoned overall to flap open, giving glimpses of her athletic figure and long, shapely bare legs. She too knew how to tantalise and get attention. The expressions on Mr Black and Mr Green's faces had desire written all over them. Suzie now had one more small piece of the jigsaw; the Harrier's unique hovering ability was to be used to lift something very heavy. But what, and why?

She declared, 'If it's lifted centrally, and isn't too wide, keeping it out of the way of the hover jets and enabling the plane to stay on an even keel, it should be no problem. That's providing it's not too heavy for the plane to lift and it doesn't have to be held for too long.'

'The plane will be used to carry the weight only a short distance,' Mr Green declared.

'How short? What sort of distance and in what conditions?' Suzie asked.

'The distance is not great, probably no more than a few yards in fact. I've calculated that the plane is capable of carrying the load much farther if it was required, according to the figures I have. The distance is so short that fuel load and weather conditions don't really come into the equation, unless there's a force ten gale blowing, and that's not likely.'

'Weather conditions. Somewhere could be very windy,' thought both of the women, desperately trying to calculate what the job may be from the additional pieces of information.

'It would be heavy on fuel, but if that is not a problem, then there's no reason why it cannot be done,' expressed Suzie.

'Good. That's excellent,' Mr Black enthused. 'Mr Green has worked out a way to reproduce it on the simulator. Tomorrow you will both try it out to see how you fare.'

Staring at Tanya, who was descending the stairs after grabbing her overall and handbag, he asked, 'Meantime, perhaps you would like a rest, my dear?'

Tanya knew what he was angling for, and was not in the mood. 'Thanks. I'd rather have a bit of fresh air and a smoke, if you don't mind,' she said, oblivious of her contradiction in terms. She went outside for a smoke.

'You're not going to disappoint me as well, are you?' Mr Black asked, turning to Suzie.

'Of course not,' she replied with a smile, linking her arm through his, while inwardly thinking, 'God, I hope I don't have to put up with this for much longer.'

Outside, Tanya wanted to think more about the latest piece of information she had been given. If only she could speak to Ryall, even for a few minutes, he might have a better idea of what this was all about. But that, she knew, was unlikely, and she would have to bide her time and wait until he made contact with her again. She hoped that it would be soon – or it may be too late.

15

The Courier

On Thursday morning, following the evening of his unmasking, Harry Mortimore spent most of his time with Special Branch detectives, giving details about the information he had passed on to Mr Black. He was closely questioned about the case that Inspector Williams was working on when he disappeared and was eventually found with bullets in his back. Harry Mortimore denied passing any information to Mr Black at that time or about that case. He told them that if he had done so and then found out that it had led to the death of a policeman, he would not have been able to keep quiet about it, despite the consequences, and would have spoken up straight away. He may have been in a difficult situation, but he still had his pride, and his conscience would not have allowed him to cover up the death of a policeman, whatever the personal cost may be.

When the first interview was over, and with lunchtime approaching, he was allowed, with supervision, to continue his job in Records. Brooke was anxious that he should be available as usual to answer Mr Black's call should it come, and knowing the villain's need for information, he was sure that it would arrive. All of Harry Mortimore's incoming telephone calls were monitored and after a frustrating afternoon, the call they were waiting for eventually came at 5.20 p.m., shortly before he was due to leave for home.

'Yes, I did ... Yes, there is. It's got something to do with you looking for pilots,' Harry Mortimore replied to Mr Black's questions, giving the answers he had been briefed on. 'Yes, I've got copies of the file ... Yes, that's okay. About eight-thirty. Goodbye Inspector,' he said, calling him by his old rank the way he had always done, ever since the day that he was dismissed.

'Good,' pronounced Brooke, stopping the tape recorder and replacing the telephone extension. He checked to see if the boffins had time to trace the call, but it was a short call, made from a mobile telephone, making it impossible to trace.

Brooke called Sir Joseph's office with the news. '... and the two undercover motorcycle policemen are ready. I've got a couple of unmarked squad cars tagging along as well,' he informed him. 'I've picked DCs Green and Teal for that job, they make a good team.'

'Well done, Colin. It's important that we don't lose the courier and that he doesn't spot your men.'

'I understand that, sir. It'll be a tricky job, but we'll do our best.'

'Keep me posted with your progress,' he directed.

At their small two-bedroomed mid-terraced house in Streatham, Lucy Mortimore wondered what was going on. Why were policemen invading their home? One was upstairs in the bedroom and others were waiting outside. She knew nothing about her husband's unauthorised dealings, and Sir Joseph had agreed to keep the problem a secret from her for the moment, because of Lucy's poor health. She had been told that her husband was cooperating with the police in order to catch a criminal that he had become aware of.

He looked more nervous than she had ever seen him before, despite it not being the first time that a courier had called at their house for a package. Instinctively, she knew there was more to it than DI Brooke had told her. Not that she would let it show. Her husband had struggled for years to pay for all the treatment that she had required, and she was not about to upset him any more than he clearly already was.

At 8.30 p.m. precisely, a motorcycle revved up before stopping outside the house.

'Okay, Harry. This looks like it. Just act normally and we'll do the rest,' Brooke told him.

He grabbed the large padded envelope and answered the doorbell when it rang.

'Collection for Inspector Black,' informed the rider, in his full-face crash helmet with tinted visor, which he left pulled down, making recognition impossible.

Harry thrust the package forward and said nothing. The rider whipped off his leather glove, took the package and stuffed it into a bag, which he then strapped on his back. He left the gate wide open, shoved his fingers back into his glove, and with a roar set off on his motorcycle down the centre of the road, lined with cars parked on both sides.

Brooke, peering from behind the curtains in the upstairs bedroom, spoke into his communicator. 'He's off, Jeff. For Christ's sake don't lose him.'

'Okay,' replied the first motorcycle policeman, moving off behind him. 'Tim and I are going to follow him in relays. That way we should avoid him spotting us.'

The courier turned into Streatham High Road, made his way along the crowded A23, then turned towards Wandsworth. The road was jammed with cars and he weaved his way through the traffic, followed at a short distance by the first motorcycle policeman. There was too much congestion for them to do anything but trail behind, leaving what they thought was a safe gap. The courier was travelling at normal speed and did not seem to be in any hurry. At one set of traffic lights that were red, the first policeman could not avoid catching him up and parked behind him on the outside lane as they waited for the lights to change. When they did, the group set off again, with the squad cars in the rear staying in touch by radio and following as close as the heavy traffic would allow; though they were now already several hundred yards behind.

After passing through Wandsworth, the courier sped along the less crowded and faster A3, and took the road to Richmond, where the traffic became heavy again. He negotiated Richmond town centre, then turned left on a side road and accelerated fast. By the time the first police motorcyclist rounded the corner, he was nowhere in sight. Gathering speed and searching frantically to both his left and right, the policeman screeched to a halt after passing a building site and catching a glimpse of the courier charging across the unmade road, throwing clouds of dust into the air.

'He might have spotted us tailing him; either that or he's being very cautious,' radioed Jeff to his colleague. 'He's ducked into a building site. Hang around outside Tim, I'm going to follow him in.'

Entering the site quietly, with his bike revs low to keep the noise to a minimum, the policeman followed the dust cloud. He glided around the corner of an unfinished brick and concrete structure with metal rods sticking out in all directions, and saw the courier's motorcycle lying on its side in the dust. Close by was a stack of 3-feet-diameter concrete pipes, end on, all blocking the way through to the other side of the site. The roar of a motorcycle revving up on the far side confirmed what the policeman feared.

'He's scrambled through a pipe to the far side and has another bike waiting for him,' Jeff informed his colleague. 'Tim, circle around the site and see if you can pick him up on the other side. I'm on my way.'

By the time they found another entrance to the site on the far side, there was no sign of the courier. Jeff informed the trailing squad cars about their problem, and the two police motorcyclists split up to cruise the nearby streets, but their man was nowhere to be seen. Both squad cars were still in the main road trying to catch them up when Ray Teal saw the courier racing down the outside lane going in the opposite direction and moving at a reckless speed.

'I've spotted him. He's heading back through the town centre, Jeff. I'm turning round.'

DC Ray Teal, followed by DC John Green, both did a dangerous U-turn, which annoyed several motorists they were forced to cut up, in order not to lose sight of the courier before their motorcycle colleagues could get back on his trail.

'It's no good,' Teal decided, seeing the bike disappear into the distance, beyond two sets of traffic lights that were now red.

Jeff pulled up beside him. 'I'll continue to search for him. Which way did he go?'

'North,' said Teal, pointing straight in front of him. 'My guess is that he's making for the M4 motorway. I'll ask control to check the motorway junction cameras. With that bag on his back he shouldn't be too difficult to spot if he uses that route.'

Jeff acknowledged his line of reasoning and sped off when the lights changed to green, leaving Teal and the others to return to base and explain what went wrong to DI Brooke.

'Oh, great!' said Brooke, when he heard the bad news. 'Four coppers and you can't even keep a watch on one motorcycle courier.'

'We're not sure that he even spotted us. It's possible that he'd already decided to take elaborate precautions. Black is bound to have told him to be careful,' explained DC John Green.

'I hope you're right,'

Brooke informed Sir Joseph, now at his home in Woking, of their inability to keep the courier under surveillance.

'That's a pity, Colin. It's another lead we've lost. And it

means that Mr Black might know that we're on to him, and searching.'

'We think it's possible that the courier didn't spot any of our men, but was simply being very careful.'

'If he did spot the tail, then Mr Black will realise that we've discovered who his contact is. If so, we must hope that he thinks we've found his informant by accident Colin, as indeed we did, and doesn't suspect that we've planted an informant on him. If he thinks that Suzie's involved, I wouldn't like to imagine what he'd do to her.'

16

Delivery

In Mr Black's caravan, both Suzie and Tanya, lying in their beds, heard the roar of a motorcycle arriving late at night. They were not allowed to venture out after Mr Black's curfew time of 10 p.m. and could only wonder at what was happening.

'Were you followed?' Mr Black questioned the courier, taking the envelope from him and tearing it open.

'I'm not sure. I might have been. There was a motorbike behind me for several miles, so I thought I'd better play safe and use the escape route. If he was following me, I lost him at the building site.'

Mr Black thumbed through the papers. He and Mr Brown stood outside the barn in dim shadows with only a single light, hanging from above the door, to see by.

'So, you are sure that you lost him?'

The young courier looked anxious, fiddling with a tassel on the bottom of his leather jacket. He had run errands for Mr Black before, and knew how strict he was about the rules he had to abide by and what was expected of him.

'Yes. I'm not even sure that he was following me, but I thought it was best to take your advice and make absolutely certain,' he said, trying to convince his employer that he had taken as much precaution as Mr Black had instructed him to.

After a brief look at the papers, Mr Black stuffed them

back in the envelope and looked up. 'And you came here by only A roads and didn't use the motorways?'

'No, of course not. You always tell me not to if there's been any suspicion of a problem with the pick-up,' he maintained, with more than a hint of nervousness in his quivery voice.

Glancing at his watch, Mr Black enquired, 'How did you manage to get here so quickly? It's only a little after ten-thirty. You must have driven very fast.'

'I did. I thought you'd want to see the package straight away, and at this time of night there's not a lot of traffic on the roads. I was able to get a move on. I kept an eye out for the police and slowed down until they were out of sight. No one stopped me.'

Mr Black took an envelope out of his pocket and handed it to the courier. 'Good boy,' he said, tapping him on the shoulder. 'I shan't be needing you any more tonight.'

The young rider thumbed through the notes, satisfied that it was okay, and stuffed them in his pocket.

The tap on the shoulder was a signal to Mr Brown, standing behind the courier. He took out his silenced gun and barely a sound was heard when the weapon spat out its lethal piece of lead which ploughed into the young man's back. His face turned to horror as the bullet tore through him and came out the front. His anguish lasted only a brief moment before he fell to the ground and his motorcycle clattered down with him.

'Get rid of him and the bike, Mr Brown, and double the guard for tonight – just in case. These papers are old and not what I was expecting to receive,' he said, holding them up.

'I'll see to it straight away. Do you think he was followed?'

'No, I don't think so, but I'm sure he used the motorway. All the same, keep checking on the guards at the entrance throughout the night. You'd better do it now as well.'

Pressing the button on his communicator, Mr Brown

confirmed that the guard was alert and had seen only the courier that evening.

Mr Black listened then announced, 'Good. It's time I went to bed. Goodnight.'

He retrieved his envelope from the rider, full of counterfeit notes, then entered the barn and left Mr Brown to clear up and dispose of the body.

By morning, all traces of the previous evening's visit were gone and nothing further was said about the courier or the package he had delivered.

Later that Friday morning, Suzie and Tanya put all the skills they had learnt to the test, and between them accomplished take-offs and landings on the simulator with the heavy weight slung below the fuselage. The whole feel of the aircraft changed. Much more power was needed to achieve a vertical lift and the Harrier swayed more from side to side. Suzie coped better with the change of method, and managed to get the plane airborne and back down again with reasonable ease. Tanya, however, needed Suzie's help to achieve lift-off, and struggled to master the change. That afternoon they went through a full rehearsal, and made extensive use of the cannon and missiles that the Harrier carries, slung below the wings. Tanya enjoyed that part of the training much more and did a lot better at target practice.

Handling the plane proved to be a good deal more difficult when they donned their full anti-g flying kits, but they were familiar enough with the aircraft controls now to overcome the awkwardness that it produced. Both women went through all the manoeuvres they had previously learnt, and handled the aircraft with adequate competence, considering the short time they had been given to master it. Suzie's actions were quicker and smoother, showing that she had a clear edge on Tanya in flying skills.

When the exhaustive tests were over, the women were glad

to get out of the sweltering heat of the simulator cabin. Descending the steps, Tanya removed her helmet, brushed away beads of perspiration from her face and pulled down the zip on her flying suit to the waist. The men all stood and stared at her bright red bra and her bulging bosoms, bouncing back and forth as she swaggered down the steps. Even Mr Green cast her a sideways glance, looking longingly at the breasts he would love to get his hands on. It was Tanya's way of letting Mr Black know that not all the manipulation belonged to him, and she was still capable of exerting some influence.

Mr Black stepped forward. 'Well done both of you!' he enthused, a broad beam crossing his face, puffing his cheeks up into two red balls.

'I've sweated like a pig in there today and I want a proper bath or shower, and tonight. I'm fed up with making do with a strip-down wash in lukewarm water,' asserted Tanya.

'Of course. I think you are both more than ready for the task in hand, and I've arrange for us all to have a night in comfort at a hotel this evening.'

Mr Black's readiness to agree to her demand left Tanya a little surprised. 'Good. Thanks,' she muttered.

'Ready for what task?' Suzie asked, focusing on the job. 'And when?'

'I will come to that all in good time, my dears. For the moment, get changed and bring some fresh clothes with you.'

The women returned to the caravan and packed their bags. Both saw this venture as giving them the possibility for outside contact, though each had a very different reason for wanting it. A little over half an hour later the MPV with the blacked-out windows was brought to the front of the barn. They were shown into the back seat, again with a guard beside them and three more in the centre row of seats in front of them. Suzie was well aware that this was a deliberate act to prevent them from seeing the direction they were taking and knowing what their destination would be.

After, what Suzie assessed, was about 20 minutes, the MPV pulled into a small country hotel with the impressive name of The Country Grande. Trees surrounded the hotel and the tarmac car park, and it was obviously chosen by Mr Black for its isolated location. Even the public road passing it was screened from the hotel by rows of conifer trees, flanking a winding gravel driveway.

Mr Black escorted the women into the foyer and asked them to sit and wait while he spoke to the receptionist and confirmed their booking. He was a careful man and made certain that he gave the women no clues as to the whereabouts of the hotel. Suzie carefully scanned the place, while trying hard to conceal her actions, but frustratingly could see nothing that gave her any indication of where the premises were located. She did, however, notice Mr Black showing the receptionist something that looked like an ID card. The notion came to her mind that Mr Black was declaring that he was still in the police force, and had probably told the hoteliers that the two women were being escorted by him and his men. This would explain why the receptionist was giving them furtive glances, and also why Mr Black was able to keep the women so tightly in his grasp without arousing any suspicions.

The rest of the men joined them, carrying their bags, and they all climbed the stairs to their first-floor rooms. The five guards shared two rooms between them, situated on either side of the rooms with Mr Black in one with a double bed, and the women in the adjacent room with single beds.

All the hotel rooms were en suite, and Suzie and Tanya had been in their room only a couple of minutes before Mr Black entered through an adjoining door.

'I trust the arrangements are to your liking?' he asked.

'Yes, thank you,' was the joint reply.

Suzie questioned. 'Why did we have to spend so much time learning how to use the guns and rockets on the simulator? You aren't going to start a war, are you?'

'No, of course not. As I told you, it is merely a precaution in case of unforeseen problems to use as a warning. We want you both to be ready for any eventuality. Before then, we have to get our hands on one of the Harrier aeroplanes.'

'How on earth are we going to do that? I don't imagine the Royal Air Force are going to let us walk into one of their bases and fly out with it.'

'No, nor do I, though that was one of my considerations. Instead we are going to Dunsfold.'

Suzie creased her brow. 'Dunsfold? What's that?'

'Dunsfold is a British Aerospace establishment on an airfield in Surrey where, among other aircraft, they repair and update Harrier Jump Jets. Once a year they hold an open day airshow and invite members of the public in. They even allow employees, along with their families and friends, to look around the factory before the show starts. I have acquired the necessary Personal Identity Tag and car passes to get in, and we will steal an aircraft that has been checked and made ready to fly in the display, and you will fly it out.'

'Who will fly it out?' Tanya asked.

'All in good time,' replied Mr Black, with his now familiar response, as usual giving little away.

'And when is all this likely to happen?' Suzie asked, seeing this trip as a good opportunity to get a message out to Sir Joseph.

'Tomorrow.'

17

The Hotel

Saturday morning dawned. In their hotel, Mr Black pulled the curtains apart, letting the bright early morning sun penetrate the bedroom. He was already washed and dressed, eager for the day's important events to begin.

Tanya stirred from beneath the bedcovers and blinked at the overwhelming magnitude of light that cascaded into the room. 'What time is it?' she asked.

'It's past six o'clock.'

'Oh God, is that all. It's still early.'

'Yes, but we have a lot to do today, and we must get an early start.'

Lifting the telephone, Mr Black punched the buttons. When the caller replied he asked, 'Is everything ready? Good. Tell the rest of the men that I will see you all at breakfast in about half an hour. Don't be late,' he instructed, returning the telephone to its cradle.

Tanya slipped out of bed, and grabbed her dressing gown from the floor to cover herself up, before stepping into the bathroom to run the shower. Although she had showered the previous evening, she was prompted to move into Mr Black's bedroom and submit to his advances once more, and wanted to shower again. Not that she disliked sex, but, he was an older, fat, balding man who had little idea about how to please her and only thought of his own gratification, and with him it turned into a chore instead of a pleasure. Having a shower helped her to feel clean, to feel that she had washed away his grubby hands after he had fondled and slobbered over almost every part of her body the previous night.

'Don't be long,' he shouted, through the open doorway. He went into the adjoining room, where he was surprised to see Suzie already dressed and waiting, reading a magazine.

'Did you sleep well?' he enquired.

'Yes, thank you, I did. At least, I did after my bad headache settled down,' Suzie politely answered.

'Has your migraine completely gone?'

'Yes, it has. I'm sorry about that. I'll … try to make it up to you.'

A smile crossed Mr Black's face. What a fortunate position he was in, to have two lovely females at his beck and call, with both wanting to stay in his favour – for the moment at least. He returned to his room.

After her shower, Tanya dressed in a beige skirt and jacket, and a white blouse. Mr Black commented favourably on her appearance, before they all wandered down to the dining room to partake in the tradition of a full, English, fried breakfast.

Tanya had not been out of Mr Black's sight since they had left the barn, and she was beginning to wonder if he harboured second thoughts about picking her, and was about to back out of their agreement. Worse still, had he somehow found out that Ryall was alive and they had met? Then again, it might be that he was smitten with her, and simply wanted to make sure that no one else entertained any thoughts of making a move towards her. If only Ryall had got in touch with her. She now desperately needed to talk to him.

Suzie, too, had noticed that she was watched carefully and found that outside telephone calls from the hotel room were not allowed – at least, not for her. Added to that, her room and windows were locked, and Mr Black made it clear that at least one of the guards would be on duty outside throughout the night, making it impossible for her to sneak out to use a telephone.

The rest of Mr Black's group were all waiting in the dining room when he and his two glamorous pilots arrived. The women were shown to a separate table where a waitress, dressed in an appropriate black outfit with a white pinafore, took their orders. While the other members of Mr Black's entourage tucked into the full fried breakfast, both the women ordered a healthy start to the day of coffee, fruit juice and toast.

Quiet murmurs filled the air with Mr Black and his top three men, Mr Green, Mr Brown and Mr White, sitting together discussing their plans in lowered tones. There was no further room at his table, so the other two members of his group shared a separate table. The quietness of the dining room was only broken by the rustling of newspapers as two smartly dressed businessmen ate their breakfasts while scrutinising early editions of the *Financial Times*. The smell of fried bacon, mixed with the odour of cigarette smoke blown into the air by one of the businessmen, filled the room, to Mr Black's annoyance. The bright morning sun, glistening through the net curtains, graphically lit the smoke as it drifted towards the yellowing ceiling.

With breakfast almost finished, Tanya glanced over Suzie's shoulder and had a job to conceal her surprise when she saw Ryall, peering round a corner at the far end of the room. He mouthed the words 'Ladies loo', which Tanya understood and acknowledged with an almost imperceptibly small nod, closing her eyes for a moment as she did. Suzie was observant and noticed the nod, wondered what it was for, but said nothing.

Tanya licked the toast and butter from her fingers, wiped them on a serviette and stood. 'I won't be a minute, I'm going to the Ladies,' she informed Mr Black, picking up her handbag and dropping the serviette on the table.

'I'll come with you,' Suzie suggested.

'That's okay, I'd rather go alone,' Tanya hurriedly replied.

'Okay,' Suzie said, now knowing there was more to it than a mere call of nature. She returned to her seat.

Mr Black acknowledged Tanya's need and watched her leave the room, before tipping a head towards Mr Brown, who understood his gesture and followed her. She entered the Ladies, went through an inner door and approached Ryall, waiting for her.

Observing Mr Brown following her, Tanya put a forefinger to her lips to indicate silence from Ryall. He perceived the danger and moved quietly into a cubicle, with Tanya following.

'There's one of Black's men outside, keeping an eye on me,' she whispered.

'Okay,' he replied, while undoing the buttons on her blouse and lifting up her bra to run his hands over her breasts.

'Can't you wait?'

'Not for you,' he insisted.

She held his face and they kissed. 'Where on earth have you been? I wanted to talk to you earlier,' she rebuked.

'I had things to attend to. I wanted to see the wives and girlfriends of my men before the police got to them, so that I could explain what happened and make sure that none of them said anything they shouldn't. I promised to get the man that did it, and offered them a share of my proceeds when we turn Black over. That's the least I can do,' he lied.

A guilty look came over Tanya's face. 'That's very noble of you, and I'm sorry about your men.'

'That's okay. What have you found out?' he asked, sucking at her nipple and making it erect.

'Wait a minute, I can't concentrate,' Tanya said, drawing away.

She gave him the details that she had learnt, and told him

about the uneasiness that bothered her. 'We got rid of one woman only to find that Black's got another one up his sleeve.'

Ryall thought about Paula, but decided not to tell Tanya that she was still alive, thanks to him. 'She wouldn't understand my motives, or maybe she would understand them only too well,' he considered. 'It's best that I say nothing about her, or her friend Mike.'

'Suzie has done really well at flying the Harrier, and it could become a bit of a problem if Black thinks that she's a better pilot than me,' Tanya explained. 'I'm doing what I can to keep him sweet on me and he makes promises to pick me, but it's awful having to let him maul me all the time and take what he wants.'

'I know, baby. But I'm sure it won't be for much longer. If he's snatching the plane today, then the job must be soon. He won't want to hang on to it for a long time, because he'll guess that the authorities will probably mount a big search for it. And a big search is what I'm sure they're gonna do, make no mistake about that. If someone nicks a fighter plane, all the stops will be pulled out to find it, otherwise they're left with egg on their faces. So, just hang on a little while longer, baby.'

'Okay, if you say so. Have you got any ideas on what I should do about Suzie?'

'We can't pull the same trick as last time, so we'll have to discredit her some other way. Has she said anything to you that we can use?'

'No, nothing that I can think of.'

'Then we'll have to make something up.'

'Like what?' Tanya asked. 'It'll have to be plausible or Black's bound to get suspicious.'

'Has he talked to you about anything that he fears?'

'No, not really. Though, strangely enough, he did tell me that he used to be a policeman, before he turned to a more profitable life of crime.'

155

'So I've heard.'

'How do you know that?' asked Tanya, frowning.

Ryall suddenly realised that he had inadvertently given away something that Mike and Paula had said to him when he had told Tanya that he was visiting his men's wives and girlfriends.

'I … err, was told that by Mr Brown when he first hired me to steal the simulator,' he quickly stated.

'Oh, right.'

'You can tell him that Suzie casually mentioned to you that she was once a policewoman. That ought to make him think twice about using her.'

'Okay. When should I tell him?'

'Wait until the robbery is imminent. That way he won't have any time to check it out, or get another replacement.'

'Good idea.'

Ryall sat on the toilet lid and lifted Tanya's skirt up and slipped his hands into her knickers. He nuzzled his face into her breasts, and she put her arms around the back of his head, squeezing him against her. He ran his hands to the top of her knickers and gave a sharp wrench, ripping them off.

Tanya looked surprised, but delighted. 'Do we have time?' she asked.

'We've time,' he insisted, pulling his zip down.

Nuzzling her breasts had excited him and he was ready for her. She gently lowered herself upon him, enjoying increasing satisfaction as he slowly penetrated her. This was so much better than submitting to Mr Black, as she had been obliged to do for the last two nights. He was a wham-bam type of lover, who thought only about taking what pleasures he could get for himself and had no concern for his partner's needs. Movement was difficult, and could only be performed by Tanya, with Ryall sitting, his hands grasping her shapely smooth backside, helping her with the action. Her arms enfolded his head, while he enjoyed rubbing his face against her breasts, and teasing her nipples to erection with his tongue and lips as he moved gently in and out of her.

Their actions were slow, but smooth, providing a sensuous pleasure for both of them. Tanya stopped for a few seconds, sitting on his lap, relishing the feeling of Ryall inside her and allowing it to heighten their bodily enjoyment, while giving her legs a chance to recover from the ache that balancing her weight over him was producing. She began slow movement again and could feel the excitement building up in Ryall to a pitch where he could hold out no longer and climaxed, before her, the intoxication of the moment filling both of them with heady pleasure.

The knowledge that Mr Black's man was outside the door and close enough to discover them, increased their anticipations. Tanya reached a high spot and started to cry out, when they heard the inner door bang open. She stifled her cry, and they abruptly stopped their movement and listened closely.

The cubicle doors were being shoved opened one by one. Tanya extricated herself from their entwined position and stood to face the door; Ryall lifted his feet and put them on the toilet. The door rattled.

'Yes, who is it?' Tanya asked.

'Just making sure that you're okay. You've been a long time,' suggested Mr Brown.

Thinking quickly, Tanya said, 'I've got a bit of a tummy ache and had a touch of diarrhoea. It must be something I ate last night. I'm just coming.'

'Okay,' Mr Brown said, making for the exit after he had looked underneath the cubicle door to reassure himself that all was okay.

The inner door closed. 'You *were* just coming!' Ryall joked.

Tanya looked at him, his desire quenched and his energy diminished. He was sitting on the seat with his trousers around his ankles, and his knees resting under his armpits.

She giggled, 'You look like you've just been! And I know where.'

'When this is over, and we're loaded, I'll go there again and again,' he promised, stuffing her ripped knickers into his pocket. 'I'll keep these as a reminder of pleasures to come, if you get my meaning.'

She did.

Tanya gave him a kiss, straightened her clothing, and left. Mr Brown was waiting by the outer door and escorted her back to the dining room, unaware of the inner excitement she felt at the pleasant ache that was still within her, coupled with the feeling of naughtiness she had at knowing she wore no underwear. She was also smirking inwardly at having put one over on Mr Black and his constant sexual demands.

'You were a long time,' suggested Mr Black.

Rubbing her stomach, Tanya repeated her plight of having a slight upset. Suzie's intuition told her there was more to it than that, but what? Perhaps she also was trying to get a message out.

Picking up her handbag, Suzie excused herself and went to the Ladies. She knew there would be someone following her because she had watched it happen when Tanya left. Back in the Ladies, Ryall carefully peered round the doorway and saw Suzie approaching, followed by Mr Brown. He ducked back into a cubicle, locked the door and waited silently. Suzie entered a cubicle, tore off a strip of toilet paper and scribbled a message on it using her lipstick. It was difficult, because the paper was thin and kept tearing. She tried several times before managing to complete a short note that was legible, then flushed the rest down the loo and waited to make sure that all traces of the message were gone.

Folding up the note she stuffed it into her bra. 'All I need now is a few moments on my own when we're at Dunsfold, and a bit of luck that someone finds the note and gives it to Sir J,' Suzie muttered to herself. She was unaware that Ryall was close by listening intently, trying to assess whether she was doing something that he wanted to know about.

Suzie returned to the dining room and when everyone had finished eating breakfast, their bags were loaded aboard the MPV and the group of eight checked out of the hotel, with Mr Black smiling a thank-you to the receptionist when he settled the bill and returned the room keys. Tanya wondered if he had paid with his counterfeit notes and thought that he probably had. She was right.

The MPV was revved into action and the group set off down the twisting driveway to the main road, on the start of their journey to Dunsfold. Ryall, with a satisfied smirk on his face, watched from the dining room window as they left.

18

Dunsfold

After leaving the hotel, Mr Green was returned to the barn before the rest of the group continued to Dunsfold. The journey ahead was a pleasant, unhurried drive through the New Forest and over the green rolling hills of the South Downs. Traffic was light, with more vehicles heading in the opposite direction towards the West Country and the many popular holiday resorts there.

In less than three hours their vehicle approached the main entrance to Dunsfold Aerodrome, along what seemed a rather narrow, winding road to such a prestigious site. Mr Black slipped a PIT pass, clipped to a chain, around his neck and gave a similar one to Mr Brown who was chauffeuring. Each pass showed a colour photograph with their name, personnel and pass number indicated below. He stuck an orange disc in the vehicle's front window, showing a large letter D printed above a serial number. They all looked genuine enough, and would fool anyone unless any of the numbers were checked. They were not.

'It looks like a good day for the show,' announced Mr Black, as he and Mr Brown held up their passes for the guard to see. He knew the value of distraction. The guard agreed, took a quick glance at the occupants, lingering slightly longer on the two attractive women, and waved them on, telling them to follow the signs to the car park, and pointing the way.

They drove into the British Aerospace Dunsfold Aerodrome, which had nestled deep in the heart of the Surrey countryside for more than 50 years, built mainly by the Canadians during the Second World War as an aerodrome for the allies. This was the birthplace of the Harrier and the Hawk aeroplanes, from conception to first flight. Dunsfold Air Day was held each year, and up to 7,000 people were expected to visit the show, making the perfect cover for Mr Black and his group.

After parking their vehicle, they picked up a map indicating where the various exhibits were located for their tour around the hangars. Visitors had only a couple of hours before the show was due to start, and Mr Black and his group mingled with the ever-increasing numbers of people wandering through the massive production hangars. There the Harriers underwent their mechanical refurbishment and upgrades before they were painted, tested and returned to the RAF.

Continuing through the second hangar, where much of the rewiring was done, they saw a young employee demonstrating on a computer the 3Dimensional solid modelling techniques that were employed to produce the assembly and production drawings. Mr Brown was fascinated by the demonstration and stopped to watch the model of an aircraft being spun around to view it from all angles. The demonstrator then went on to show the 4D Navigator techniques of moving throughout the aircraft interior, showing all the structure, wiring and electronics in position. Mr Black halted his group for a moment before coughing politely to remind Mr Brown of what they were there for. He smiled a 'sorry' to him and caught them up, but he wished he had seen a lot more of the demonstration and had the opportunity to ask questions.

They were there to execute a daring robbery, and remaining unobtrusive until it was achieved was a necessary part of their plan. The police would be questioning people afterwards, and it was preferable that none of them remained prominent in any one's mind, though in the case of the two attractive women, that was not so easily accomplished.

At the far end of the hangar, the group walked towards the west end of the site, which was out of bounds to visitors. Mr Black, with his British Aerospace pass hung prominently around his neck, strolled into a hangar where a two-seater Harrier T10 trainer was in the process of having its pre-flight checks done by ground crew technicians. Dressed in a smart suit and with a large cigar smouldering away, purely for effect, Mr Black looked the part of an important visitor.

'This area is out of bounds, sir,' one technician declared meekly, looking up from within the front cockpit, 'and there's no smoking allowed here.'

'Of course, I understand,' replied Mr Black, with a wave of his hand in acknowledgement, dropping his cigar to the ground and stubbing it out with his foot. 'You carry on, I shan't encroach any nearer. Tell me, who's flying this bird today?'

'Flight Lieutenants Reginald Charles and Stephen Gary, sir.'

'Charles and Gary eh? I hear they're good chaps.'

'Yessir,' agreed the technician, watching Mr Black turn and start his walk back with a friendly wave of his hand. He had discovered the information he required; now he intended to put it to use for his evil purposes.

Not far from a canteen, was a small, whitewashed, single-storey brick building with the obliging name of 'Pilots' Quarters' written in large letters on a sign planted in the grass outside the entrance door. Two of the gang changed into ground crew overalls in the MPV before they entered the building in their search for Charles and Gary. A dozen or more pilots were relaxing in a waiting room, chatting about the demonstration they were about to give to the crowds now flocking into the show, and talking through their routines. There was much arm-waving as hands with pointed fingers cut arcs through the air, the pilots engrossed in trying to impress on their colleagues the complexities of their routines and the skill they needed to perform them. Little notice was taken of the two men who entered the room. Each pilot had his name tag sewn to the top pocket of his shirt, and a quick glance was all it took for Mr Black's men to identify the two they sought. On the wall was a large flight operations board with the details of each demonstration. It gave the aircraft type and the times to get ready, to enter the cockpit and finally when take-off was planned for. The two gang members checked the times for Charles and Gary, and left to report to their boss.

'They're in the waiting room chatting to the other pilots and are due to get changed at two-thirty, Mr Black. At three they get in the plane and at three-thirty they take off.'

'Are there any other rooms where we can hide until we are ready to move?'

'Yes, sir. There's a small locked office near the front of the building that we can use.'

'Good. Do the pilots have separate changing rooms?'

'No, sir. There's a waiting room, and across the corridor is a small locker room with a washroom attached which they all seem to be using one or two at a time. The first pilots are already in there getting prepared.'

'Then we must wait until two-thirty and catch them in the locker room,' said Mr Black, glancing at his watch. 'We've less than an hour to wait and the security men will be checking to see that everyone, apart from the invited guests, leaves this side of the site. Mr Brown, see if you can find somewhere to hide our vehicle until we need it.'

Mr Brown nodded and left to undertake his task, while the rest of the gang entered the pilots' quarters and hid in the office until they were ready to make their move.

The Compass Gate, on the far side of the runway to the hangars, was the entrance used by visitors and was the area from which they would see the show. This was except for a few privileged personnel and potential customers, who were able to watch in comfort from a VIP marquee erected on the grass verge and situated on the factory side of the runway. It allowed them freedom from the hustle and bustle of the spectators and enthusiasts on the far side, and provided the salesman with a venue where they could wine and dine their customers from the bar, where free drinks and food were available. The show was held to attract funds for a local charity, but the opportunity was also used to advertise the ability British Aerospace has to build and maintain fighter and trainer aircraft.

Amongst those thronging their way through the Compass Gate was Ryall. This was the one show that he did not want to miss. Wandering through the crowds of visitors, he made his way close to the edge of the runway and sat on a small folding garden chair that he had brought with him. From there he could see the hangars and VIP marquee across the far side through his binoculars. Behind him the car park was quickly filling up, and the fun fair was in full swing with the roundabouts and big wheel turning to the hurdy-gurdy of the organ music blaring out. Visitors were enjoying all the events, including helicopter rides, and a display of classic motorcycles, cars, Land Rovers and traction engines.

The clock in the pilots' quarters showed nearly half past two. The air display had now begun with a Vampire jet car roaring down the runway, entertaining the vast crowd. Mr Black and the rest of his party waited, huddled in the office, listening to the cheers and clapping from outside resounding in the air.

His men knocked on the office door and showed them all into the locker room. It was a small, stark room with whitewashed walls, a wooden bench in the centre and a row of dark green lockers covering one wall. Tanya drew a sharp breath when she saw the two dead pilots. Each had a small bullet hole in their forehead and, after removing their flying suits, they were unceremoniously crammed into a locker. Her time in the RAF had brought her into contact with death on several occasions – but at a distance. It somehow seemed much more real and brutal this close up. Suzie, though, had been more used to seeing death when she was a mercenary, and felt more anger than shock at the waste of two young lives.

'Put the sign on the door,' Mr Black instructed one of his men. 'And you two can get your flying kit on,' he said to Suzie and Tanya.

'The GR7 is a single seater. Where's she going to sit – on my lap?' questioned Suzie.

'We are not taking a GR7. I had planned all along to take a T10, if there was one flying in the show, and there is. It's the two-seater trainer version of the GR7. It has the same capabilities and carries the same weapons, but has an extended cockpit that seats a pilot and an instructor. That's the plane we are going to steal. It is what I was hoping we would get, and will serve my purposes admirably. Taking a single seater GR7 was only a back-up plan.'

'But the whole plane will feel and react quite differently to the one we've been training on,' complained Suzie. 'The two-seater cockpit must make the plane larger and heavier, and we're already expecting it to carry a heavy load.'

'That's true, but you won't feel any difference,' Mr Black stated, with a smile. 'Mr Green modified the program to simulate the T10 when I found out that one was flying in the show. You've been training on that one for the last few days.'

'No wonder we've been having problems coping with the training,' stated Tanya.

The women were surprised by this latest revelation, and wondered if Mr Black wanted both of them to be in the plane when he carried out his robbery. This change only threw more confusion into the equation.

'I can manage the plane on my own,' Tanya insisted, trying to gain the upper hand.

'I'm sure you can, Miss Lilac, but I want both of you there in case of any problems, and it will be good practice for the pair of you. I want you to take turns in flying it.'

Suzie commented, 'I also know the correct procedures for making sure the aircraft ground locks are removed by the ground crew before we enter the cockpit, as well as removing the five locking pins before take-off. Do you?' she asked, already knowing what the answer would be. She could also play one-upmanship, and was not short of experience at that either, thanks to the tussles she had with Mike.

A surprised pout came over Tanya's face. 'No, but I could have if I'd been shown. I haven't,' she complained, glancing at Mr Black.

'It wasn't necessary to bother you with trivial details that Miss Ochre could handle, and was already familiar with.'

This was an unexpected twist, engineered by Mr Black. Tanya did not want to appear too hostile to the move, but felt more and more that he was stringing her along, and was favouring Suzie. This only reinforced the idea that he had other plans for her, either before or after the job was completed.

'Okay, that's fine. I just wasn't expecting both of us to fly, that's all. You could have told me.'

'You had enough things to worry about with all the complicated techniques of learning to fly a very difficult plane in such a short space of time. I didn't want to burden you with things that were of no consequence to the training you were doing,' Mr Black gushed, putting a fatherly hand on her arm. 'And besides, before we got here and assessed the position, I couldn't be absolutely certain that we would get the chance to steal a T10.'

'Sure, okay. So does Miss Ochre go in the pilot's seat in the front, then?' Tanya said, pointedly to Suzie.

'No, that's okay. I'll fly in the instructor's seat at the back. I believe the controls are more or less the same for both. You can take the pilot's position, it's bound to be identical to that on the simulator.'

'Good. That's settled then,' Mr Black stated, turning his attention to a clipboard he had been handed. 'This is the pilots' itinerary. It confirms that you have less than thirty minutes to get to the plane. You'd both better get your flying suits on straight away. I want you to take off all your make-up and put these on first,' he said, producing two corsets, dropping them on to the table.

'What the hell for?' demanded Tanya.

'I would have thought that was rather obvious. Especially to one who is so well endowed, my dear. We don't want the ground crew to see a shapely bouncing figure getting into the plane when the pilot is supposed to be a man, now do we?' Mr Black chided.

'No, I suppose not. I'll change in the washroom,' said Tanya.

'Nonsense, my dear. I've already seen that you're not embarrassed to let us see you in your underwear,' he said, recalling the way she had bounced down the simulator steps while undoing her flying suit zip. 'It'll only be for a few seconds while you get ready.'

'No, of course not, only ... I don't have any knickers on.'

Mr Black was unable to contain his surprise. 'Why not? You were wearing them earlier this morning.'

Tanya had to think quickly, and she did. 'When I had my tummy ache at the hotel ... well I ...'

Raising his hand to stop her, and closing his eyes in an acknowledging gesture, Mr Black interrupted, 'That's quite all right, my dear. I understand. You go into the washroom and change.'

Tanya gave him a thank-you smile and took her anti-g suit into the washroom. Suzie had to suffer the leers, changing in front of the men. Not that it worried her; she was used to seeing men drool over her shapely body whenever she sunbathed topless – and that was her usual way of sunbathing. Her problem was that she needed to be alone in order to hide the note somewhere. She turned her back on the men for a moment when zipping up the flying suit and deftly retrieved the note, concealing it in a pocket on her thigh.

Within 20 minutes both women were ready, and they sat waiting patiently for the hands on the white circular clock to slip past the last few minutes and show the time for them to begin the most audacious, and potentially disastrous, part of their plan so far.

'This bloody girdle's killing me,' Tanya complained, fidgeting and trying to get more comfortable. Suzie smiled. She had a trim, athletic figure and did not suffer the same discomforts as Tanya, plus, having fought in the jungle had hardened her to uncomfortable conditions, unlike the relatively softer life that Tanya had led.

While they waited, both women familiarised themselves with details of the start of their display. They needed to be sure they took off in the correct order without raising any suspicions or risking a collision. Once they were in the air, nothing could prevent them from achieving the initial objective of Mr Black's plan, and delivering the plane to his hideout by a round-about route that was designed to fool the authorities.

'The Hawks and Harriers traditionally lead the finale,' explained Mr Black. 'But the Harriers fly off 45 minutes earlier to run checks and practise manoeuvres after flying a few circuits. We don't want to arouse the suspicions of the ground crews by taking the aircraft out too early. It will be far better that you start the display in the correct position and, when you get into the air, keep going straight ahead instead of circling around the airfield like the rest of them. By the time they twig something is wrong, you'll be miles away.'

'We may have to lower our altitude before we pull away from the formation, to avoid a mid-air collision, but supposing someone tries to follow us?' Tanya asked.

'I doubt if they will. They've all got a routine to stick to. They are unlikely to follow you without permission. They'll probably think you've got a fault of some kind and are going to return to base. It will take them time to figure out what has happened. By then you'll be long gone.'

A pilot who had finished his flying tried to come into the locker room but was stopped by a 'cleaner' showing him a sign telling him that the floor had been washed.

'Someone had an accident in there and we're cleaning it up. We won't be more than a few minutes,' the cleaner told him. He shrugged and moved off.

The roar of aircraft, going through their displays, penetrated the building and rattled the windows with the vibrations they generated. Mixed with the echoing reverberations of the announcements booming from the tannoy system, the crowds gasped at the daring aerobatics of the wing-walking girls, and clapped enthusiastically at the skill all the pilots exhibited. The air filled with the smell of aviation fuel, and with the display in full swing, the time to make a move was reached. Tanya lifted her long red hair and tucked it into the helmet, helped by one of the guards. Suzie did the same with her shoulder-length black hair, then pulled two papers from her pocket. She put her chewing gum in the silver paper, screwed them up and threw both in a rubbish bin before leaving the room, followed by Mr Black.

The group made their way towards the hangar. All the aircraft for each display were lined up outside, along the tarmac, in the order they were to taxi on to the runway. Two

Hawks led the way, followed by a Sea Harrier with a GR7 Harrier next and the T10 Harrier at the rear.

Tanya's visor was down to mask her attractive face, and Suzie kept her head low as she looked around the aircraft, checked that the essentials were all in order and checked that the technicians had removed the locks. She pulled down her visor before she and Tanya climbed into the Harrier, helped by a ground crew technician who strapped Suzie in with the four pairs of harnesses clicking into a large buckle over her stomach. She dialled her weight into the controls and plugged in the connector with her radio and oxygen coupling. When this was done, she gave the technician the thumbs-up to show that she was now ready, having taken things slowly to give Tanya the opportunity to get her harness on.

Mr Black and his men were waiting to step in, shoot the technicians and snatch the aircraft by force, if it became necessary. This would entail activating his back-up plan, with the T10 having to take off vertically to get past the other aircraft waiting in the queue to start their display. Meanwhile, he and his men would make their escape during the confusion this would create. They anxiously watched the proceedings from a safe distance.

Disguising Tanya's shapely bosom had not been an easy task, even with the girdle. She had been given sufficient time to secure her straps, dial in her weight and plug in the lead before the ground crew technician checked on her. He glanced in both cockpits to reassure himself that everything was okay before pulling the canopy shut, cutting out the rest of the outside noise. Tanya gave him the thumbs-up, which he acknowledged before stepping down from the aircraft, removing the flight crew steps and wheeling them away.

Tension was high in both women. So far, all had gone smoothly, but they were only at the start of their daring robbery. Everything seemed strangely quiet, after the roar of the aircraft on display, as they sat in the cockpit and waited to get started, listening only to the control tower giving out instructions. Both could feel their hearts pounding and after a delay that seemed ages long, Tanya, following the ground crew's instructions, pressed the starter button to switch the engine on and moved into line with the other aircraft taxiing along the approach road towards the runway. Suzie talked to her constantly, giving her help and encouragement. Their lives were on the line, and one small slip could spell disaster for both of them.

One by one the aircraft took off, watched by Ryall perched on his seat on one side of the runway, and by Mr Black and his men standing on the other. All their eyes keenly watched the progress of the Harriers, with Ryall staring hard through his binoculars at each pilot, trying unsuccessfully to spot the plane that Tanya, or Suzie was due to fly.

The aircraft moved to the end of the runway with the T10 alongside the GR7, and Suzie started the pre-flight checks. 'Flaps to auto, Tanya,' she said. 'Check engine rate – steady at fifty-five per cent, nozzles down to forty per cent to check duct pressure – that's okay – return nozzles to ten per cent, check IGV – inlet guard veins at fifteen per cent, checks all done and everything okay. We're ready for take-off,' she declared. 'Are you okay?'

Breathing in heavily, with her nostrils flaring, Tanya was more nervous than she could ever remember being before. Not that she was going to let Suzie know that.

'I'm fine,' she replied. 'I just wish we didn't have to keep waiting for such a long time.'

'There's a lot of aircraft flying around. They have to be very careful and follow strict rules. It won't be long now. Keep calm.'

The tower announced to the two Harriers that they were cleared for take-off and should start their run. The GR7 blasted away, rumbled down the runway and took to the sky, but the T10 remained on the tarmac.

A voice broke in over the radio from the control tower. 'Have you forgotten what your routine is Flight Lieutenant Charles, or is there something wrong? You're supposed to have taken off in formation with the GR7. Do you have a problem? Please report immediately.'

A security car, with a flashing amber beacon on its roof, came charging along the sliproad towards the runway. Mr Black and his group were unsure what was going on. Was there something wrong?

Suzie talked to Tanya over the radio. 'Come on, let's go – now,' she shouted.

'Oh, God, what do I do?' Tanya said, in a state of panic. 'My mind's gone completely blank.'

'I'll take over,' announced Suzie, grabbing the Harrier's tandem controls.

She eased the throttle levers forwards. The T10 quickly gathered speed along the runway, and when it reached 125 knots Suzie raised the nose and the aeroplane lifted gracefully into the air, with the car left trailing in its wake. The bemused spectators wondered at first what was happening, and then applauded at what they thought was all a part of the display. The T10 shot over the treetops and into the bright blue expanse of space.

'Tanya, retract the undercarriage,' instructed Suzie.

She pulled the lever to retract the undercarriage while they were still gaining speed, streaking into the sky, and they were no more than a tiny dot within a minute. Suzie took the Harrier up to 50,000 feet, blasting her way into the ether.

'Christ, this thing moves like lightning,' she exclaimed, pushing the aircraft almost to the speed of sound.

She found the experience exhilarating, watching the clouds shoot past and disappear way below her, before she throttled back and levelled the aircraft off into a smoother, more silent flight, way above the height of any commercial aircraft that might be in the vicinity. They were instantly surrounded by an eerie silence, coupled with sunlight splitting into a cascading shower of light and colours as it streamed across the canopy. Suzie checked their heading and banked the aircraft round to fly in a southerly direction. They were encompassed by an almost incandescent blue sky, lit by sunlight, which was so bright that even behind their dark sun visors they found themselves squinting. Below, banks of white fluffy clouds, looking like a sea of cotton wool, gently rolled along in an ever-changing formation of exotic shapes.

Tanya, now over her flush of nerves and thinking clearly again, grabbed the controls. 'Let me have a feel of it,' she demanded.

'Okay. Are you sure you're all right?'

'I'm fine. There was just a few seconds where nerves got the better of me. Please don't tell anyone.'

'Okay. Have you got it?'

'Got it,' she said, pulling the throttle open once again and feeling the full force of the controls under her grasp. 'Oh God! This is amazing, especially after lumbering along in big old transporters. The feeling of speed and power is fantastic. The simulator is fun, but it's only make-believe and you know that you don't actually get off the ground, it's not like the real thing. This is almost as good as sex!' she exclaimed, pushing the aircraft speed almost to its limits.

'I now understand how a pilot can get caught up in the euphoria of excitement that a plane like this generates. It's like being drunk on the power of speed,' remarked Suzie. 'But we must drop down to below radar height to avoid detection. The RAF won't be very happy at losing one of their planes and are sure to scramble as many aircraft as they can to try and find us.'

'We can't let that happen,' stated Tanya, 'or we won't get our pay-off,' she proclaimed, taking the T10 down in a sharp dive to level off at treetop height.

Both women took several turns at trying out different manoeuvres, to familiarise themselves with the feel of the plane. They took an evasive route, out over the sea, before bringing it round in a wide arc to complete their task of delivering it to Mr Black's hideout at the barn.

Meanwhile, after watching the T10's successful take-off, and by the time it had barely disappeared in the distance, Mr Black and his men departed from Dunsfold. They left by the main entrance in their MPV, getting out of the airfield before security became aware of what had happened and closed the exits.

Delighted at the successful execution of his plan, Mr Black was in a relaxed mood on the journey back to his hiding place, unlike the rest of the visitors, including Ryall, who had to endure a frustrating time until they were allowed to leave the site. All in all, it had been a good day for Mr Black and his group.

19

Raid

Cradling an SA-80 sub-machine gun, the soldier held up his right hand and the two 4-tonne RAF trucks trundling up the approach road one behind the other, slowed to a halt at the barrier gate. It was a little after midday and although the sun was shining, at this height way up in the Brecon Beacons, the wind usually whistled across the RAF base at a high rate of knots, taking the edge off any warmth that it provided. Today was no exception. The first guard approached the driver of the leading truck as he wound down his window, while his colleague stood by the hut, his sub-machine gun at the ready.

'Afternoon, Sarg. I'm here to deliver some weapons and ammunition,' said the flat-nosed driver, yanking the hand-brake on.

'Where's your Form 1250?' asked the guard.

The driver looked blankly at him.

'Your ID cards and your orders,' he advised, shaking his head in disbelief.

'Oh, right. Yes, of course,' said the driver, handing over his and his escort's identity cards and their orders, pinned to a clipboard.

'How long have you been in?' the guard asked, as he perused the documents.

'Oh, not long,' replied the driver.

'It shows,' he said.

'Our truck's got the weapons, and the one behind has the ammunition,' the driver stated, anxious to take the guard's mind off his apparent lack of knowledge about how ID cards are referred to in the RAF.

The guard said nothing, read through the orders and glanced at the driver and his passenger, comparing them with the photos on their identity cards.

This was a military base where arms, vehicles and combat aircraft were kept. The base had stepped up security earlier in the week after a general alert had gone out from Whitehall following the simulator robbery. The sergeant on guard duty was mindful of this and determined to make the proper checks.

He walked to the back of the lorry, pulled the canvas apart and stared in at the stack of wooden boxes, all stamped with RAF part numbers. He compared the numbers with those on the order sheet and wandered to the rear truck. Taking the ID cards from the driver and his escort, he scrutinised them before handing them back and looking in the back of their truck. He strolled back to the first driver, waiting with his elbow leaning on the open window.

'You've not been here before, have you?'

'No, Sarg. This is the first time I've done this run.'

'I thought I didn't recognise you.'

'It makes a nice change to drive out here to the middle of nowhere, though I have to say it's a bit barren and secluded.'

'That's the way we like it,' announced the guard, handing the orders and ID cards back to the driver. 'Wait here.'

He wandered into his guard hut, past the second armed soldier, who was watching the proceedings, and picked up the telephone. The driver saw him speaking to someone and nodding his head in confirmation, before he finished the call and returned to the lorry.

He handed a small card with a number and date on it to

the driver. 'This is your day vehicle pass. Display it in the front window at all times while you're on the base and hand it back in on your way out. You will proceed directly to the armoury, and not make any diversions. When you've finished unloading, you will come directly back here, no wandering off to other parts of the base at any time. Is that understood?'

The driver nodded, 'Okay, Sarg. I understand. Which way do we go?'

As was the usual practice on military bases, the armoury was not signposted anywhere. The guard pointed to a crossroads a little over 100 yards into the base. 'Follow the signs to the canteen over to the right there. The armoury and ammunition stores are on the first turning to the right after the canteen, situated behind the wire fence. I've rung them to check on the delivery and told them you're on your way,' he said, lifting the barrier.

'Right, Sarg. Thanks,' said the driver, handing the clipboard to his passenger, sticking the vehicle pass in the window and crunching the lorry into first gear. It chugged slowly into the base, followed by the second lorry after the guard handed the vehicle pass to the driver and gave him the same instructions. The lorries gradually gathered speed until they reached 20 mph, the maximum speed allowed around the narrow one-way roads on this RAF establishment. The base was built in this secluded area at the beginning of the Second World War, and was now used mainly as a service and repair centre for aircraft, and for training new personnel.

'It's a good job we organised that phone call and the paperwork in advance of arriving here, Dave,' said the driver to his mate.

'Yeah, Ken,' he replied. 'Security's tight. We'd have never got into the place otherwise. Getting that inside info was essential and should make this job easy.'

'Even so, the quicker we get out of here the better I'll like it. The place is swarming with guards.'

The lorries wound their way past the canteen, turned right and slowed to a halt outside the brick-built, barbed-wire fenced armoury and ammunition store. An armourer approached the gate and unlocked it. The lorries were backed into the compound and the engines chugged into silence as the ignition was turned off. The lead driver and his passenger stepped down from the vehicle.

'I got a call from HQ saying that you would be delivering some weapons and ammunition, but I didn't get all the information and I can't find any paperwork about the delivery. That's just typical! What is it that we're supposed to have requested?' the armourer asked.

The driver's mate, Dave, dropped the tailgate down and jumped aboard. 'It's all in here,' he explained, pulling the canvas flaps apart.

The soldier glanced into the lorry then felt a knife jab him in the back and an arm clasp him around his throat.

'How many men are there in the armoury?' the driver asked, prodding the knife a little deeper into his side.

'Just me,' he shakily answered.

'And the ammunition store?'

'Nobody. It remains locked at all times.'

'Who has the key?'

'It's in my office.'

'Good. If you behave yourself, you'll live. If you don't, I'll kill you. Is that clear?'

'Crystal clear,' the armourer stated.

The ammunition store was unlocked. Four more men appeared from the lorry and moved fast to unload several empty crates. They dumped them in a corner and exchanged them for other, full crates that were much heavier, evident by the grunts and groans that preceded them being stacked in the lorry. The armourer was held at knife point and could only watch helplessly as the driver checked his list, and pointed out which crates were to be taken and which were to be ignored.

The telephone rang in the ammunition store.

'What should I do?' the armourer asked.

'Leave it,' growled the driver, 'you've gone for a pee.'

In less than 15 minutes, the men had loaded up all the crates they had come for into both lorries, and the four men hid back inside the empty crates.

'Let's go,' the driver announced to his mate Dave, still holding the soldier captive.

'Okay, Ken. What about him?' he asked.

'Kill him,' was the cold reply.

The armourer soldier's eyes opened wide in astonishment and fear as a hand clamped across his mouth and the knife was thrust into his side. He slumped face down on the floor with blood oozing from the deep wound.

The doors were shut and locked, and the driver glanced furtively round to see if he was being watched before closing the compound gate behind them. The lorries set off for the main entrance along the one-way system.

'Which way to the exit, do you reckon, Dave?' the driver asked of his passenger.

'Search me! That bloke I killed was probably supposed to tell us.'

Back at the armoury, the Engineering Officer in Charge, who was puzzled at being unable to get a reply from the armourer on the telephone, arrived to find the door locked. He opened it, found the armoury empty and went across to the ammunition store. That door was also locked, and he assumed the armourer was inside checking the ammunition and being careful about security. He unlocked the door and stepped inside to find the soldier, close to death, lying in a pool of blood.

In the lorries, after explaining to a soldier they had taken a wrong turning and were lost, the driver and his mate were given directions to the exit. The two vehicles at last got back to the crossroads.

'There's the exit. We're nearly home free,' stated Ken, winding the steering wheel round and swinging his lorry towards the barrier.

At the ammunition store, the wounded soldier gasped out his message. 'Two trucks – raided the ammunition store – fake soldiers, got to stop them,' he said, before collapsing.

Grabbing the telephone, the OC jabbed the button, 2,2,2. The emergency calls operator swiftly came on the line.

'Wing Commander Winterbourne here. Fake soldiers have raided the ammunition store. Close the base immediately,' he instructed.

The base tannoy system burst into life and announced, 'Operation roundup is now in progress. Would the duty guard please report to the guardroom immediately.'

This instruction told all RAF personnel on site that a suspected intruder had infiltrated the base, and that all gates were to be shut by the guards. Everyone was to have their ID cards checked and their identity confirmed; a check that was particularly applicable to anyone who was a stranger or a visitor to the site, and one that was very thorough.

The alarm rang out as the guard lifted the barrier and stepped forward to collect the vehicle passes from the lorries approaching the main gate.

'Close the gate,' he instructed, turning to the second guard.

The barrier dropped back down and the guard held up his hand to stop the lorries.

'Your IDs will have to be checked before you can leave,' he insisted, releasing the safety catch on his sub-machine gun.

'What's the problem, Sarg?' asked the driver, noting the release of the safety catch.

'I don't know yet. It may simply be an exercise drill. Wait

here until I find out what's happening and give me your ID cards,' he said, extending his hand to receive the cards.

'Not a hope,' claimed the first lorry driver, putting his vehicle into gear and drawing his gun. The guard lifted his sub-machine gun only to be met by a burst of shots from the driver, firing at him through the open window as the trucks moved off towards the barrier. Hit in the chest, the guard was propelled to the side of the road. Their accelerators pressed to the floor, both lorries gathered pace. The second guard rushed out and dropped to the ground as a fusillade of bullets from the passing lorries smashed the windows in the guard hut and tore lumps out of the woodwork.

The vehicles crashed through the barrier and sped off down the road. The guard dashed to his colleague, who was hurt, but still breathing.

'Stop them,' he insisted. 'I'm okay.'

Steadying himself with an open stance, the second guard let loose with a volley of shots at the disappearing trucks. Bullets raked the rear lorry as two men appeared from behind the canvas and began firing back. The guard moved to the centre of the road, ignored the shots peppering the ground around him, dropped to one knee to steady himself, and fired a continuous wave at the back of the vehicle, emptying a full clip and hitting one of the men. He yanked the clip out, threw it to the ground and stuffed in a full clip. Snapping it home with the heel of his hand, he slid back the cocking lever and resumed firing while the rear lorry was still in range, peppering it with bullet holes as it sped away.

Suddenly there was a violent explosion. The blast threw debris and bodies into the air as rounds of ammunition ignited, spraying bullets in all directions. The shell of the lorry, ripped and burning, span out of control, slewed sideways on to the verge and plunged headlong down an embankment. It careered on, ploughed into a ditch and overturned, crunching to a halt on its side.

The front lorry, with part of its canvas still smouldering from the impact of the blast, beat a hasty retreat and disappeared down the winding road.

The base ambulances were in demand, and took both the armourer and the guard to the hospital operating theatres. Surgeons began their work, operating on both men in an attempt to save their lives. Others sped to the burning truck, but there was nothing for them to do there, except collect the remains of the bodies.

Group Captain Laurence Cheshire, the Base Commander, was informed of the theft and gun battle at the main entrance, and set Operation Hunt in progress immediately. The tannoy system rang out the announcement of the operation and men scrambled to a pre-arranged assembly point where they were briefed on the robbery.

After receiving search areas for each of the six groups, they dashed to their Land Rovers and set off in pursuit of the fake soldiers. Two helicopters also took to the sky to assist, and the local police were informed of the theft and asked to set up roadblocks in a 20-mile radius around the camp.

Many of the airmen had heard the blast when the truck exploded and were curious to know what it was. Now they knew, and they also knew that two of their comrades were in a critical condition. All service personnel viewed attacks on their comrades severely and this made the men a lot more eager to search diligently for the truck and its occupants. Now, almost half an hour after the shootings, they streamed out of the base and sped down the road, each one peeling off towards their appointed area.

Meanwhile, the remaining fake soldiers were using the time to put as much distance between them and the base as they could. They thrashed the truck down narrow country lanes, blasting the horn at every bend to avoid a collision, and taking dangerous risks in order to escape their now inevitable pursuers. The area around the base was mainly wild, open countryside and sparsely populated. Their luck held, with no vehicle approaching at a critical bend in the road.

Near the outskirts of a small hamlet, the truck turned off the road on to a dead-end dirt track that led towards a small coppice. Hidden among the trees were a supermarket delivery van and two cars; a VW Golf and a Ford Escort. All were stolen the previous day and placed there in readiness for their getaway.

'Let's get these boxes into the van and quickly,' the driver stated.

They started loading them when the sound of an approaching helicopter filled the air. The men stopped and looked skywards. Between branches of the trees, they could just make out the dark outline of the helicopter, its rotor blades spinning in a blur. It passed overhead and the roar faded as it disappeared into the distance across the hills.

'Do you think they were looking for us, Ken?' asked one man of the driver.

'Maybe. But it doesn't matter. They didn't see us and we'll be away from here in a few minutes. C'mon, let's finish loading up and get out of here.'

The four men moved the stolen weapons into the van, stashing them in the back and hiding them behind crates of tinned fruit. More crates were stacked in front of them before they closed the doors and locked them.

'Get rid of this RAF gear,' ordered the driver, stripping off his uniform.

'What are we going to do with these vehicles? Burn them?' he was asked.

'Don't be stupid! They'd see the smoke for miles. We'll leave them.'

'My prints are all over the truck and I've got a record. They'll soon trace me,' his colleague argued.

'Then you'd better get out of the country before they get to you.'

'I didn't bargain for us having to shoot our way out of the camp. I though we'd have plenty of time to disappear before they came after us.'

'And me. You two take a roundabout way to the flat and I'll meet you there with the cash when Dave and I have delivered this little lot to Mr Black and got our money. Then we'd all better lay low for a while until the heat dies down.'

They all changed into civilian clothes. Ken and his mate Dave each donned a light brown overall and climbed into the delivery van cab. The other two men jumped into the VW and they motored back to the road. After checking that no other vehicles were in sight, the VW turned right and the van turned left, each going their separate ways and disappearing into the rolling Welsh hills.

20

Hide

The Alsatian dog gave several gruff barks, and sprinted ahead for a few yards before stopping to turn and check that his master was still in sight. He was.

Sir Joseph Sterling strolled slowly along the woodland footpath beside the common, chatting to his son Jim, who held the hand of his attractive wife Jenny. Her parents had immigrated to England from Jamaica before starting their family, and Jenny brought them great joy when she was born. Her mother's happiness was cut short when it was discovered that she had cancer, and most of Jenny's memories of her were of the struggle she had to beat the disease while keeping a happy face and promoting a philosophical view on her chances of succeeding. She eventually lost the battle when Jenny was ten years old. Her father, Ken, saw to it that their daughter continued to get a good education, and after leaving grammar school she started work as a clerk for a Foreign Office Special Operations group. Jenny progressed to becoming a field operative and was transferred to a department under Sir Joseph Sterling. Through her work for him she met his son, Jim. Their relationship grew and, after a disastrous wedding day that kept them apart for nearly two weeks, they were eventually married.

Today, they joined Sir Joseph in his regular Saturday afternoon walk with his dog, Oliver. It was a walk that was as regular as his demanding job and full life would permit, though he had recently made attempts to cut down on the hours he worked, without a great deal of success. Weekends were the only time when he could usually rely on having an hour or two to exercise his faithful dog, since the death of his wife three years earlier. During the rest of the week he often came home late and Oliver had to be satisfied with a short stroll before settling down for the night.

Jim knew that Mike and Suzie were carrying out a job for his father because, not only were they friends, but they were also his partners in their boat building company. Before leaving, they explained to him why they would not be available for a while to help him and Jenny with the business.

Jenny had become a partner in SMJ Boatyard when she married Jim, but declined to have the boatyard name changed to include her initial. What Jim was now attempting to do was extract some details from his father about the job that Mike and Suzie were on, and more importantly, to find out how long they were likely to be away. He discovered that his father was reluctant to say too much about their work, and refused to commit himself to a rigid timetable, even to his enquiring son.

'At the moment, Mike is out in an army helicopter looking for the hideout where Suzie has been taken,' he told Jim.

'Taken? Does that mean she didn't go willingly?' he asked.

'No. She went willingly, but unexpectedly, and without us being able to track her movements. Our problem is that we've only got an approximate indication at the moment of where she's gone. It's like searching for the proverbial needle in a haystack.'

'And how long is Mike going to be searching for this needle? And why is it that you don't have a better idea where Suzie is? Is she in any danger?' Jim asked, his fondness for her apparent.

'Suzie is level-headed and resourceful. I am sure that she is all right and we will find her soon.'

'I'm pleased to hear that. She is more than a business partner. Both Mike and Suzie are very good friends of ours as well. Jenny and I can manage the business without them for a while, but it's obviously more difficult.'

'I appreciate that, Jim, and I'm sure that it won't be much longer, perhaps another day or two. We're pulling out all the stops to locate her. I can't really tell you much more than that.'

Sir Joseph picked up a stick and threw it for his dog. Despite it landing only a few yards away, Oliver eagerly raced after it, gathered it in his jaws and bounded back to his master, dropping it at his feet and furiously wagging his tail, hoping for a repeat chase. Sir Joseph was about to throw the stick again when his mobile telephone rang. It usually meant business. He shrugged his shoulders and handed the stick to Jim, who threw it a great distance for the dog to chase after.

Jim and Jenny walked on ahead, not wanting to eavesdrop on his father's conversation, knowing that many things Sir Joseph dealt with were highly classified. He spoke for a few seconds, slapped the mobile shut and caught the pair up.

'I'm sorry, but I'm going to have to end our afternoon walk rather abruptly. There's a bit of a flap on and I must go in to work.'

'What, on a Saturday afternoon, Dad?' Jim asked.

'Yes, I'm afraid so. This is a problem that I feared might occur. It's connected to the job that Mike and Suzie are dealing with, so they may not be back with you quite so soon after all. I'm sorry.'

They all turned around and headed back to Sir Joseph's plush Woking house.

'That's okay. What's a few more days and a few more lost orders,' Jim sarcastically bemoaned.

'That's very unfair,' commented his father, stopping to

face him while he spoke. 'Mike and Suzie are engaged in something that's very important, and I know they are relying on the pair of you to hold the fort,' he admonished. 'Come on, Oliver,' he shouted, and the dog came charging back to his side.

Jenny tugged Jim's hand and frowned, giving him a 'please don't complain' look, which he acknowledged.

'I didn't mean to sound bitchy, Dad. I know it must be important, or you wouldn't have asked them.'

Sir Joseph smiled at his son. 'That's okay, Jim. It *is* important, and if there were anyone else that could do the job for me, I would use them. Sadly, there isn't, and until I can crack this case, I'll have to go on asking them to help me.'

Back at the house, Jim and Jenny said goodbye and left in their Rolls-Royce, heading for home, a detached house in Weybridge in a quiet cul-de-sac near the river. The car and house were among the many nice things that Jim was able to purchase after he became the fortunate winner of a rollover jackpot lottery win, two years earlier.

After dashing up to London, Sir Joseph met DI Brooke in the lobby of his Whitehall office to discuss the loss of the Harrier.

'Hello, Colin, do come on up,' Sir Joseph said, tapping his arm and wandering up the stairs to his office.

The building was quiet on this Saturday afternoon, with most of the staff off work for the weekend, enjoying a sunny summer's day. Sir Joseph rattled his keys as he searched for the right one to open the door to his office.

'Come in, Colin. Take a seat,' he said, pointing to the chair in front of his desk. Sir Joseph pulled up the blind and pushed the window open a few inches. The roar of London traffic seeped into the office and the level of noise prevented the window from being opened any further if their conversation was not to be disturbed too much.

'That was a clever move, stealing a Harrier from a small air show, Colin. I should have anticipated that, then perhaps those two pilots would still be alive. I am certain that our ruthless Mr Black was behind it. It fits the pattern we were expecting.'

'Yes, I agree. But you mustn't blame yourself for not thinking of it. Black is, as you said, ruthless, and would have found some way to get what he wants, even if it meant killing a lot more people. The next question is, what do they want the plane for?'

'And can we locate it before they either sell or make use of it? The RAF have scrambled all the planes they can spare and they and the police are using their helicopters to search for it, but I gather the T10 dropped off the radar screen very quickly after it was stolen. Was it armed?'

'No, thank goodness, not for an air show. I've asked for a general alert to be put out to all the bases where arms and amunition are stored, and also the factories where they're manufactured. I'm still waiting to hear from them, but hopefully nothing is missing,' Brooke advised.

'Good. How long do you expect that to take?' Sir Joseph asked.

'Not too long. Certainly, some time this afternoon for the bases. It might take a while longer for the factories to respond because most of them are shut for the weekend, though there's usually a security man on guard. If not, the local police have been asked to find the keyholder, normally the manager, and get him to check the place out.'

'We could be in for a bit of a wait, then. Would you like a cup of tea or coffee?'

'Yes, a coffee would be nice, thank you. I'll put the kettle on,' said Brooke.

'I didn't have the heart to ask Miss Wilson to come back in again this afternoon,' Sir Joseph stated. 'I wonder where she keeps the biscuits.'

DI Brooke and Sir Joseph drank their coffees while discussing the motives that Mr Black may have for wanting a Harrier Jump Jet, while at the same time checking on progress in the search for the missing aeroplane.

'Good. Thank you very much for your splendid efforts, Dennis,' praised Sir Joseph, returning the telephone to its cradle. 'The Major has as many men out and about in a search as he can muster and, along with the police, is checking small flying clubs and abandoned airfields. He will ring me straight away if they find anything; however, I think it's unlikely the thieves will chance landing the Harrier in one of them, but we have to check them all the same, just to make sure. So far there have been no reports of any sightings,' he informed Brooke. 'Before they went off the screen, the radar showed them heading towards the coast, then they disappeared from view. So my guess is they've either crashed, which I think is unlikely because we would have found the wreckage by now, or they've gone down to a very low altitude and out to sea to escape detection. I imagine they intend to sneak back in, low over the coast.'

'That's very clever. It means we've got no way of telling where they're heading for unless we get a visual sight of them,' Brooke acknowledged.

'Do we know how much fuel was aboard and what sort of distance the aircraft is capable of flying?'

'Yes, sir, we do. I spoke to the ground crew at Dunsfold and they informed me that the aircraft is filled with enough aviation fuel to do a forty-five-minute practice run and complete the air show display, plus some in reserve in case of an emergency. It was due to be airborne in total for almost an hour, and has full tanks with enough fuel to travel to Land's End and still make a vertical landing. Vertical landings take a lot of fuel,' he added.

'Hmm. They're unlikely to make a conventional landing – it's too risky. Someone might see them, and it would have to be an existing airfield, or at least a temporary runway and that would be easily visible from the air. A vertical landing in a secluded spot in the middle of the countryside is much more likely.'

'Yes, I agree,' said Brooke. 'It's one of the plane's distinct advantages, and one of its strong selling points.'

'Do you have any information from the site about any witnesses to the theft?'

'Only preliminary reports so far. But the guard on the security gate clearly remembers a MPV arriving with two good-looking women in it, but doesn't remember seeing them leave, though he may have missed them, of course.'

'That could be Suzie and her pilot friend Tanya. There's a good chance they were piloting the Harrier.'

'Could they be flying the plane across to the Continent?'

'That's possible, but I think unlikely. Mr Black feels safer on home territory. And, as we think that Mr Black's headquarters are in this country, I am inclined to believe that the aircraft will be brought back here via a stretch of deserted coastline.'

'So, they must have already picked out an isolated site where they can land. Motorway cameras caught the motorcycle courier that my men lost the other day, on the M4 and M5 making his way towards the West Country. They were unable to track him any further when he pulled off at junction 28.'

'The West Country is where Mike Randle has been concentrating his search. He was already of the opinion that it was the most likely area, and it certainly looks as if he's right. He's got a good nose for detecting things like that; especially when it's crucial for him to find Suzie. They seem to have a sort of telepathy with each other. A very useful feature, which I understand has got them out of scrapes on more than one occasion when they were mercenaries.'

'Right. In that case I'll get the boys to check the map for possible southern coastline areas in the west that are sparsely populated, and ask them to search the surrounding areas. We can only hope that we get lucky,' said Brooke.

'Assuming they bring the plane back into this country and land, their options then are what? They could hide it, load it on to a trailer to transport it somewhere else, or even refuel it to fly further on.'

'But we don't think that's likely. My guess is, they already have a place to hide the plane waiting for them, sir,' Brooke maintained.

'Yes, I tend to agree with you. Mr Black always plans things well in advance. However, I still want to be in possession of all the details about any possibilities that are open to them. If they don't hide the Harrier straight away, that leaves transporting or refuelling it. Get in touch your man at Dunsfold, and find out how difficult it is to do either of those will you, Colin?'

'Right away,' said Brooke. His hand was hovering above the telephone when it began to ring. 'I'll use Miss Wilson's phone,' he declared, rising from his seat and heading for her desk in the adjacent room.

Sir Joseph nodded and answered his telephone. By the time Brooke returned with the answers to his questions, Sir Joseph was staring hard at the file on his desk and tapping his teeth with the end of his pen. Brooke knew this was a sign that he was thinking more deeply and had a problem on his mind that needed sorting through. He sat and waited for him to speak.

Looking up from his file, Sir Joseph removed his glasses and said in a quiet voice, 'An RAF base in mid-Wales has just reported a break-in, early this afternoon, by an audacious group of men posing as soldiers. They arrived in two trucks and collected several hundred rounds of twenty-five millimetre cannon ammunition, and a quantity of Maverick and Sidewinder missiles. They're still checking to find out exactly how many are missing.'

'Bloody hell!' exclaimed Brooke, sinking into the chair and running his hands through his thick crop of slightly wavy, dark hair.

'The alarm was raised as they were leaving the camp and shots were fired. Two RAF personnel were hurt, both seriously, but one of the trucks was hit by the duty guard after it crashed through the barrier, and it exploded, killing all the occupants.'

'What a mess! Do they have any clues as to who they were?'

'No. But they've located the lorry that got away. It was found only a few miles from the camp along with another stolen car, which was presumably the getaway car intended for the men who died in the explosion. Needless to say the vehicles were empty, of course. The police are examining them, and the burnt-out wreck, for clues. We badly need a break in this case, Colin, so let's hope the unplanned confrontation with the base guards has made them careless enough to leave a few clues lying about.'

'I didn't realise we had a base in Wales that held those sort of armaments.'

'No, not many people do. It's supposed to be restricted knowledge that only a few top brass and some RAF personnel were privy to. Even many of the soldiers on the base aren't aware of it.'

'I suppose it's silly to suggest that it may not be anything to do with Black?'

'Oh, I'm sure it's Mr Black all right. Our erstwhile inspector does seem to have the knack of getting hold of information that is not intended for his ears,' remarked Sir Joseph.

'How soon can we find out exactly what's missing?' Brooke enquired.

'Quite quickly I think. I know the Base Commander there; he's a friend of mine. That's how I managed to get Paula on to our team. I've already telephoned him. They're running an inventory check right now, and he'll ring back when it's complete and they know how many missiles were taken. Some may have been destroyed when the truck exploded, so it may not be possible to confirm exactly how many they actually got away with.'

'Do you think that Black wants to sell the Harrier as an armed aeroplane to someone?'

'Perhaps, but that merely shifts the problem of what they want it for, from one person to another. What did you find out?'

Brooke glanced at his notes. 'Well, refuelling the plane is not difficult if you've got access to a standard NATO refuelling point – probably also not that hard to obtain. Moving the plane by road is more tricky. The wings need to be removed. That in itself is not a problem, because there are only six bolts holding it on. The difficulty is that the outriggers – the stabilisers – are on the wings, and a special cradle is needed to support the fuselage to prevent it from falling over when the wings are taken off. The aircraft also needs to be de-fuelled first, because the fuel tanks are in the wings. Even with the right equipment it would take an expert at least three hours to achieve this.'

'That all sounds a bit messy to me. I think Mr Black is more likely to go for the refuelling option. He could then either use the aircraft or move it to almost anywhere. Meanwhile, he needs a place to hide it. Unfortunately for us, the Harrier can be easily hidden from the air. All he needs is camouflage netting and a tree to hide it under.'

'Is there anything that we can do to stop him?'

'Yes, I think so. I'm considering the idea that we should put out a nationwide appeal for anyone to get in touch with us who thinks they've seen a Harrier land in a remote spot away from any airfields. Even clipping treetops can't hide it completely,' Sir Joseph asserted. 'And it makes quite a noise.'

'Good idea,' Brooke stated.

'This has to be the work of Mr Black, Colin. It all fits the pattern. First he steals a simulator to train two pilots, then he uses them to steal the plane, and meantime raids an RAF base to obtain the armaments he needs. So, not only does he now have a sophisticated combat aircraft, but also the weapons to arm it with.'

'I assume that you've still not heard any good news from Mike Randle?'

'No, not yet. He is, as I said, scouring the countryside by helicopter and moving further west all the time. If he's in the air and the Harrier is flown anywhere near him, he might see it. But that's like hoping for a miracle.'

'Yes. Still, miracles do happen sometimes and we could do with a bit of luck.'

'I wonder if it was Suzie who was flying that aeroplane,' Sir Joseph pondered.

'My men are at Dunsfold searching the area for clues, but I'm not hopeful of finding anything useful to us,' Brooke confessed.

'We must double our efforts to find him, Colin. I shan't rest while that maniac's on the loose with such a devastating weapon at his disposal.'

21

The Plan

The T10 Harrier roared overhead in hover mode then drifted down, swaying a little from side to side. Swirling leaves were thrust into the air and performed a dance before floating back down to the dusty surface. The aeroplane landed with a gentle bump on a small square of cleared forest, alongside the barn that Mr Black now used as his new temporary headquarters. His back-up premises were adequate enough for his plans, but a lot less comfortable for his men; not that this was ever a consideration that he worried about. To him, the only drawback was the more distant journey from Dunsfold would take a little longer, but that was a small price to pay for the safety and isolation that he required. The weeks of planning and searching for suitable premises were now showing their value.

Mr Green opened the large wooden doors and Tanya was happy to let Suzie land the plane, taxi the Harrier into the straw-laden barn and switch off the engine. She parked it close to the simulator, sitting on its shiny hydraulic ram jacks, looking quiet and still, like an alien monster from *War Of The Worlds.*

'Congratulations on getting away with the plane. Did everything go okay?' Mr Green asked Suzie, as she descended from the aircraft by the wooden steps that he had pushed into place.

'Stealing the T10 went like clockwork, Mr Green,' she related, removing her helmet and shaking out her hair. 'Though I thought that killing the two pilots was unnecessary.'

'We can't leave any witnesses to incriminate us.'

'That's what I'm worried about,' thought Suzie.

'How was the flight?' Mr Green asked, watching Tanya climb from the cockpit.

'The whole journey was exhilarating.'

'And how about you, Miss Lilac? Was it exhilarating for you as well?' he asked, offering a hand to help her down, which she declined.

'Very. The treetop flight on the way back was particularly thrilling. I enjoyed that. It's a cracking plane to fly, once you've mastered the controls.'

She looked at Suzie, wondering if she intended to say something about her panicking before take-off and taking control of the aircraft away from her. Suzie smiled and said nothing. Having Tanya indebted to her was a good position to be in, and may pay dividends at a later date.

'You might as well relax for a while. It'll take Mr Black another hour or more to get back,' Mr Green concluded.

'Good. I can't wait to get this bloody girdle off,' Tanya moaned.

'On the way down I noticed there's a big motor mower sitting by the edge of the field now,' stated Suzie.

'How very observant of you. Yes, later this evening we plan to have all the long grass cut down in a wide strip through the centre to make a runway,' Mr Green divulged. 'We shan't do it before dusk in case it's spotted from the air. When you leave to carry out your part of the job, the plane will be too heavy to take off vertically with a full tank of fuel aboard, so you'll make a conventional take-off.'

'Presumably you'll fashion a runway.'

'Exactly.'

'Won't the ground be a little rough for the take-off?' Suzie asked.

'No. Mr Black has acquired the runway plates that the armed forces use to build temporary runways in jungle conditions.'

Suzie lifted her eyebrows. 'He thinks of everything, doesn't he?'

'We try to,' he agreed.

Mr Green's assessment of the time Mr Black would return was right. It was past six o'clock before his PSV pulled into the rough, tree-flanked, winding lane that led to the barn. He was delighted that the second part of his plan had gone so well, and congratulated everyone on a job well done. Nothing was said about the delay in taking off. Perhaps he had not realised there was a problem, and Tanya had no intention of telling him.

'You should all be proud of your achievements. Did both of you fly the plane and get a feel for it?' he asked, wandering around the aircraft and patting it like a baby.

'Yes, we did,' announced Suzie. 'It was an exciting experience.'

'Good. Two of the first three hurdles have now been successfully negotiated and the final part of my plan goes into action tomorrow,' beamed Mr Black.

'Three hurdles?' thought Suzie. 'I can only think of two. I wonder what the third is.'

She was soon to find out the answer.

Tanya thought, 'Tomorrow! That's quick. I hope Ryall's keeping a good watch, in case I don't get to speak to him.'

'Get that hook welded into place straight away,' Mr Black instructed.

A boiler-suited man was shown by Mr Green what he required. He dragged a trolley, holding two gas bottles, up to the aircraft and started his work.

'Are we going back to the hotel tonight?' Tanya asked hopefully.

'No, my dear. We will all stay here tonight and set off on the final leg of our adventure early tomorrow morning. I am expecting two visits tonight. One will be a truck to refuel the aircraft, and the other will be a delivery van, loaded with weapons.'

'Weapons? Don't you have enough guns already?' suggested Suzie.

'These are weapons for the Harrier. You will be armed with both cannon and missiles. The other team was instructed to obtain them earlier today.'

'That must be his third hurdle,' thought Suzie. 'And he's got another team working for him. That's a lot of people to pay off. Surely he can't pay them all with fake money and then bump them off, so this job must be really big.'

'When you and Miss Lilac fly out of here tomorrow, you will go fully armed and ready for the task in hand,' boasted Mr Black.

'What task?' Tanya asked bluntly. 'You keep talking to us about this job without telling us what it is we have to do. And why do we need all those weapons?'

'Patience, Miss Lilac. Everyone will know what is expected of them before this night is over.'

The barn door creaked open a short distance allowing the roar of a vehicle, slowly chugging its way up the difficult narrow lane in low gear, to filter through. A guard poked his head through the gap. 'The fuel tanker's arrived, Mr Black,' he shouted.

'Good,' he replied, turning to Mr Brown. 'Get the plane refuelled, immediately the man's finished welding that hook into place. Miss Lilac and I will be in the caravan having a chat if you need me – but knock first.'

He beckoned Tanya to follow him and shuffled his way to the caravan at the rear of the barn. She trundled after him, wondering what he wanted, and praying that it wasn't sex, though thought it was most likely.

It was obvious that Suzie's presence was not required. Why? Was he so elated at their success that he fancied having Tanya at that moment, or was there something more sinister on his mind? Suzie sat at the bench next to Mr Green while she waited to find out and watched the man in the boiler suit holding the large black welding mask to shield his eyes from the bright, arcing light. It lit up the whole barn in a blue-white glow as the specially manufactured hook was argon gas welded on to the centre pylon on the underside of the fuselage.

Climbing the caravan steps first, Mr Black plonked himself down on the kitchen-diner settee and patted the seat next to him. Tanya heeded his request and sat beside him.

'At least he hasn't gone straight into the bedroom,' she thought, 'though this is where he first had Suzie. I hope he's not kinky enough to want it here again.'

'I wanted a quiet word with you, my dear, because tomorrow will be a significant day for you.'

'And for Miss Ochre as well, I imagine?'

'You no doubt recall that I said only one of you would be selected to fly the Harrier when the big day finally arrived?'

'Yes, but now we've got a two-seater plane. Though, I think you ought to know that Miss Ochre told me, in confidence of course, that she was once a policewoman. I don't like to break a trust, but I felt that it was too important not to tell you, considering why we are all here.'

'Thank you, my dear. That merely confirms what I had in mind. It so happens that I had already decided that she will not be a part of my plans. But you don't need to worry about that. My men will deal with her in the morning. All right?'

'Yes. Okay.' Tanya was pleased, but also very surprised. 'I can fly the plane on my own with no problems,' she assured him, while feeling slightly worried that she would now have to, without the help that Suzie had given her.

Mr Black continued, 'I promised that if you were to co-operate, I would pick you when the big day comes. Well, tomorrow is the day and I'm keeping my promise to you. It's going to be the most important, life-changing day of your whole existence so far.'

'But not nearly as important as it must be for you,' she probed.

He visibly swelled up with pride. 'Yes, I think you could safely say that tomorrow will be the crowning glory in my distinguished career of crime. And one that will leave the authorities wishing they had listened to me much closer, instead of merely scoffing at all my methods and ideas, and humiliating me by insisting that I leave.'

A small piece of the complex jigsaw that was Robert Black fell into place for Tanya. He was driven by the need to show those who had rejected him that he was better than they were, and he intended to show them by staging a big event that none of them could ignore. He had already grabbed their attention by stealing the Harrier, though the question still remained, what was that all-important event?

'You're going to show them all, aren't you?' Tanya delved.

'Yes, I am. They will rue the day that I was forced to resign.'

'But what is it that you're going to show them?'

'I am going to demonstrate how to commit the world's greatest robbery, and use a stolen RAF aeroplane with its armaments to achieve it. The authorities will look stupid for allowing it to happen. Then, I am going to sell that plane, with the remaining missiles, for a very tidy sum to a Middle East terrorist group. That will make them all sit up and take note. They won't laugh at me after that.'

Tanya now saw Mr Black in a new light. It worried her. She had always looked upon him as determined and a little eccentric, but now she thought of him as unstable as well.

'How safe will it be for me tomorrow?' she wondered. 'I must play an important part in this plan of yours?' she asked.

201

'Yes, you do. When the task is complete I shall reward you very handsomely, as I've told you before.'

'How handsomely? After all, it seems that I really am your only pilot now.'

Mr Black was not naïve, and knew exactly what she was pressing for. 'That is partly why I wanted to talk to you in private.'

'Go on.'

'Well, although we should be scooping a massive haul tomorrow, there are quite a few hirelings and minor workers, apart from the close members of my consortium, that we have to share the spoils with. I was thinking that, if you were to become a sleeping partner with me, we could eliminate some of the recipients, and then your share would be increased quite considerably. What do you say?'

He was even more ruthless than Tanya had thought, and she needed to be convinced that her safety was assured. 'That sounds okay, but what's to stop you from doing the same to me afterwards?'

'Have you not enjoyed our evening get-togethers?'

'Why, of course I have,' lied Tanya, putting a friendly hand on his knee for a few seconds.

'Then how could you possibly think that I would do you any harm?'

'I saw how you dealt with those other people, including Miss Pink.'

'Ah, yes. But she was a traitor. You told me so yourself.'

Tanya had to acknowledge that fact. 'And money is also a powerful incentive.'

'That's very true, but there will be more money for each of us than we could possible spend in the rest of our lives. Even for someone as young as you.'

'Even so, it doesn't mean that you won't want all of it.'

'At my age, the odd million or two doesn't make that much difference,' Mr Black casually threw in.

Tanya's eyes widened. 'The odd million or two? How much do you expect to get in this robbery then?'

'Around forty million dollars worth of gold bullion, plus another ten million pounds for the Harrier.'

'Forty million dollars. How much is that in pounds?'

'About twenty-one million pounds sterling, give or take a few hundred thousand.'

'That's a lot of money, and a lot of gold. No wonder it's such a weight.'

'Exactly. That's where you come in.'

Things were beginning to fall into place for Tanya. 'So that's why you need the Harrier, to lift the heavy load of gold.'

'That's right,' Mr Black declared, putting an arm around Tanya's waist. 'The other thing you need to consider is, of course, that after the robbery we will all be vigorously hunted by the authorities. I can whisk you off to a safe haven, where we can live in luxury and remain free. It's all arranged, and my hideout villa in a sunny climate is there waiting for us. We will be king and queen of the district with everyone clamouring to befriend us. They will all be jealous of our wealth, and money talks.'

'It all sounds too good to be true.'

'Trust me, my dear. For you and me, it can be true.'

'With that much stolen gold, you might have difficulty trying to dispose of it,' she said, trying to consider all aspects of likely problems that could affect the outcome.

'You've no need to worry your head about that. I already have an international buyer lined up to take the ingots off my hands, and a representative of PLOY, the Peoples Liberation Organisation of Yalon, to purchase the Harrier. All the details have been taken care of. We can be out of the country in a matter of hours after the robbery.'

A smile crossed Tanya's face. She allowed him to undo the buttons on her blouse, but her mind was elsewhere, going through the options open to her, now that she knew what the full plan was.

'I think we should adjourn to the bedroom and talk over any little detail that you may have questions about,' he suggested.

22

Two Into One

After Mr Black had confided his plan to Miss Lilac and satisfied his lust for her, which as usual did not take him very long, he summoned Mr Brown and quietly gave him some instructions. Mr Brown returned to the caravan with Suzie.

'Ah, Miss Ochre, do come in,' Mr Black enthused.

Suzie stepped inside the caravan with Mr Brown following her.

'It has come to my attention that you are a police spy.'

Suzie opened her mouth to speak as Mr Brown's gun came crashing down on the back of her head. She slumped to the floor in a dark haze, peppered with flashing streaks of light as unconsciousness swamped her, like a dark blanket dropping over her head, drifting down to envelope her in a black mist.

'Tie her up, gag her and put her in the bedroom. See that a bolt is fitted to the door, and lock the window. Make sure that she doesn't escape. Is that clear?' Mr Black instructed.

'I'll see to it straight away,' maintained Mr Brown, grabbing Suzie's arm and dragging her along the corridor towards the bedroom.

'When we leave here tomorrow, Mr Green will tidy up and destroy all traces of our visit, along with our meddling informer here.'

Tanya looked shocked. 'Can't you simply leave her behind?

After all, it's too late for her to do anything about your plans now.'

'No, it's not sensible. The least information the police have on us, the easier it will be to get away and remain undetected. I thought you'd be pleased that I've chosen you.'

'I am, very pleased,' defended Tanya, not wishing to upset him.

'We'll say no more, then. Miss Ochre will disappear like the others.'

Mr Black was showing his ruthless streak and his total unconcern about the death of anyone who interfered with his plans.

This worried Tanya. 'What if he found out about me and Ryall?' she thought, 'but then, how could he?'

While Suzie was being bound and thrown on to the bed, Mr Black and Tanya left the caravan. Mr Green was supervising the intense activity that was taking place. The hook was now welded into position and the plane had been refuelled.

The main doors were opened to allow the supermarket van to enter, arriving after a long journey from the Welsh hills, to deliver the stolen weapons. Two men stepped down from the vehicle.

'How did your operation go?' enquired Mr Black.

Ken, the driver, stepped forward. 'We ran into a bit of trouble, Mr Black. We got hold of the arms okay, and were about to leave the base when the alarm was raised. Someone must have discovered the theft. The guards tried to stop us and we had to shoot our way out. Only our vehicle and four of us got away. The other two have gone straight to the flat to wait for us.'

'That's very unfortunate. What happened to the other truck?'

'It took a long burst of fire from one of the guards. He

must have hit a box of ammunition. The whole truck went up – blown to smithereens.'

'And the men?'

The driver shook his head. 'No chance. None of them could have survived the blast.'

'Including the driver?'

'Including Roy,' he confirmed.

'So, no one was left alive who could give away this location?'

'No. The location of your hideout is still safe.'

Mr Black drew a deep breath. He did not like failure of any sort and made no attempt to hide his feelings. 'I suppose that is something to be grateful for. What weapons have you managed to salvage out of all this mess?'

The driver looked slightly miffed by Mr Black's dismissive attitude at the death of his friend and the other men. 'They were good blokes. They died doing a job for you.'

'Yes, yes, quite so. But what weapons have you got?'

'Six Sidewinder missiles, four Maverick missiles and ten boxes of twenty-five millimetre ammunition.'

'Good. At least that is sufficient for our use. I was hoping to sell the plane with plenty of spare armaments, but they'll have to make do with what I give them. Right, get them loaded on the plane,' he instructed, turning immediately to thoughts of his plan and ignoring any hurt feelings he may have caused with his uncaring attitude. His men started unloading the weapons.

'What about our money?' enquired the driver.

'Give the man his money, Mr White,' he directed.

'Are we paying for eight men, or only four?' he asked.

'Those men had relatives who'll need to be compensated for their loss,' sneered the driver, angry at the thought that his men wouldn't get paid for not only risking, but giving their lives.

'Pay them what we agreed, Mr White,' said Mr Black, in an

apparent show of generosity, knowing the money was counterfeit anyway.

The driver and his mate took the attaché case, looked at the contents and left in their empty stolen van.

The six Sidewinder missiles were loaded into place on the pylons underneath the Harrier's wings and the two 25 mm Aden guns were stocked with 100 rounds of ammunition each. When arming of the T10 was finished and the aircraft was fully operational and ready to fly, those men who were not needed any more by Mr Black were paid off. They left, with bundles of counterfeit money, after receiving a solemn warning to keep their mouths shut about what they had seen. The hideout would only be required for a few more hours, so secrecy about its location would only be necessary for one more night. The remainder of the missiles and ammunition were delivered by lorry to the client's headquarters as a gesture of their intentions, under the accompanying watchful eye of Mr Brown.

The men who remained in the barn were those who had a part to play in the following day's robbery, and they gathered to listen to Mr Black give details of what was expected of them.

He stood on a wooden crate to make the all-important address to his men. 'Tomorrow is the day we have all been waiting and planning for. Tomorrow we will pull off the biggest robbery this country has ever seen, and all of us will be *very rich* afterwards,' he declared, emphasising the important words.

The men looked at each other and smiled. They all liked the bit about being very rich, and a gentle murmur erupted.

'Now pay attention, men,' Mr Black announced. The barn went quiet again and all eyes turned to him. 'I will accompany Mr White and his party. We will drive to the coast near Sidmouth tonight, where there is a fishing boat, the *Passado*, waiting to take us into the English Channel. Mr Brown will meet us at the boat after completing his delivery; Mr White has all the details. There are guns aboard, and we will set sail and make for the rendezvous point. Some time tomorrow morning we should see the *Amazon*, a small cargo ship that is making for Hamburg. It will be about a hundred and fifty miles out to sea. When we locate it, I will radio Mr Green, and Miss Lilac will take off in the Harrier to intercept it.

'On the deck of this ship there are several containers. One of them holds the goods that we are going to steal. The ship will be armed with guards, and their job is to protect that container at all costs. We have a nice surprise in store for them, one they are not expecting – the Harrier. They will be told to surrender, and if the sight of the Harrier doesn't persuade them to comply, then a burst from the plane's cannon probably will. If they are stupid enough to continue resistance, they will face the full force of the Harrier's guns, which will eliminate most, if not all of them.

'Then, you men in Mr White's party will earn your keep and board her, to do any tidying up that is needed. The ship will then be in our control and we will hook up the container to the Harrier as it hovers above the ship. The container will be lifted on to our boat, then you men will return to the *Passado*. The *Amazon* will be sunk by the plane's missiles. The Harrier will then be delivered to our client at a location that I will give to the pilot later. We will make for the shore in our boat and transfer the container to a lorry. You men will be handsomely paid for your services and then disappear. I hope that I don't need to remind you all to be careful what you say to anyone else, and not to splash the large amount of money that you each receive carelessly around. Is that clear?'

Heads shook and one or two men mumbled an almost indistinguishable 'Yes'.

'Good. Any questions?'

'Yes,' Miss Lilac spoke up. 'Do you know what sort of weapons the men on the *Amazon* have to guard it with?'

209

'I am informed they have a heavy-calibre machine-gun mounted on the deck.'

'What happens if they don't surrender, but start shooting at me? They might hit the Harrier,' she suggested.

'I'm sure that the Harrier's weapons are far superior, and I am confident that you will not have any problems taking care of it. However, should the Harrier be damaged in any way, I do not expect it to stop us achieving our objectives. Is that clear?' Mr Black warned, with a hint of the anger he foresaw would be evident in him should this occur. 'If by chance the plane was so badly damaged that it could not return to shore afterwards, because for instance it had lost a lot of fuel, it could then be ditched in the sea and you would be picked up by our boat.'

'I'm not keen on ditching the plane in the sea. I could drown before I got out,' protested Miss Lilac.

'That's not likely. Our boat is standing by, and we have a couple of divers at the ready in case of problems. As a matter of interest, a Harrier GR7 ditched in the Mediterranean Sea last year and it took more than a half an hour to sink. There's plenty of time for you to leave the cockpit and be picked up. If this happens, we will have to waste time opening all the sea cocks so that both the plane and the ship will disappear to the bottom of the sea. This will leave the authorities scratching their heads wondering what has happened, and we will all lose a share of the money that selling the plane would have brought.'

'It's also an ideal time to get rid of me,' thought Tanya.

What Mr Black failed to make clear was that the GR7 that had ditched in the water, turned nose down very quickly, and only the tailplane was above the surface for the length of time that he stated.

'What happens if the ship radios for help?' asked a voice from the rear of the group.

'Unlikely. The cargo they are carrying is one they wish to keep secret from the authorities.'

'But another ship could be nearby and call them,' he insisted.

'That's possible. If there is an attempt to call for assistance by anyone, we are ready to jam the airwaves. In any case, it will take far too long for anyone to reach them in time. Even if the coastguard is contacted, we will be finished and long gone by the time they get there, which is why we need to complete our task and sink the vessel quickly.'

'I'm not a very good sailor. What happens if it's choppy out there?' asked a flat-nosed, heavily built man with tattoos covering both of his arms.

'Whatever the weather, the robbery will still go ahead. The *Amazon* will only be in range of our boat and plane for a short time as it proceeds up the English Channel,' Mr Black asserted, slipping back into the style of police jargon that he used when addressing similar meetings at the Met. 'However, the weather forecast for tomorrow is good, so there should be no problems.'

Mr Black looked around his mixed bag of thugs and waited for another question, which did not arrive.

He continued, 'Right then, Mr White and his group can start their journey to the boat. I will follow in a few minutes in the MPV. Mr Green and his men will look after things here at the barn in my absence, and he will ensure that the Harrier is ready for take-off tomorrow morning when I call him. Thank you gentlemen.'

A gentle murmur rose from the men, discussing the plan as they wandered towards their cars. For many of them, this was the first time they had been given an idea of what it was they would have to do. Most were hardened thugs, dredged from the lowest level of the country's criminals. Many had already killed, and were unrepentant about the deaths and misery they had caused. None had ever encountered this type of robbery before, or the rewards they were promised when it was successfully concluded.

When the men had left, Mr Black took Miss Lilac to one side and said, 'The only change to the plan that I announced will be that you are to sink the *Amazon* before the men are taken back aboard our boat. Mr White will give you the instructions. I will meet you at the location where we will hand the Harrier over to our clients, and once I've completed the transaction for the gold, we will disappear. Is all that clear?'

'Perfectly. I presume Mr White is aware of your true plans?'

'Of course. You, me, and Messrs Brown, Green and White will be the only survivors. They are trusted men who have worked for me before, and will be paid for their services and go their own way, and we will go ours.'

'What about the other men on your boat? The divers for instance?'

'Mr White will take care of them.'

Tanya looked at Mr Black and smiled. He was certainly cold-blooded, and had worked out all the details very carefully but, she still was not sure how much to trust him. Was he telling her the truth when he offered to make her a partner, or was he still using her and intending the same fate for her as the others? Was it better to tell Ryall, if she got the chance to speak to him, and hope they could outwit Mr Black and snatch the gold for themselves? Sharing between two was better than sharing between five. But was Ryall using her to get at Mr Black for his revenge, and possibly to steal the gold for himself? She had known him only briefly and could not be sure. So many options, so much to consider, including the ultimate one – sod them all, and take the gold for yourself. The trouble with that one was knowing how to turn that much gold into cash. Tanya had much to ponder on before making a decision.

Before he left, Mr Black had a few quiet words to say to Mr Green, who listened and nodded. The noise of departing vehicles faded into the distance, and everything went strangely quiet in the barn, with only Mr Green, two guards and the women left behind.

'Nothing to do but wait now, I guess,' Tanya commented to Mr Green.

'Yes. We should all get some rest soon. Tomorrow is a big day.'

'I think I'll go out for a smoke first,' she said, picking up her handbag and smiling at him.

'Sure. There's a guard outside to see that you're okay,' Mr Green declared.

'Thanks,' Tanya replied, thinking, 'That's a shame. I want to contact Ryall. I wonder if he's close by still.'

'And your curfew time has been lifted by Mr Black,' he mentioned.

Tanya gave him a 'thank-you' smile, but was thinking, 'Bloody cheek of the man to insist on it in the first place.'

In the caravan, Suzie awoke on the bed with a thumping headache, and a lump on the back of her skull. She wondered what Tanya and Mr Black had talked about and guessed that it was probably about her not being a part of his plans. She was still hoping that someone at Dunsfold had found her note, but as time passed with nothing happening, she was becoming less confident they had.

'If it was found, someone should have discovered this place by now,' she reasoned. Her hands were tied very tightly behind her back and her mouth was covered with sticky tape. She started testing her bonds in a desperate attempt to undo them.

Dark clouds rumbled across the sky, adding to the gloom outside the barn, and a slight chill had returned in the air. Only a small stream of light, seeping through the partly open door and one single, dull lamp mounted above the door, lit the outside area. Tanya fished in her handbag and took out a packet of cigarettes and her lighter. Her face shone in the dark for a few brief seconds when she lit the cigarette, before it faded back into the gloom of the night. Folding her arms, she stood close to the bushes. The guard wandered up and down, treading a path in the same way he had ever since she had arrived. With her back to the bushes, Tanya smoked, and watched him reach the end of his route. She was about to try whispering as loud as she dared, to find out if Ryall was nearby, when an unseen hand caressed her backside.

'You've a lovely bottom, and I want to kiss it,' Ryall quipped.

Raising a hand to her mouth as if to take another puff of her cigarette, Tanya was intent on masking the smile that covered her face while allowing her to whisper.

'Ssh, the guard will hear you. Stop it! You're putting me off, and we haven't much time to talk. You can kiss me later. I've some important things to tell you.'

Ryall stopped messing around, melted back into the bushes and listened to Tanya's whispered details, between stops when the guard came close. Even Ryall was amazed when Tanya told him how much the robbery was estimated to net.

'Wow! That's some haul. No wonder he's kept the details a secret until now. It'll give me great pleasure to relieve him of his "crowning glory", and we will be the ones who spend the rest of our lives living in luxury.'

'That sounds good to me,' Tanya declared.

'It doesn't look as if you'll be needing my little go-to-sleep cylinder after all,' Ryall stated.

'What's that?' asked Tanya.

'It's a cylinder of sleeping gas with a remote controller, that I thought you might need to put the other pilot bye-byes. If the other pilot's not going ...'

'I'll take it anyway. I don't trust Mr Black. He might have told Mr Green to accompany me, and I'm not keen on that. I'm still not sure what he's up to, so it might come in useful,' said Tanya, holding her hand out for the cylinder and control unit. She surreptitiously stuffed them into her handbag.

'To activate it, flip the switch on the controller to "On", and press the red button. Okay?'

'Okay.'

'Only a couple of breaths and he'll be out for the count.'

'Right.'

'By this time tomorrow, we will be rolling in it – literally,' enthused Ryall.

'Are you sure you can sell the gold ingots?'

'That's no problem. I know a London fence who will be only too happy to take them off me, for a price. Right, here's what I want you to do ...'

Tanya listened to Ryall's plan while puffing away at another cigarette and smiling at the guard each time he passed nearby.

When he had finished, Ryall asked, 'You got all that?'

'Got it. I'll see you tomorrow then.'

It began to spit with rain as Tanya threw her cigarette butt to the ground, trod on it, nodded at the guard and returned to the barn. She was happy that Ryall was still there, and that she had been able to talk to him and sort out their final plans. The die was now cast.

23

No Escape

Turning over in bed, Tanya pummelled the pillow into shape and tried to get back to sleep. She could not. The bed was strangely empty without Mr Black, and the prospect of the action she would be involved in later that day span round and round her head, and would not go away, no matter how much she tried to put it to the back of her mind. This, coupled with thinking about what Mr Green was going to do with Suzie, prevented her from getting any further shut-eye. Though Suzie was her rival, she had helped Tanya a lot, and had not grassed on her to gain an advantage, when she could easily have done so. Why, she did not know. Her rival was tied up in the next room, but there was no sound coming from there any more. Earlier she had listened to Suzie struggling to get free of her bonds. She must be sleeping now.

'It's better to not think about her,' she decided. 'Instead, think about all the money that me and Ryall will have in only a few short hours.'

Light was beginning to creep into the barn at the dawning of a new day. Tanya, still unable to sleep, got up to smoke another cigarette. Mr Black did not like her smoking in the caravan, and usually only capitulated if he got his sex first, but he was not there to complain. She sloped into the kitchen-diner, switched on the light and the portable television, and tried twisting the aerial in all directions to get

216

a good picture, to no avail. She tried banging the television, but that did not produce a picture either. Flicking the switch off, she was surprised to hear a gentle knock on the door.

Pulling her dressing gown together – covering her otherwise naked body – and tightening the belt, she opened the door and looked down on Mr Green who was standing there.

'I saw your light on, and wondered if there was anything wrong?' he asked.

'No, nothing's wrong. I just couldn't get to sleep, that's all. I'm a bit excited and a bit nervous.'

'That's not surprising. Today is a big day for all of us. A little nervous tension is good to keep the mind focused,' he expounded.

Tanya noticed his eyes flicking back and forth to her ample cleavage pushing its way past the lapels of her dressing gown, and quickly saw this as a possible opportunity to discover more about Mr Black's true plans for her.

'Would you like to come in for a cup of tea?' she asked. 'I was thinking about making one.'

'Er, that's very nice of you. I'm not a tea drinker, but I wouldn't mind a cup of coffee.'

'Okay,' Tanya agreed, returning to the kitchen, leaving the door open.

In the single bedroom at the far end of the caravan, Suzie had worked on her bonds during the night and eventually managed to loosen them. The rope had cut into her wrists, which were now sore and bleeding with much of the skin rubbed off. But now, at last, the rope was sufficiently loosened for her to force it off. She slowly pulled the tape away from her mouth to prevent a ripping noise, and grimaced at the painful process.

When the last piece pulled away, she murmured, 'Thank God for that,' and rubbed her mouth on the back of her hand.

After hearing Tanya talking to someone, she quietly tried the bedroom door, and discovered that it was bolted on the outside. The door was a poor fit, thanks to the bashing it had taken when the ram jacks were forced into the caravan, and there was a gap down one edge. Suzie peered down the narrow corridor through the crack, and saw Mr Green enter the kitchen at the far end where Tanya was waiting for the kettle to boil. He sat down at the breakfast table, out of her sight, and mouthed a quick 'Thanks' when handed his cup of coffee.

There was some movement in the bedroom door and Suzie gently pushed and pulled the door handle, working the gap wider and wider until the screws holding the catch became sufficiently loose for the bolt to slip out. She was careful not to push the screws completely out, in case they fell on the linoleum floor and were heard by Tanya and Mr Green. They spoke in whispers, too quiet for Suzie to hear what was said, and Tanya was only partly visible at the other end of the corridor.

'You must have the full trust of Mr Black, for him to leave you in charge?' suggested Tanya, attempting to bolster Mr Green's opinion of himself.

'Yes, I have. I've served Mr Black for several years now, and have found that he always repays his people's trust handsomely.'

'He has asked me to join his group. Do you think that he will treat me in the same way?' Tanya asked, letting the folds of her dressing gown loosen to show more of her curvaceous figure.

'Yes, I'm sure he will,' Mr Green replied, finding it almost impossible to take his eyes off her breasts, most of which were now showing.

'We had a quiet talk last night, and he told me about his plans for all of us. Did he tell you as well?' she asked.

'Oh, yes. I'm fully aware of what Mr Black's plans are. We

discuss them together and make joint decisions about our next move,' maintained Mr Green, who was well aware of what Tanya was attempting to do.

He may only have been an electronics expert, and not very successful when it came to wooing women, but he was not stupid. He also knew how to take advantage of a situation, especially when he had a good idea of what Mr Black's real plans were for all of them, and knew that he would be safe. Normally, he would not dream of going anywhere near one of the women that Mr Black was associating with and bedding – but today was different. Today he could take advantage of the attractively curvaceous Miss Lilac, and not get into any trouble because of it.

'Is he really going to take me with him when he gets his hands on all that money?' she asked.

'Well, I'm not really supposed to talk to anyone about Mr Black's plans,' he maintained, giving Miss Lilac the opportunity to persuade him to confide in her.

'But if I'm one of the group now, and he is going to look after me, surely there's no harm in you telling me,' she said, turning to face him on the bench seat and undoing her belt. She opened the dressing gown wide, revealing her ample naked figure. 'I'd be very grateful to you and won't tell a soul that we've spoken … or about anything else.'

Mr Green's pulse, among other things, rose sharply. This was an opportunity that he had only dreamt about previously, and he was not about to miss this chance. He placed his glasses on the table and pushed Tanya down on to the seat and grabbed a breast in each hand.

'Okay, I'll tell you, but afterwards,' he agreed, putting his lips to her nipples.

A satisfied look crossed Tanya's face. This man was easy to manipulate, and after a few brief minutes of letting him have his way with her body, he would tell her what she needed to know. She could then make up her mind whether to go with

Mr Black or stick to the plan that she and Ryall had agreed on.

Tiptoeing barefooted down the narrow corridor to the kitchen, Suzie peered around the corner and watched Mr Green quickly divesting himself of his trousers. He looked like a man who thought this was all a dream and wanted to rush at it with speed to get what he wanted before he woke up. He held Tanya's ample breasts and nuzzled his face into them as he penetrated her. Before he could even begin to thrust in and out he reached a climax and had to stifle his cries of enjoyment.

Tanya held on to him as he lay on top of her, thinking, 'That was even quicker than I expected. It should be easy to handle him now, he's like a baby in my arms.'

'Did you enjoy that, Mr Green?' she asked.

'I did. It's been a long time since I've been with a woman, and never with one as lovely as you, Miss Lilac.'

'You did get overexcited rather quickly.'

'Yes. I'm sorry about that. My feelings of passion got the better of me.'

'Never mind. If we're all together after the robbery we could do this again.'

'Oh, I doubt that, and anyway Mr Black might have something to say about it,' he suggested.

'We don't have to stay with him once we've got our cut. We could go our own way. What are his plans for all of us?' Tanya enquired.

'After the robbery we'll all meet to divide the spoils, then Mr White, Mr Brown and myself will disappear on a long holiday. You will go with Mr Black to his overseas retreat where the police can't touch either of you, he told me so.'

'Perhaps he is planning to go away with me after all,' she thought. 'So are we going to get bars of gold each?' she asked, to test him.

'Oh, no. Mr Black has already got a buyer lined up. He takes the gold, we get the cash.'

'Cash?'

'That's right. Each of us has got an international bank account set up, ready and waiting. After Mr Black gets the funds, he will transfer our shares into these accounts, so you won't be getting counterfeit money, if that's what's worrying you.'

'That sounds good,' commented Tanya, feeling Mr Green slip out of her now that his ardour had diminished. He was comfortable with his face buried in her breasts and stayed put. 'What is going to happen to Miss Ochre?' she whispered.

At the mention of her name, Suzie's ears pricked up as she strained to hear what was discussed.

'Mr Black has given me instruction on how to deal with her, you've no need to worry about that,' Mr Green informed.

'So that means you're going to do away with her, in the same way that Mr Black had the first pilot, Miss Pink, killed?'

'Of course. None of us wants to have someone left alive who can identify us all. Why, does killing her bother you?'

'What bothers me, is wondering whether he's got the same thing planned for me after he no longer needs my flying skills,' Tanya confided.

'No, of course not. You shouldn't think like that. He will look after you as promised, and you'll both be very rich and live in the lap of luxury.'

'Mr Green certainly knows how to say the right things,' thought Tanya. 'But is he telling me the truth? It all sounds too good to be true and I still have my doubts.'

She commented, 'I hope the weather is okay. I'd hate to ditch in the sea, especially if it's rough.'

'You won't have to worry about the sea. Today's forecast is for a bright start to the day with only light winds, though they are due to get worse in the Channel later on, but we should be finished and gone by then.'

'Good. I don't fancy flying the plane in a high wind and rain.'

A distant clatter of the barn door closing, as one of the guards went outside, disturbed the pair.

'I'd better get back before I'm missed,' Mr Green declared, extricating himself from Tanya's arms, pulling up his zip and fastening his belt. 'Thanks for everything,' he said, taking a last look at Miss Lilac's figure before she closed her dressing gown.

Suzie crept back to her bedroom; she now had the last piece of the jigsaw and knew that the robbery was to be on the high seas, somewhere in the English Channel. Escape was now a priority for her if she wanted to stop them.

Tanya smiled at Mr Green, who stepped from the caravan. Her ploy had given her all the information that she had asked for, but she was still unsure what Mr Black's true plans for her were.

She decided, 'I think I'll go along with him – for the time being. Ryall can be my back-up plan. After all, Mr Black always seems to have one, now it's my turn.'

Suzie, hearing the caravan front door close, quietly opened the bedroom door and was startled to see Mr Green standing there with a gun pointing at her.

'I thought I heard someone in the corridor. You weren't thinking of leaving us, were you Miss Ochre?' he asked, stepping into the doorway. 'Or should I say Miss Suzie Drake, emissary of Sir Joseph Sterling.'

'Well, now that you come to mention it…' Suzie replied, slamming the door shut on his gun hand.

He screamed as she put her body weight behind the door, crushing his wrist and forcing him to drop the gun. Releasing the door allowed him to fall into the room. Suzie put a foot to his backside as he got up, sending him flying over the bed and crashing into the flimsy wall, smashing a hole in it with his head. She strode down the corridor, glanced at a startled Tanya and jumped from the caravan, sprinting towards the barn door.

Mr Green staggered to the caravan door, not knowing whether to hold his injured wrist or his battered head, and yelled, 'Stop her!' to the guard on duty outside.

The guard heard the yell and pushed open the barn door as Suzie reached it. She shoved the door straight back into his face, crashing it against his forehead and propelling him rearwards, where he collapsed on the floor. Suzie stepped over him and dashed into the wooded area, knowing Mr Green would not be far behind.

She ventured deeper into the wood and hid behind a tree, unsure which direction to take. The barn door crashed open as Mr Green came out and helped the guard to his feet. He pointed agitatedly in several directions before they split up and started to search for her. Suzie moved away, then tripped over something that was buried under leaves. She brushed them away and found a motorbike dumped on its side. She picked the bike up then noticed another strange mound nearby. Brushing the leaves aside revealed the body of a young man in a leather jacket. It was the dead courier.

The key was still in the ignition, the way it had been when the young man was shot. Jumping on the bike, Suzie turned the key and the engine turned over and over but was reluctant to start.

'C'mon, start,' pleaded Suzie, knowing that her two pursuers were bound to hear the motorcycle.

Not until the petrol had reached the carburettor did the bike's engine cough once, and then burst into life. Jamming it into first gear, Suzie revved it for all it was worth. She let the clutch out and the wheels, spinning on the damp leaves, propelled her forward. She ducked and dodged her way around the trees and headed for the edge where she could see daylight. Shots splintered the trees around her as she weaved through. At the edge she faced the wide open expanse of field covered in 2-feet-high grass, but with a smooth runway cut through the middle, and now covered in the temporary runway sheets of metal.

Behind, Mr Green was racing after her through the woods as fast as the terrain would let him. Suzie heard the roar of a vehicle approaching and turned to see a jeep speeding towards her with the guard behind the wheel. The driver stopped to pick up Mr Green, then charged after Suzie, racing along the makeshift runway. Both bike and car sped over the sheets, which were locked together to fashion the flat, temporary surface. All too soon the runway came to an abrupt end and Suzie was forced to scramble into the wet grass. Motorcycles were no strangers to her – Mike owned a Triumph Bonneville which she had ridden on many occasions, but on tarmac roads, not like this, thrashing through long grass over rough terrain while being pursued by a madman in a jeep.

The motorcycle crashed up and down the ruts as it cut a path through the field. The four-wheel-drive jeep, more suited to the uneven surface, quickly caught up with Suzie. She twisted and turned the bike as the jeep closed in and they tried to knock her off. To elude them, she performed a race track skidding turn, leaning the cycle over at a steep angle and roaring off, only to come face to face with a fence and gate. The gate was padlocked. Cursing, Suzie drove off, with the jeep fast closing in on her as Mr Green fired wildly at her, missing his target.

The field was encompassed by the wooded area to one side and on the others, the fence, stretching around the whole of the remaining perimeter. The only clear exit was back past the barn. Suzie revved up the engine and was tearing towards the barn when the jeep caught up with her and bumped into the back of the bike. Accelerating a little more, Suzie put a few yards between them, but the jeep caught her up and again bumped into her, but harder this time. The back of the motorcycle slewed round and she fought to control the bike as the handlebars jerked back and forth. The wheel caught a dip in the ground and she was thrown headlong over the handlebars. The jeep narrowly avoided colliding with the bike and ground to a halt a few inches from Suzie as she rolled over and finally came to a stop. Mr Green and the guard jumped out and stood over her with their guns pointed at her head.

'Your little escape attempt is over, Miss Drake. One more move like that and I'll put a bullet in you myself,' asserted Mr Green.

Suzie was driven back to the barn and marched into the caravan.

'Killing you is going to be a pleasure,' Mr Green spat, holding his injured wrist.

Tanya watched the men again tie Suzie's hands behind her back and secure her feet. This time when they bound her, she was conscious, able to tense her arms and keep them slightly apart, allowing her more movement when she relaxed her muscles. Suzie looked at Tanya and their eyes met for a brief instance before Tanya averted her gaze, not wanting to look into the eyes of the woman who had helped her yet who she was condemning to certain death.

'Find something to jam the door with,' Mr Green instructed the guard.

'What are you going to do with her?' Tanya asked, still wishing there was a way that her rival could be stopped without the need to kill her.

'Never you mind. Get dressed in your anti-g suit. We're leaving here soon,' barked Mr Green, who was now an angry man and showed no warmth towards the woman he had lusted after, and casually had sex with, only a few minutes before.

Tanya went to her bedroom and dressed. She was showing some tension at the turn of events, and was in turmoil, not knowing who to trust. Seeing Suzie bundled on to the bed in the small bedroom had not helped matters. The off-handed way that anyone who stood in their way was got rid of, worried Tanya. She could not help thinking that she may be next in line to suffer that fate, if she was not careful.

'I hope you had a good sleep last night, Miss Drake, because it was your last one – unless you want to count forever,' Mr Green joked.

'Why are you doing this? Why does Mr Black think I'm a police informer?' she asked.

Mr Green opened a scrap of paper and held it up. It was the note that Suzie had written to Sir Joseph.

'Look what Mr Black found in the rubbish bin in the pilots' quarters at Dunsfold. It's from you, I believe?' he inferred, flapping it in front of Suzie's face.

'It's got nothing to do with me,' she maintained, trying to bluff her way out of a situation that she knew was hopeless.

'We know better, and Mr Black knows only too well who Sir Joseph is,' he retorted, slamming the door. The guard produced a length of wood and jammed it through the bedroom door handle and across the door frame to secure it.

'Get the Harrier checked and ready to start,' Mr Green instructed Tanya. 'We should hear from the men on the boat quite soon.'

The words had hardly left his lips when his mobile telephone rang. 'Right. Yes, we're all set and ready to go.' He snapped the mobile shut. 'It's time to fly,' he announced.

A guard returned from protecting the entrance to the lane and the two guards opened the barn doors wide, while Mr Green opened a case and took out several devices.

'What are they, bombs?' Tanya asked.

'Incendiaries. This old wooden barn will burn nicely. There won't be any evidence left to identify, including the meddling Miss Drake. Now get in the plane. I'm coming with you.'

Any lingering doubts that Tanya had about her safety were all confirmed by Mr Green's attitude towards her. Why only now did he tell her that he was going to accompany her? It could only be for one reason, she decided – they did not trust her and he would be there to keep an eye on her, and may even be there to kill her. That settled it! Ryall was definitely the best bet; she would go along with his plan.

'Can you fly a Harrier?' Tanya asked Mr Green, with doubt colouring her every word.

'A little,' he explained, ignoring her tone of voice. 'I'm not an expert, but I can take off and land it in an emergency. I've been trying it out on the simulator during the night while you've been asleep, as part of my busy programming. I'm getting quite good at it, if I say so myself. And with the computerised auto-lift facility, even I can get the plane to make a stabilised lift-off.'

'You've been a busy boy, haven't you,' thought Tanya, then added in a sarcastic tone, 'But we're not taking off vertically. Are we?'

Mr Green ignored her cutting remark, but threw her an angry glance. 'Don't forget, we've got to keep low to avoid being seen on radar,' he warned.

The guards placed the incendiary devices in strategic places around the barn, while Mr Green donned his anti-g flying suit. Tanya picked up her handbag and climbed the waiting steps to the plane. She checked that no one was watching her, before hiding the gas cylinder in the front cockpit underneath the pilot's seat. The men were too busy placing the devices to notice her, and Mr Green was still struggling to get into his flying suit. Tanya settled down in the rear cockpit, buckled up, fastened on her helmet, and connected her radio and oxygen lead. She placed the controller in a leg pocket, and with butterflies starting to well up in her stomach, she waited for her passenger and the start of what could be a dangerous but very profitable job.

227

'After we've left, set the timers for five minutes, then go to the rendezvous point. I'll see you there,' instructed Mr Green to the men. He was revelling in his new-found authority and enjoyed being away from the domineering presence of Mr Black for a while.

The guards nodded their compliance and Mr Green climbed into the Harrier while Tanya went through the aircraft checks. After removing the ladder, one guard jumped into his car and towed the plane out of the barn. Once the checks were complete, Tanya started the plane's engine. The men covered their ears to block out the roar from the T10 as she taxied it around to the cleared area behind the barn.

The deafening sound of the plane's engines increased in volume and it slowly rumbled along to line up in front of the makeshift runway. Although Tanya had flown the plane, she had not taken off or landed it. Suzie had achieved that, and now, with slight trepidation and butterflies in her stomach, it was time to ignore her nerves and not freeze in the way she had done at Dunsfold. A least she had now flown the plane, and the controls felt more familiar.

With the T10 standing at the beginning of the temporary runway, Tanya increased the revs until the plane vibrated and shook so much that it felt as if it would shake itself apart. She released the brakes. The plane charged down the runway, gathering speed all the time, and Tanya wondered if it would ever get off the ground. It accelerated relentlessly on, rattling over the iron plates, towards the fence looming larger by the second, getting closer and closer. Gradually the 12-tonne, sophisticated fighter plane reached 125 knots, lifted from the ground and took to the heavens, rocking a little from side to side and clearing the gate by only a few feet.

Birds sprang into the air and fluttered away at the sudden, unwelcome disturbance of this ear-shattering plane blasting into the sky. The power was gently increased, Tanya moved the nozzles fully to aft and the T10, fully loaded with fuel and weapons, moved gracefully up and away. The guards watched the plane skim the treetops and bank round in a southerly direction before disappearing into the distance. Quietness returned once more to this tranquil countryside area. They dashed into the barn to activate the timers.

Locked in the caravan, Suzie heard the roar of the plane taking off and rolled off the bed, falling to the floor. With her supple limbs, the little movement that she now had allowed her to squeeze her backside through her bound arms, pull them under her legs, bringing her tied hands in front of her. She hauled herself to her feet and hopped to the window. Outside in the barn, she saw the men splash petrol around the walls and switch the timers on. One of them looked up, noticed Suzie at the window and waved goodbye, before they jumped into their waiting car. It sped down the narrow lane, creating clouds of dust swirling in the air, and was only a distant memory within a few seconds.

They left the timers ticking away the seconds before the incendiaries would explode into a deadly fireball which would engulf the whole barn.

24

Fire

Locked in the caravan, there was not time for Suzie to untie the bonds around her legs, and the door refused to budge when she yanked at the handle. She charged it with her shoulder and it gave a little, but was jammed tightly shut and resisted her attempts to break it open.

'Sod!' she exclaimed.

An idea came to her. Suzie lay on the floor and used the strength in her legs and feet. After several kicks, she heard a crack and the flimsy caravan frame, reinforced by the broom handle behind the door, started to break. One more kick opened up a split, and a final hefty one broke the frame in two. The top hinges of the door tore off as it crashed open, smashing against the caravan wall and sliding to rest at an acute angle. Suzie hopped her way along the corridor and twisted the front door handle. That door was also locked, and the narrow corridor did not afford her enough room to lie down and attempt to open it in the same way. She hopped into the kitchen to look for a knife to cut herself free.

At that moment, a large explosion rocked the caravan, knocking her to the floor. She grasped the top of the sink and slowly hauled herself to her feet, and looked in horror at the fire quickly spreading up the walls of the wooden barn. A second explosion on the far side started a fire there, which likewise raced up the wall. The two fingers of flames rapidly travelled towards each other. Soon the wooden beams and thatched roof burst alight. Burning thatch dropped to the floor, falling on both the low-loader and the caravan roof.

Yanking a kitchen drawer open in haste, all the utensils crashed to the deck. Suzie scrabbled on the floor, found a knife with a serrated edge and cut at the rope around her ankles. The fire spread quickly through the tinder-dry wood and thatch, setting the whole barn ablaze, bringing timber frames crashing to the ground and torching parts of the caravan, as Suzie frantically cut away at the bonds.

She screamed out loud when a roof truss crashed down on top of the caravan making her jump. 'Oh shit! Bloody hell, Mike! If ever I needed you, it's right now,' she exclaimed.

The rope finally broke and, getting to her feet, she stared with despondency through the kitchen window at the fire, which had now engulfed most of the barn. Suzie grabbed a frying pan and with her wrists still bound, swung it two-handed at the window. The glass shattered into a million pieces and flames shot through the opening, forcing her back and setting the curtains alight. Suzie looked around for another way out but the caravan was parked tightly up against the back wall of the barn, which was now also starting to burn.

The inside of the caravan was filling with smoke, Suzie began to cough and choke. She grabbed a tea towel, ran it under the tap and held the wet cloth to her face to block out the acrid smoke.

Suddenly, through the haze and fire, a figure came into view, dodging a way through the burning debris. The smoke-filled barn made it impossible to see who it was, but it looked as if someone from the gang had returned, or perhaps a local farmer had seen the blaze and arrived to help. Suzie screamed out at the top of her voice and battered on the sink with the frying pan. Was the man here to rescue her? And would he hear her cries and be able to get through the fierce flames? The heat was intense, and time was short. Within a few minutes the fire would engulf the caravan and consume everything inside, including her.

The figure side-stepped burning debris and was forced to jump clear of a burning roof truss as it crashed to the ground. The shadowy outline came close enough for the man to be seen clearly by Suzie, and she could hardly believe her eyes.

It was Mike.

It felt as if an enormous weight had been lifted from her shoulders.

'Mike, Mike,' Suzie bellowed, with tears welling up in her eyes, at sight of the man she loved, the man she thought might be dead.

Mike heard the cries and saw her in the caravan as he dodged another chunk of blazing roof joist that crashed to the floor in front of him. It blocked his way to the caravan, now well ablaze, and he could see there was very little time left to get his lovely Suzie out.

Alongside him was the low-loader, with the wooden floor of the trailer burning furiously. Mike jumped into the cab and gave an ecstatic yell of 'Yes!' at finding the keys still in the ignition. He twisted the key and the engine turned over and over but the vehicle refused to start.

'C'mon you bitch, start!' he yelled, stamping on the accelerator pedal. The engine coughed twice then roared into life. Mike revved it up, shoved the vehicle into first gear and crunched it forward, driving over the burning wood and moving up to the side of the caravan, gently bumping into it. Slipping the clutch and pushing the revs up to screeching point, Mike inched the low-loader forward, shoving the caravan along in front of him as more burning debris crashed down on its roof and his vehicle. The tyres screamed their complaints at the sideways movement as the caravan was pushed into the now fragile, burning rear wall of the barn. Mike kept the vehicle moving relentlessly forwards. Suzie clung on to the taps in the sink to stay on her feet with the caravan shaking violently at its rough passage of travel.

More sections of wooden roof joists fell on top of both vehicles, but Mike kept inching the low-loader forward. Inside the caravan, Suzie was forced to dive for cover under the kitchen table as cupboard doors swung open allowing crockery and utensils to fly around the room. The caravan juddered along sideways on its burning tyres, screeching along the concrete floor and was pressed into the ancient daub and wattle timber-framed barn wall. Keeping the vehicle moving, Mike forced both caravan and low-loader through, demolishing the wall, and causing more burning timber supports to crunch down on the roof. The 100-tonne vehicle pressed on, and by the time the cab had cleared the barn, the caravan wheels had jammed in the long grass and it began to topple over. Slowly it overturned and smashed down on its side with Suzie screaming as she was tossed around inside. Mike jumped from the lorry, leaped on top of the caravan and grabbed the door handle.

'Shit! That's hot,' he swore, flapping his scalded hand at the locked door. 'Get back out of the way, Suzie,' he yelled.

Mike drew his pistol and pumped three bullets into the lock, then gingerly grabbed the handle and smartly swung the door open. He dropped inside and found Suzie lying among the shattered pieces, cut by broken glass and coughing uncontrollably from smoke that filled the room. Mike lifted her up, threw her over his shoulder, climbed from the smouldering caravan and raced towards a large, corrugated-roofed outbuilding packed with bales of hay. He dived into the hay seconds before the caravan's gas cylinder exploded, hurling chunks of smouldering debris into the air.

The burning thatched roof of the barn collapsed to the floor with a muffled thud, throwing up clouds of smouldering reeds, and what remained of the sides came crashing in. The tyres on the low-loader burst with a sharp bang, sounding like a shotgun blast, when fire burnt through the rubber. Flames licked the vehicle's petrol tank and an almighty explosion erupted, blasting chunks of burning wood and debris in all directions.

Mike held Suzie close to him, sheltering her from falling lumps of barn and roof raining down on them. He moved quickly to stamp out the tufts of burning hay and when the dust finally settled he brushed the hair away from Suzie's bruised and blackened face and they embraced, kissing with a passion that only lovers do after a long absence from each other.

'I thought you were dead, Mike. You don't know how pleased I am to see you,' Suzie declared.

'Oh, yes I do! I feel exactly the same. Trying to find you these past six days has been a nightmare,' he insisted. 'Are you okay?'

'Sure, I'm fine, but would you like to untie my wrists?'

'Not until I've had my evil way with you,' he said, pinning her arms down above her head and lifting her scorched T-shirt. He kissed each breast lovingly.

'I'm glad to see they're not damaged.'

'Is that all I mean to you?'

'No, of course not. I haven't inspected the other bits yet.'

Suzie smiled, pleased that neither of them had lost either their lives or their sense of humour during the ordeal. She lowered her arms over Mike's head and they kissed again as he undid their belts. They made love in the hay with renewed passion and reconfirmed their commitment to each other. The dangers they had faced, and their spell apart, ensured their lovemaking was delightfully reassuring for them both, if a little rushed.

'Are you in a hurry?' Suzie asked.

'Not really. But I'd rather the pilot didn't come looking

for me and find us here like this. He's bound to wonder about all the noise.'

'Pilot? What pilot? And how did you find me?'

'I've been searching the county, a small area at a time, in an army helicopter that Sir Joseph put at my disposal. I spotted the smoke rising from the fire, and when we got close I could see what looked like a hastily fashioned, temporary runway. That clinched it. We came to investigate and parked the helicopter in a field behind the back of what's left of the barn.'

'Then I guess we'd better not keep the pilot waiting, and get going. Before they set off explosives to torch the barn, I overheard Tanya talking about the sea and the Channel. I'm sure they are using the Harrier to rob a ship of gold bars.'

'Gold bars?'

'Yes. I heard her mention them. We should make for the coast straight away,' suggested Suzie.

'I'll tell the pilot,' Mike informed.

Mike untied Suzie and they dressed, and hurried back to the field where the helicopter was sitting, but the pilot was nowhere to be seen. Mike looked around and saw him standing by the gate into an adjoining field of cattle. He was talking to an attractive young woman with long blonde hair.

'Is he a young pilot?' Suzie asked.

'Yes, quite young. Late twenties, I should think.'

'Then he'll probably stay there chatting for a while. We haven't got time to waste.'

'No,' said Mike, putting two fingers into his mouth and giving a loud whistle.

The pilot turned, saw them, waved and hurried back to the helicopter.

'Sorry. I didn't know you were back. Is this the lady we've been searching for?' he asked.

'Yes, it is. Didn't you hear all the explosions from the barn?'

'Well, yes. Now you come to mention it, I did hear a bit of a bang.'

'A bit of a bang?' questioned Mike, with incredulity. 'It was more than a bit of a bang. It was a bloody great explosion and we could both have been killed.'

'Well, you certainly look as if you've been near a bonfire,' he remarked, looking at their blackened faces and clothes, 'and I can see a bit of smoke over there.'

'Near a bonfire! A bit of smoke? We've been in a raging barn fire that's now burnt the whole place to the ground. I see you were busy and didn't rush to help.'

'No, certainly not. My job is to stay by the helicopter to guard it, not go chasing across the countryside at the sound of any little bang.'

'Any little bang! I'll have you know that the barn was blown to smithereens to start the fire.'

'We don't have time for this discussion, Mike,' interjected Suzie.

'No. We've got to get down to the coast fast. We think that Black is committing a robbery with the Harrier, somewhere in the Channel, right at this moment.'

'My instructions were to help you look for Miss Drake, and now we've found her. Nothing was said about charging off to a robbery. I'll have to contact base first to see what instructions they give.'

The pilot radioed base and talked to his commander, telling him they had found the woman they were searching for. He was instructed to return to base.

Mike and Suzie were adamant that they could not afford to lose the time.

'I'm sorry,' said the pilot, 'but those are my orders.'

'I'm sorry as well,' said Mike, taking a swing at him and catching him with a right hook. The pilot dropped to the ground unconscious with Mike shaking his bruised fist.

'Shit! That hurt.'

'Never mind. Let's get going,' insisted Suzie, climbing into the cockpit and donning the headset.

The helicopter's rotor blades turned slowly, then quickly gathered speed taking the aircraft into the air. The downblast fanned the pilot and he opened his eyes.

'You stay with your lady friend. We'll get someone to pick you up,' shouted Mike, watching the bemused pilot stagger to his feet and check that his jaw was still in one piece.

He stood and watched the helicopter fade to a tiny spot, and disappear from view over the southern horizon.

25

Time To Fly

With the barn hideout now way behind, the Harrier sped towards the coast. Fields and hedgerows below shot past in a blur of greens and browns as the T10 clipped the treetops at more than 200 mph. Tanya was not sure what Mr Green, sitting in the pilot's seat in front of her, was feeling, but she guessed that he was probably petrified, and that pleased her. She was savouring the enjoyment of getting her own back on him for all the problems he had put her through during her training in the simulator. She deliberately flew as low as she dared to scare the living daylights out of him, and succeeded in scaring herself at the same time, though she again found the experience exhilarating as the adrenaline coursed through her body. Now, more familiar with the controls, she was feeling a lot happier at flying the Harrier.

Towns and villages quickly appeared then disappeared, to be replaced by others that vanished in the same brief moment of time and were forgotten in seconds. The rugged cliffs of the English coastline blasted past and quickly receded into the distance behind them, bringing the diminished sense of speed that the vast expanse of blue sea and white surf below them created. The Harrier zipped past boats, tossed by the churning waves, ploughing towards their destinations. Tanya checked her heading and made a slight adjustment. Dark clouds rolled along in the distance, and the weather was looking as if it could turn a good deal rougher than the forecasters had predicted.

'It's quite windy and the sea's a lot choppier than I thought it would be,' grumbled Tanya. 'It'll make the operation a lot more tricky.'

'Yes, I agree, but it's too late to back out now. I'm sure you'll manage okay. Mr Black's boat should be in sight soon,' Mr Green blurted over the intercom.

'Okay,' Tanya replied, slowing the plane by decreasing the power, bringing the nozzles down gradually and increasing the flaps.

A small fishing vessel came into view riding up and down on the dark, unforgiving waves. The name *Passado* was clearly visible in large white letters painted on the side of the faded blue wheelhouse. Men stood around the deck, watching the Harrier approach.

'That's them,' said Mr Green, 'We're right on track,' he announced, switching frequencies to contact the vessel.

'The *Amazon* should be in sight now, somewhere in the distance in front of you,' Mr White informed him, standing in the wheelhouse doorway, staring up into the sky at the approaching plane.

The T10 shot past the vessel and headed towards a larger ship looming on the horizon. They overflew the *Amazon* to check it out and noted the increased activity at their presence. The ship tossed up and down on the waves, and to Tanya it looked likely that hovering above it would be far more difficult in reality than it had been during training on the gently gliding simulator. At the sight of the Harrier taking an interest, a menacing looking machine gun was brought out and lowered on to its deck mounting.

'That must be the *Amazon* all right. That's a nasty-looking gun they've brought out. I'll bring the plane around and stay out of reach of that thing,' Tanya said.

She flew the T10 around the ship in a wide arc, selected

hover stop, and brought the plane gently to a mid-air hover, less than a mile from the dark rust-covered craft that had their complete attention.

The *Passado* closed in and Mr White radioed a message to the *Amazon*, telling them to surrender or suffer the consequences. Their reply was to send a salvo of bullets from the deck-mounted machine gun, but the fishing vessel, like the Harrier, stood off, well away from the reach of their weapon. The message was repeated, and so was the answer.

'They don't seem to think that we mean business,' Mr White stated over the radio to the Harrier's pilots. 'I want you to blast the ship into submission, without sinking her. We can't take our cargo off if she goes to the bottom, so use only the guns at this stage. Do you understand, Miss Lilac?'

'I understand. This should be the interesting part,' announced Tanya, getting into the swing of things. 'Let's see what this baby can do in a real combat situation.'

The Harrier gathered speed and prepared to attack broadside at sea level. Skimming the waves, the jet held steady with the ship in her sights. At 500 yards the on-board display showed convergence of the Harrier's weapons, and Tanya squeezed off a half-second burst from each of the 25 mm Aden cannons. In that short time the guns spat out more than 30 rounds. Her aim was slightly off target, and the lethal weapons demolished half of the wheelhouse, leaving the ship with no steering mechanism.

The fighter blasted over the vessel and climbed into the sky, rattling the few windows in the ship that were left unbroken. The men manning the machine gun fired continuously and swung round at the Harrier as it flashed past. A shot peppered the outside edge of the port wing with bullet holes. The damage was slight, and not enough to prevent the Harrier from making a wide sweeping arc and positioning for a second attack.

On this approach the aim was good and a further half-second burst of cannon fire demolished the deck gun and the soldiers manning it. The rest of the crew ran scared when they saw the devastation that a 25 mm diameter bullet did to the structure and to a man, blowing a hole clean through him. They all dashed for cover, retreating below deck. A final burst from the Harrier's guns and what was left of the wheel-house totally disintegrated. The bullets ripped large holes in the side and deck of the ship, showering splinters of decking in every direction.

'These guns are lethal,' exclaimed Tanya. 'Look at the damage they've done with one short burst. Those men didn't stand a chance; the rest of them might as well give up right now.'

'They're mainly African soldiers from a rebel army. Nobody will miss them,' declared Mr Green, with no concern.

'African rebels,' thought Tanya. 'Interesting. That must be where the gold comes from. I bet they aren't moving it legally. That's probably the reason why Black's got to hear about it.'

The remainder of the men on the *Amazon* feared, with good reason, for their lives. The officer who was command-ing them on their trip had been killed, along with the gunners, and they were now leaderless. Panicking, they ignored their strict orders to remain silent, and tried to put out a Mayday call. The *Passado* radio operator was checking the emergency frequency, heard the call and blocked it with a band of interference before any location could be given.

Whilst the Harrier's devastating attack was on, and with the only effective weapon against them reduced to scrap iron, the *Passado* raced towards the *Amazon*, pulling along-side her.

The small fishing vessel was tossed back and forth by the rolling waves and high swell of a rough sea that was getting increasingly worse with each passing minute. The men, struggling to stay on their feet, slung grappling irons up to the deck of the ship. They clanged over the railings, and after a sharp tug to make sure they were secure, the boarders began their dangerous clamber up the ship's side. One man lost his grip and yelled as he dropped towards the boat, crashing into the *Passado*'s railings and plunging into the sea, disappearing below the waves. The rest of the men swarmed on to the *Amazon*'s deck.

Mr Black's orders were to leave nobody alive on the ship, and his gang of cut-throats carried out the order with ruthless efficiency. Sub-machine guns rattled out their death song, with little fire being returned from the ship's guards, in their state of disarray. The crew, despite being unarmed and surrendering, were all shot. Mr Black's group had the vessel under their control within a few minutes and counted only three casualties among their men – one injured, one shot dead and one drowned.

Mr White waited until he was sure the vessel was completely secure, and every cabin and hiding place had been searched thoroughly to eliminate anyone who might be concealed, before he ventured aboard. Once on deck, he checked the containers and located the one he was looking for.

'This should be it,' he pronounced, banging the side with his fist.

The container was smaller than others on deck, measuring only 10 feet square by 6 feet high. Mr White hauled himself on top, inspected the padlock securing the container shut, and promptly put two bullets into it. The lock shattered and he opened the lid and glanced inside. A wooden crate filled most of the container, and prizing off the lid revealed the contents. It was full of gold bars, neatly stacked. He closed the lid and jumped back down on the deck.

'That's the right one, okay. Get those chains around it, and hurry,' he ordered. 'The weather's starting to close in. It's getting a lot rougher,' he stated, returning to the *Passado.*

A man climbed on top of the container and chains were looped underneath from both sides, then passed up to him. He locked them together through a lifting ring and signalled to the pilots in the Harrier to close in and hover nearby.

Tanya moved the plane in gingerly, taking her instructions from Mr White over the radio. The sea swell rocked the ship back and forth, shooting spray over everyone and making it difficult for the plane to remain close enough for the ring to be threaded on to the lifting hook. Tanya tried several times to close in a little nearer and hold the plane steady, and almost knocked the man off the top of the container as he fought to grab the hook and locate the ring.

'Careful,' shouted Mr Green, over the radio, 'You're going to get us killed if you don't watch out.'

'I'm trying my best. With this bloody raging wind, this isn't easy, you know,' snapped Tanya, fighting hard to stop the Harrier swaying from side to side.

'I know. But it's not a raging wind, it's just a little gusty. Take it slowly, just like you did in the simulator.'

'In the simulator! Huh! That's a laugh. Suzie helped me with most of this. I couldn't get the bloody hang of it.'

'What!' cried Mr Green. 'Well, Miss Lilac, you'd better get the hang of it now, and quick.'

'Or what? What are you going to do about it?' challenged Tanya, her outburst more a sign of frustration than fear. She was greeted with silence. 'That's what I thought, Mr bloody Green, so just shut up and let me concentrate.'

Mr Green seethed, but knew there was nothing he could do or say at that moment either to help the situation or alleviate the anger burning inside him. He was unable to fly the plane well enough to take over, especially in these weather conditions, and had to simply sit and watch. He would get his revenge later and it would be all the more sweet because of her contempt for him. She was just like all the other women he had known, no respect for him or his intellect.

The man on top of the container finally managed to slip the heavy ring over the dangling hook. Tanya immediately felt the impact of the extra weight on the controls and boosted the power. The container lifted slowly from the deck and swayed an alarming amount, unbalancing the man on top and sending him crashing into the sea.

'Oh, don't worry about him,' Mr Green snapped. 'Just get this load clear of the ship before it takes us down with it.'

The wind was increasing and waves rocked the small fishing vessel, tossing it back and forth. A storm was fast approaching from the open sea and dark thunderclouds swirled across the sky towards them, bringing stronger winds and rain.

The container was heavy. Much heavier, it seemed, than was calculated on the simulator. Controlling the Harrier in hover mode was difficult.

'It looks like you didn't quite get your sums right, Mr Green,' Tanya crowed. 'This thing's a bloody sight more difficult to hold than it was on the simulator.'

She took the plane up and gently swung it round to face the English coastline.

'What are you doing?' screamed Mr Green.

'The load is too heavy to manage and there's a storm coming. I can't land this thing on a small boat that's tossing up and down like a rocking horse. I'll have to take the container and drop it ashore.'

'What about the ship? We are supposed to sink the ship.'

'Tell them to pull the damn plug out. I'm having a job to hold this plane steady as it is. Do you want to chance firing a missile with this load hanging below us?' Tanya asked.

'No, I guess not,' agreed Mr Green. 'But I want to inform Mr White what we are doing first.'

'If you want to inform Mr White, then go ahead. I'm not hanging around here to drop into these damn waves.'

Mr Green radioed the *Passado* and explained their predicament to Mr White. He understood their problem and could see the struggle Tanya was having to keep the plane steady.

'Mr Black has already anticipated the possibility of difficulties because of bad weather, Mr Green, and has selected a landing site on the coastline,' Mr White explained, passing the new coordinates to the Harrier pilots. Tanya was instructed to head for the alternative landing site.

'Have you got all that?' Mr Green asked her.

'No. I mis … some of …,' Tanya, replied switching frequencies as she spoke to make it appear as if their communications were breaking up.

Removing his face mask, Mr Green craned his neck round to look at Tanya behind him and yelled out that he would set the new coordinates himself. She could not hear him, but this was the opportunity she was waiting for. Tanya flipped the switch on the remote control and pressed the button to release the gas. The hissing noise alerted Mr Green. He turned back to see wisps of smoke drifting from below his seat, but by the time he reacted, it was too late. He scrambled to put his mask back on, but dizziness overtook him and he fell into unconsciousness before he could clip it in place. His head rolled to one side and Tanya saw that he was out for the count.

She reset the coordinates, adjusted her heading and swept away from the *Passado*, leaving behind the storm-tossed vessels that held Mr Black's men, riding the increasingly rough waves. She wondered what they would do about their plans to kill off all the men. Would they now have to change their mind about doing that? Not that Tanya cared about any of them.

Mr Green was asleep, she had control of the T10, with a

container full of gold bars slung beneath the aircraft, swaying gently, and she was heading towards the coast. Things were going rather well.

26

Surprise

The Harrier's wing tip was peppered with bullet holes. The damage was slight, much to Tanya's relief, but a small amount of fuel was beginning to seep from one of the openings, and anything that might prevent her from reaching the landing point, she viewed with alarm. Above the deep blue, inhospitable sea, interspersed with dashes of white foam, the sight of the English coastline looming large in front of the plane filled her with delight. She held the Harrier at a steady speed to avoid the heavy load swinging from side to side, and if she had got her directions correct, the rocky face before her should be Dowlands Cliffs. There, Ryall would be waiting for her with a lorry to transport their prize. The storm clouds were way behind her in the distance and things were beginning to match the weather ahead, and look much brighter.

Tanya glanced at the rock face looming before her. 'I've got to take her up a bit. I don't want to smash this lot into the cliffs. God, I hope he's there,' she muttered.

Her worry was unfounded. The Harrier responded and slowly climbed higher towards the deep green headland, coming into view above the chalky cliffs. There, standing beside an open-backed truck on a clifftop pathway in front of a backdrop of tall trees, was Ryall. He waved furiously to Tanya, as if she would have difficulty in seeing him, and indicated that she should lower the container straight on to the open-backed lorry.

That task proved to be every bit as difficult as it was to remove the cumbersome weight from the ship. The wind gusted over the headland cliffs at an alarming rate, rocking both the container and the plane, pushing it perilously close to the nearby trees. It was far too heavy for Ryall to manoeuvre the container into position; he tried and it easily brushed him aside, knocking him to the ground. He indicated to Tanya that he wanted her to put the container down on the ground first. She lowered it on to the grass, crunching it down with a force that made a deep indent in the soil.

While the Harrier hovered above, Ryall jumped on top of the container and tied a rope around the hook. Instructing Tanya to lift the load back aloft, Ryall looped the rope around an upright on the lorry and pulled for all he was worth to guide the container into position while yelling and waving instructions to her. She could not hear him, but understood his gestures, and between them they positioned the container over the lorry and it thudded down on to its back, with a force that severely tested the vehicle's suspension. Leaping back on top, Ryall unhooked the chain and the Harrier moved away, traversing backwards and landing on the ground with a thud.

Tanya shut the engine down and breathed a sigh of relief. Ryall raced to the plane and jumped up on the wing. Opening the cockpit, Tanya undid her harness, threw her helmet away and stood triumphantly. They smiled at each other.

'How did I do?' she asked, arms aloft, asking to be congratulated.

'Brilliant. I never thought you'd fail,' said Ryall, offering Tanya a helping hand. This hand she accepted and he assisted her to step out on the wing, and they slid to the ground.

'It looks like you had a bit of trouble,' he suggested, fingering the bullet holes in the wing.

'That's nothing. You should see what the gun and wheelhouse on the boat look like. There's nothing left of either of them, or any of the soldiers who got in the way,' she stated, squeezing out of her anti-g flying suit.

'Did you sink Black's boat?'

'No. The weather was getting much too rough. I had enough trouble controlling the plane with that great weight hanging below it. If I'd let loose with a missile, there's no telling what would have happened, so I gassed Mr Green and hightailed it back here. He's still sleeping like a log in the front cockpit. How long will he be out for?'

'Forever. The sleeping gas is poisonous.'

Tanya looked slightly miffed. 'You didn't tell me that.'

'It didn't seem important, especially as you didn't expect to use it. But that's another one of Black's men that we won't have to worry about. What happened to the other woman?'

'They tied her up in the caravan and set the barn alight. She must be charcoal by now. I felt a bit sorry for her after the way she helped me, but she's in the past,' maintained Tanya. 'With this gold, we've got a future.'

'Such a waste of a good-looking woman,' reflected Ryall.

'She was in the way. If Black's men hadn't killed her, then your gas would have.'

'True.'

'So stop worrying about her, you've got me now,' Tanya said, walking to the truck with an arm around Ryall's waist. 'We've now got our hands on gold worth about twenty-one million pounds.'

He gave a gentle whistle. 'Wow! That should be enough for us to live the rest of our lives in luxury. It's a pity that you couldn't sink Black's boat, but no matter. This'll show him that he's not the mastermind he thinks he is, and with all this gold, we can afford to hire a good hitman to knock him off.

That's the only way we can be certain that we're rid of him, once and for all. Otherwise, we'll be looking over our shoulders for evermore, wondering if he's still chasing us.'

'Do you know any good hitmen?' asked Tanya, realising there was still a lot she did not know about Ryall.

'I've heard of a guy who lives in Russia somewhere,' he said, his arm around her waist, but with his hand a little lower down on her backside. 'Zenon Horak or something-or-other. He's supposed to be the best. I've got underworld contacts; we'll find him. Meanwhile, we'd better get out of here. If Black's not dead, he'll be after us. We need all the head start we can get.'

Ryall opened the lorry door and stepped back sharply. Pointing at him from inside the cab was a gun, held by the chubby fist of Mr Black, who had Mr Brown alongside him behind the steering wheel. He sounded the horn and two more men appeared from among the trees. One wore a suit and had tanned features, the other was dressed in a pilot's anti-g flying suit.

'Ah, Mr Ryall, welcome. And you too, Miss Lilac. Thank you for delivering my goods to me. I'd like you to meet Ahmed, an emissary of PLOY, who have purchased the Harrier, and this is his pilot. They will be relieving you of the plane. I get the gold and a handsome purchase price, they get the plane, and you two get ... not a lot for trying to deceive me, and failing miserably,' Mr Black sneered. 'Ahmed, the Harrier is all yours for the bargain price of ten million pounds sterling, in cash. I believe you've already arranged to refuel the plane somewhere on the Continent.'

Ahmed nodded his agreement to the statement and the pilot stepped forward with two attaché cases and opened them. Mr Black's beady eyes lit up at the bundles of crisp £50 notes.

'It's amazing that two small cases can hold such a large amount of money,' he said, thumbing through the wads of notes to check they were all there. 'Thank you, Ahmed, you are now the proud possessor of a T10 Harrier complete with armaments, plus spare missiles which you have already received as a gesture of my intent,' he gushed, with an open hand directing him to the plane.

The pilot strode towards the Harrier.

Mr Black looked pointedly at the crestfallen Tanya and Ryall. 'And as for you two, I've got some interesting news. I've been on to your little game for quite a while.'

'How?' Tanya questioned.

'Your little tracking device interfered with Mr Green's electronics. It didn't take us long to find Mr Ryall in his camper van parked in the woods nearby. And talking of Mr Green, where is he?'

'The excitement was too much for him. I had to put him to sleep,' Tanya confessed.

'I see.'

'Permanently,' she sneered, wishing to aggravate him.

Mr Black's face did not alter, and he showed no sign of regret.

'Why didn't you capture me when you discovered that I was still alive?' asked Ryall.

'I needed a pilot and didn't want to upset Miss Lilac by killing you. I'd already lost one, discovered that another was a police informant, and was reasonably sure that the third one was going to double-cross me. I couldn't afford to chance losing her until after the robbery,' Mr Black stated. 'And as it turned out, my worries were well founded. First Miss Pink, then Miss Ochre and now Miss Lilac; all mutineers who must suffer the consequences of betraying me. Such a pity,' he said, pointedly at Tanya, 'we could have had a lot of fun.'

'You expect me to believe that you wouldn't have done away with me, like you did the others?'

'Of course. But I'm intrigued to know where you hid the tracking device. I searched your handbag and didn't find anything suspicious.'

Tanya dipped her hand into a pocket and produced her lipstick. She twisted the bottom of the holder. 'Now it's on.'

'Ah! I see. Very clever. Well, thank you for loading up the gold for me, I must be away before the rest of my men get back and want me to share it with them. Goodbye.'

Mr Black raised his gun to fire, but was rudely interrupted by an army helicopter rising over the cliff face, distracting his attention. The sudden noise and sight of it stopped him for a split second. Ryall pounced on his momentary hesitation and slammed the lorry door shut on his gun hand. Mr Black screamed in agony, dropped the gun and nursed his fingers, crushed by the door.

'Let's get out of here,' Mr Black yelled, slamming the door shut and putting his throbbing fingers in his mouth for comfort.

Ahmed went for a gun in his belt and Ryall threw himself at the man, winding him as both crashed to the ground with the gun spinning away. Getting quickly to his feet, Ryall snatched the lipstick from Tanya and threw the device into the back of the lorry as it motored away. He grabbed her hand and they dashed into the trees for cover.

After getting to his feet and sucking in gulps of air, an angry Ahmed picked up his gun and ran towards the Harrier. The T10 was the prize that he was after, and he wanted it badly. His pilot was already in the cockpit and had fired up the plane's engine.

'It looks like we've hit paydirt,' announced Suzie over the helicopter's intercom to Mike, who was sitting beside her. 'All the rats are together, and squabbling.'

Climbing on to the Harrier's wing, Ahmed turned and fired several shots at the helicopter. Suzie pulled the stick aside and took the helicopter away, out of range. The lorry rumbled off along the clifftop pathway, heading for the road while Ryall and Tanya ran for cover of the trees.

Ahmed jumped into the cockpit after unceremoniously

dragging Mr Green out and dumping his body on the ground.

Scrambling under cover of the trees, Ryall and Tanya watched Mr Black and the truck full of gold disappear into the distance, leaving a cloud of dust behind them.

Over the deafening roar of both the Harrier and the helicopter, Tanya shouted to Ryall, 'That's Suzie with Paula's boyfriend Mike, and that's an army helicopter they're in. I don't know what the hell's happening here or why they're both still alive,' she stated, 'but they certainly arrived at an opportune moment for us.'

Ryall nodded and said nothing.

The pilot increased the power in the T10 while Ahmed strapped himself into the front seat after slamming the canopy shut.

'Who do we go after?' Suzie asked, bringing the helicopter round to face the T10.

'If that pilot and his friend are going to do what I think they are, we better get out of here while we can.'

'Yeah. They're going to take the Harrier up and that thing's still got four missiles strapped under the wings. I don't fancy trying to outrun that plane. Let's hope they're only interested in stealing the T10 and vamoosing with it.'

A swirl of air surrounded the Harrier as it rose in a vertical take-off and swung its nose towards the helicopter.

'Quick, take us up,' Mike bellowed.

The helicopter shot skywards as a burst of cannon fire swept harmlessly below them and out to sea.

'Let's get after the lorry. We don't need to tangle with a fighter plane like that,' Mike said.

Suzie swung the helicopter round in an arc and they swept around the edge of the trees and followed the road, quickly catching up with the lorry, bouncing up and down the rough pathway. It skidded on to a narrow side road and began to gather more speed, but the massive weight of the container slowed it down. Mr Brown fought to hold the vehicle on the road, and was forced to ease up at each bend to avoid turning the lorry over or losing their load. The helicopter shadowed them from above and Mike leant through the doorway and let loose a volley with his P7 pistol. Bullets ricocheted off the lorry and holes punctured the container as the vehicle motored relentlessly on. Mr Black, grabbing Mr Brown's gun, returned fire through the window.

The Harrier, to Mike and Suzie's amazement, roared along behind them. 'What are we going to do about that damn plane, Mike?' Suzie asked. 'The bloody Harrier's still on our tail.'

'Search me! But I can tell you this; a helicopter's no match for the armoury of a Jump Jet. I've radioed Sir Joseph and told him about our predicament. He said that help is on the way. Meanwhile, I think we should try to follow Black and see where he's taking the gold.'

'That's okay, as long as that pilot doesn't take any more potshots at us.'

'He's not going to risk chasing after us. It's the plane they want, they can't afford to waste the time,' Mike pronounced.

The Harrier shot past them and banked round in a sweep and manoeuvred to face the helicopter.

'Got any more bright ideas?' Suzie quipped.

'Visual display set to Air-to-Air,' the pilot announced to himself, 'and when you're in the crosshairs, fire.'

Pressing his thumb firmly on the red 'Fire' button on the stick, the T10 shuddered as a Sidewinder missile shot out from beneath one wing and streaked towards the helicopter.

'Oh, shit!' exclaimed Suzie, yanking the stick hard to one side, twisting the helicopter over and dropping into a steep dive.

The missile shot past the main rotor blades with only inches to spare and hurtled out to sea.

'We've gotta get out of here,' yelled Suzie. 'They obviously want blood. Hold on to your hat.'

She took the helicopter up to full throttle and sped away at over 200 mph heading south towards the English Channel.

'We can't chance one of those missiles going astray over a populated area,' she stated. 'It's better that we lead them out to sea, and forget about Black and the gold.'

'Yeah, why not? What sort of terrain I'm above when I get blown to oblivion doesn't really make a lot of difference.'

'What's the matter? Don't you trust me any more?'

'Sure, I trust you. I just don't trust them.'

The Harrier chased after them and another missile sped their way. Suzie banked the helicopter over and the Sidewinder shot past, blasting its way out to sea.

'I don't think the pilot knows how to lock a missile on to a target – thank God,' Suzie yelled, 'or we'd have been blown into little bits by now.'

She twisted and turned the Lynx helicopter, pushing it to its limits, but could not shake off the versatile Harrier. No matter how hard she tried, the T10 remained behind them, and they knew their dangerous game of cat and mouse with a Harrier could have deadly consequences for them if the pilot found his target.

'Let's hope we can dodge the next two missiles. After that he's only got his cannon left,' stated Suzie.

'Oh, great. I now have the choice of being blown to bits by either a missile *or* cannon fire,' Mike said sarcastically.

'Not if I have anything to do with it. We're not dead yet, and I haven't been through all this to end up as target practice for some foreign renegade pilot.'

The Harrier closed in again for the kill. Suzie thrust the stick from side to side, throwing the Lynx around in a severe test of both its flying capabilities and hers. The helicopter ducked and dived, twisting and turning, with

Suzie trying everything to avoid giving the pilot a clear shot at them.

'He must give up soon,' declared Mike. 'They can't afford to hang around here much longer, surely?'

Like an answer to his prayer, and without warning, two RAF GR7 Harriers streaked over the clifftop and headed straight for the stolen T10. The renegade pilot spotted them immediately, broke away from chasing the helicopter and hightailed it out to sea, gaining speed fast from a near stationary position. The GR7s were in hot pursuit, and with their current speed, quickly caught up with the T10. One of the pilots issued a warning to the stolen Harrier to stop and be escorted back, or they would be forced to shoot it down. The warning was ignored and instead the plane climbed high into the sky and banked round in a loop, with the pilot attempting to manoeuvre his aircraft to get behind one of his pursuers. The two RAF combat pilots, who had both served in the Gulf War, were far too experienced to fall for such a simple move. They followed closely and remained behind the T10, issuing a further warning.

Realising that he was unable to outmanoeuvre or outrun the pursuing aircraft, the pilot slowed the T10 to hover mode and swivelled it around to face the GR7s. They in turn slowed to a hover, moved apart to avoid both being in the line of fire, flew backwards to keep an eye on their quarry and settled at a stand-off distance of half a mile. The three aircraft formed a circle facing the centre, with the pilots watching each other intently. For a few moments all was still and the three aircraft hovered in the air, with the GR7s waiting for the pilot of the stolen plane to surrender or make the first move. The lead RAF pilot issued a final warning, adding that the T10's position was hopeless and emphasising that they would not hesitate to shoot the plane down if forced to.

Suddenly, the T10 spun on its axis to line one GR7 in its

sights and let loose with a Sidewinder missile. The power with which the missile shot out rocked the aircraft, with the back-force triggering the onboard management system to stabilise the plane. The missile streaked across the sea with smoke and flames pouring from the rear. The intended target rose sharply and the GR7's radar automatically activated its programmed countermeasures on detection of the missile, and released chaff and flare to divert it away.

The T10 pilot's inexperience with his plane was evident by him firing the missile manually and being unaware of how to lock it on to the target. It zipped past the plane, eventually falling harmlessly into the sea. Letting such an armed, sophisticated fighter blast off missiles, and possibly getting lucky and hitting one of the Harriers, could not be allowed. Being acutely aware of the strong brief they were given on scrambling, the second GR7 closed in immediately the missile was fired. It sped towards the T10, now trying to retreat after missing its target, and with convergence at less than 500 yards, the pilot gave a full one-second burst from the Aden guns. The accurate cannon fire shattered the front fuselage and cockpit, killing both occupants and smashing the controls. The T10 careered out of control and dropped like a stone, falling nose-first into the sea as the GR7 banked, streaked overhead and shot skywards.

The fight was over. It had taken only a few brief minutes.

The lead pilot reported the outcome of their action to headquarters and, after dropping a marker buoy over the crash position and relaying the coordinates, they flew back to base. The Navy would have the job of retrieving the wreck in the coming weeks.

Mike and Suzie looked on from their helicopter, enthralled by the action they had seen.

'Phew,' exclaimed Mike. 'Those blokes sure know how to handle that plane. It's so versatile. Did you see them flying backwards?'

'That's easy,' exclaimed Susie. 'I can do that in this helicopter. Watch.'

The Lynx traversed backwards.

'Okay, okay, I believe you. But those guys don't mess about.'

'And nor must we, or we'll never catch up with Mr Black, the gold, or Ryall and his busty mate,' Suzie declared, sweeping the helicopter round in a big circle.

They signalled a thanks to the GR7 pilots and headed back for the woods where their quarry had disappeared.

'There's no sign of them,' Suzie stated, circling above the trees along the clifftop. 'It's too dense. I can't see a thing in those woods. We're gonna need people on the ground to search for them.'

'Right. I'll contact Sir Joseph and tell him what's happened. I'll ask if he can arrange for the police to comb the area.

'In the meantime, we'd better see if we can locate that truck with Black and the gold bars. He must be well on his way by now, to wherever it is he's making for.'

27

The Chase

Hidden amongst the densely planted trees, Ryall and Tanya saw the T10 pursue the helicopter, and watched as it chased the Lynx out to sea.

'With any luck, that'll be the end of those two meddlers,' Tanya sniped.

She and Ryall were scampering through the dank woodland, to look for transport that would allow them to pursue Mr Black and retrieve the stolen gold bars. Instinctively, they ducked when the two GR7s roared overhead and began their engagement with the stolen Harrier.

'I wonder where the hell they came from?' Tanya asked.

'I don't know, and it's not our problem. But I do know that we've got to get some wheels, and fast,' announced Ryall, 'or we'll never catch up with Black. The nearest village is a good couple of miles away.'

'That cagey bastard is getting away with all the gold and the money he got for selling the plane.'

'We're not finished yet. I've still got the receiver,' announced Ryall, 'and that homing device is still sending out a signal,' he said, glancing at the row of indicator lights that were getting fewer each time he checked. 'We must get a car soon or he'll be out of range and impossible to catch up with.'

'How about that one?' said Tanya, pointing to a bright red, RS Turbo convertible, parked with the top down.

'That's perfect.'

They approached the car, which was hidden among trees and parked near the end of a little-used dirt track. Closing in, they heard grunts of enjoyment filtering through from behind some nearby bushes. A closer inspection revealed the source of the pleasure came from a man and a woman stretched out on a tartan car rug under a pine tree. They were engaged in clandestine lovemaking, with the woman's blouse and bra undone and the man's trousers around his ankles. His jacket hung on a nearby branch, and they were so engrossed in each other and savouring the forbidden fruits of their lovemaking, they did not see Ryall search through the pockets, where he found the car keys. He carefully lifted them from the jacket, but then they jangled. The man heard it and looked up.

'Hey! What the hell do you think you're doing?' he shouted.

'You keep fondling the lady. We're going to borrow your car.'

Ryall threw the keys to Tanya. 'You drive, I'll direct.'

They jumped into the car, watched by the man hurriedly trying to pull his trousers on. By the time he had, the thieves and his car were disappearing down the track.

'She had a nice pair of tits,' remarked Ryall. 'But not as good as yours,' he added quickly.

Tanya gave him a sideways glance and smiled. They motored through the woods at a hasty speed, the car twisting and turning on the rutted track before sliding on to the road. Ryall took the receiver from his pocket and checked to make sure the direction finder was still registering.

It was. The pursuit was on.

In the back of the truck, the lipstick receiver rolled back and forth while sending out its constant signal. It took Ryall only a few seconds to establish the general direction and an approximate distance, and he and Tanya were soon in breakneck pursuit of Mr Black and his lorry load of stolen gold bars.

Meanwhile, in the helicopter, Mike and Suzie had also resumed their search for the lorry and radioed Sir Joseph with an update of events.

'Where did those other two planes come from?' Mike asked.

'The coastguard picked up a frantic Mayday call from a ship which described them as being attacked by a hovering fighter plane, before the call was jammed. I'd requested that any reports of possible Harrier sightings were to be relayed to me and I realised what was happening straight away. I asked the RAF to scramble two fully armed GR7 Harriers from the nearest base, with instructions not to let the plane get away at any cost, even if it meant shooting it down. Your last call confirmed what I suspected.'

'We saw them chase the T10 out to sea.'

'What happened?'

'The idiot piloting the T10 was stupid enough to fire off a missile at them, so they had no choice but to shoot it down.'

'That's too bad. Harriers are not cheap. They cost the government about twenty-three million pounds each when they were in production. Still, it's better than having a fully armed one in the hands of a terrorist organisation,' asserted Sir Joseph.

'A terrorist organisation?'

'Yes. That's what I suspect Mr Black was doing. I received a report only yesterday stating that Ahmed Dinashar had sneaked into the country. The only thing that would tempt a man like him to come out of hiding, would be a great prize – like an armed Harrier. He is the buyer for a terrorist group named PLOY, the Peoples' Liberation Organisation of Yalon.'

'Yeah. Right. Well, if it was him in the plane, you may find that he won't be buying any more arms from now on,' Mike commented.

'I'll know more when the commander of the GR7s briefs me and we sort out arrangements to get the Harrier lifted, providing it's not in water that's too deep.'

'We're trying to locate Black and the container load of gold. They shot off during the mêlée, so we're going to make a wide sweep and search for his lorry.'

'Good. I've alerted the local police. The vehicle ought to be fairly conspicuous with that load on the back and they are combing the wooded area for your two friends as well. I've also requested that an attack helicopter be put in the air, with six armed men aboard trained in anti-terrorist tactics. I want them to be ready to deal with the situation when Black is located. He's not getting away from me this time.'

'Right. I'll contact you again if we find anything,' added Mike, ending their conversation.

The helicopter buzzed over a duel carriageway while Mike was fiddling with the radio.

'While I was changing frequencies to talk to Sir Joseph I picked up a strange signal,' he told Suzie. 'Did you see Ryall throw something into the back of the truck before they fled?'

'Yes. Now you come to mention it, I did. He took it from Tanya. I wonder what on earth it was?'

'I've been thinking about that, and also about how Ryall managed to get in touch with her again so easily after we lost them at the warehouse. I'm willing to bet that he gave her a homing device to make sure he could find her, and that could be what he threw into the back of the truck,' Mike postulated, scanning the frequencies. 'Got it,' he announced.

'If you're right, then all we have to do is follow that signal. Which direction should I head for?' Suzie asked.

'It's a bit difficult to tell. I need the proper receiver to be sure. Fly around in a circle and I'll see which way gives the strongest signal.'

After circling around a couple of times Mike declared, 'West, head west,' pointing in the general direction. 'It seems strongest that way.'

Suzie nodded and pulled the stick over. The helicopter responded and they banked round and sped west over the main road heading towards the city of Exeter.

In the meantime, after checking the rear-view mirror and the sky, and seeing nothing untoward, Mr Black smiled. 'We've definitely lost them Mr Brown, we're nearly home and dry,' he stated with satisfaction, opening the case to take another look at the money. Suddenly, he slipped a note from within a wad and held it up to the light. 'The bastard!' he exclaimed.

'What's up?' Mr Brown queried.

'These notes. They're worthless forgeries. I'll kill that bastard.'

'Don't worry about him. The money from the Harrier was a bonus. We'll probably be able to pass some of it off, anyway.'

'You could be right. But I still don't like being ripped off by anybody,' Mr Black declared.

'We just need to make sure the same thing doesn't happen when you do the deal for the gold. There's plenty of money there for both of us.'

'True. I'll take care of Mr Ahmed Dinashar later.'

'Next stop Exeter Airport, then we'll fly away to the sun,' Mr Brown announced, his thoughts wandering to all the good things he would be enjoying soon with his share of the money. Mr Black would reward him well for his loyalty, and as there were now only two of them, it should be a tidy sum.

'I'll contact our buyer and confirm that we will be there as agreed. Once the money is transferred to my account, we will be on our way. A private jet is standing by to take us out of the country,' he asserted, punching the buttons on his mobile with a little difficulty because of his swollen fingers.

Nearly 10 miles behind them, and racing along the A3052 in their stolen car at a speed in excess of the limit allowed, were Ryall and Tanya.

'Keep going,' he told her. 'The signaller is still sending and it's getting stronger. We're catching them up. They're continuing in a westerly direction. I wonder where he's heading for.'

An army helicopter buzzed overhead and continued flying above the road in front of them.

'That can't be the same one, can it?' Tanya asked.

'Naa. That Harrier should have made mincemeat out of them and anyway, they can't possible know which way to go. It's probably a regular army helicopter on manoeuvres.'

'What if it is them, and they're just guessing and searching along the main roads?' she worried.

'Let them guess. They've no way of knowing we're in this car and we're the ones with the direction finder.'

'That's okay as long as they don't get lucky and spot the lorry from the air.'

'Don't worry. If they do, we'll be right behind them to snatch it away,' Ryall asserted.

In the helicopter, Mike was given the latest news from police headquarters on the hunt for Mr Black and the missing gold. He passed the information on to Suzie.

'The police say that a man was robbed of his car in the woods at the clifftop, near to where the Harrier landed. The robbers were a man and a woman, and the man called the woman by name – Tanya. That's got to be our pair of thieves, either looking for Black or making a getaway. They pinched a red open-topped Ford.'

Suzie nodded. 'We passed an open-topped red sports car

charging along the road a mile or so back. Do you think that could be them?'

'I don't know. It might be. Ryall may still have the receiver and be following the signal, so it's possible. I'm getting a lot of interference from the airport traffic and can't tell which direction it's coming from any more, so let's go back and take a better look. Make a wide circle and come in behind them. If you're right, then we can trail them without being spotted,' said Mike, grabbing his binoculars.

A few miles ahead, Mr Brown drove the lorry on to the airport perimeter road, past a couple of hangars, and stopped outside a warehouse. The shutter door opened and he drove in, cut the engine and pulled the handbrake on. A swarthy, well-dressed man sporting a dark beard and with features characteristic of his native India, closed the shutter door. Holding a handgun, he moved towards the lorry and opened the cab door as five more of his countrymen, all armed, appeared from behind wooden crates and surrounded the vehicle.

Mr Black and his henchman stepped from the vehicle and greeted the only man not clutching a gun.

'Abid, it's good to see you again,' he effused, holding out his hand.

The extended hand was ignored, making Mr Black feel slightly uncomfortable. He was among men who killed at the slightest provocation and cared little for anyone other than their own kind, and he knew it. He was vulnerable, and had to trust the man he was dealing with would stick to his part of the bargain. He had little room for manoeuvre, but was not entirely out on a limb; Mr Black always liked to have a back-up plan, and today was no exception.

His contact was Abid Ali-Khan, a man who had the reputation of being able to supply, exchange or launder any amount and any type of currency, or anything else that a customer wished for. He was also renowned for taking a large cut of the proceeds and had become extremely rich on the deals that he brokered. Wanted by almost all the major Western countries, he only came out of hiding these days for the really big deals. This purchase was big, and was the reason why he was taking charge of the exchange personally.

'You have got the gold?' Abid asked, in a manner similar to Mr Black's when he had asked Ryall about the simulator only six days previously. He too did not want to hear that there had been any problems.

'The gold bars are all here, just as I promised,' Mr Black informed him, giving an open-handed gesture towards the crate on the lorry.

A flick of the wrist to his men sent two of them climbing on to the back of the lorry to inspect the container and its contents. One of them picked up the lipstick and held it up with a questioning frown.

Mr Black's face twisted with anger when he saw the tracking device and he snatched it away, throwing it to the ground and stamping on it, crushing it to little pieces. 'Bitch,' he declared.

'What is it? Is there a problem?' Abid asked, the tone of his voice now changed to one of concern.

'No problem,' insisted Mr Black, 'but to be on the safe side, I recommend that you place a couple of men outside to watch for a man and a rather well-endowed woman who might turn up and try to cause trouble.'

A nod to two of his men by Abid was acknowledged, and the men checked their handguns and stepped through the small door in the shutters. They emerged into bright sunshine, to hear the deafening roar of an aircraft speeding down the runway before gracefully lifting into the blue sky and heading towards the horizon, carrying a cabin full of holidaymakers.

'Who are they?' demanded Abid.

'Ex-employees of mine, who unfortunately were able to make an escape after interference by a rival couple in a helicopter. If they are stupid enough to show up here, I'm sure your men will have no problem in taking care of them.'

'Let us hope not – for your sake.'

'Shall we get on with the transaction? As you can see, all the gold is there.'

One of Abid's men climbed down after inspecting the container, and spoke in his native tongue. Mr Black was unable to understand, but the half-smile on Abid's face told him that he had been given the good news, that the gold shipment was complete, as promised.

He turned to Mr Black. 'My man tells me the consignment is correct,' Abid said, turning to his laptop computer, opening it and punching a few keys.

Mr Black watched eagerly as the modem dialled out his Swiss bank. He was invited to enter his account number, which he did with eager anticipation, his bruised hand a little shaky.

'Your hand looks to be quite swollen,' Abid commented.

'Yes. I had an accident when getting into the lorry and the door banged my fingers. It was a little painful at first, but it's okay now,' Mr Black lied.

He waited for further instructions regarding the transaction.

'Forty million US dollars was the agreed price, I believe.'

'Yes. Quite so,' Mr Black effused, watching Abid enter the required amount and press the 'enter' key to begin the transfer. Mr Black watched the whole of the transaction carefully to ensure that the money was safely deposited.

Still charging along in the red convertible, Ryall tapped the receiver and got no response. 'He must have found the lipstick. The signal's stopped,' he informed Tanya, throwing the receiver into the door pocket. 'That means they must have stopped, and they can't be very far in front of us, only a couple of miles at most, I reckon. Have you got any idea where they were heading for?'

No sooner had the question left his lips, than a sign directing motorists to turn right at the next junction for Exeter Airport flashed past. Tanya spotted it.

'Yes, I do believe I know where they're going. I recall Black saying that he'd lined up an international buyer, so he must be coming in from abroad. He's also skipping the country in a private plane when he's got his money, and Exeter Airport is only a few miles ahead. That's got to be where he's gone.'

'Good girl,' praised Ryall, touching her shoulder. 'We'll show Black who's best, yet.'

Tanya signalled right, thrashed past traffic lights that were turning red and threw the car around the corner. With the tyres screeching, they headed for the airport.

In the sky above, Mike was staring at the car through his binoculars. 'That's them okay and charging along at a high rate of knots. Tanya's at the wheel, I'd recognise that pair of big … blue eyes, anywhere.'

'I bet that's not the only big things she has that you recognise,' said Suzie, curtly.

'Well, I do have to admit that she has an outstanding figure,' Mike replied, tongue in cheek, knowing that it would aggravate her in a playful way.

'And no doubt you'd like to get your grubby little mitts on them,' Suzie replied, in a mock, slightly hurt fashion, knowing that Mike would probably feel that he had over-stepped the mark with a frivolous comment and would counter-react to correct the matter. Two can play at that game, and Suzie was better at it.

'Not at all. Your figure is much more superior,' he oozed, 'much more athletic and trim and …'

'Okay, okay. I forgive you. Look, the car is stopping by the airport. Do you think that Black is attempting to fly the gold out?'

'It's a possibility. But I doubt it. It would have been easier simply to load it on to a boat and keep going.'

'Except that our curvy pilot tried to snatch it for herself.'

'That's true. See if you can find a patch of grass nearby and put us down quietly. We'll investigate. I'll let the boss know what's happening,' instructed Mike, reaching for the radio.

On the ground, after parking the stolen car in bushes outside the perimeter wire fence, Ryall stood on the bonnet and scanned the airport complex and outbuildings.

'See anything?' Tanya asked.

'Not yet.' He continued to look. 'Yes. There's some warehouses or hangars across the other side of the runway. One of them has two men patrolling up and down outside. They must be the guards. Let's go,' he said, jumping down.

Ryall got into the driver's seat and spun the car on the grass in his haste to get back on to the road leading to the far side of the airfield. He ignored the 'No Entry To The Public' sign, drove straight in and parked at the back of the warehouse. Opening his jacket, Ryall took two Beretta 93R machine pistols from the holsters underneath each arm, handing one to Tanya. He turned the selector to three-shot bursts.

'Where on earth did you get these from?'

'Always be prepared is my motto, since I met Black.'

'I'm not sure I can use this,' she said, staring at the gun in her hand. 'Getting a person killed by someone else or killing at a distance is not so bad. This will be much harder.'

'I haven't come this far to let that bastard Black get away with the gold. And besides, I can give you twenty-one million good reasons why you should be prepared to use it.'

Tanya thought about the money and all the nice things

she could buy with it. 'Yes. That's a lot of good reasons, isn't it?'

Suzie landed the army helicopter in a nearby field. She and Mike ducked low underneath the slowing rotor blades, dodged traffic as they crossed the road, and ran towards the back of the airfield.

Inside the warehouse, Mr Black took out his mobile. 'You don't mind if I ring my bank, do you? I want to make quite sure that the transaction has gone through okay without any hiccups,' he suggested to Abid.

'Of course not, only …' he produced a gun and pointed it at Mr Black, 'I'm afraid they will only tell you that there was no money transferred to your account.'

Two of Abid's men stepped forward with their guns pointed at Mr Black and Mr Brown. The third man stepped into the driver's cabin of the lorry.

Mr Black stared at the weapons. 'I see. You are just like all the rest. You have no scruples and no honour.'

'Not entirely true. I could have simply had you killed when you arrived and taken the gold. This way, I did at least try to leave you with your life, but you had to go and ruin even that. I won't say that it's been a pleasure, but at least it's been profitable. Kill them!' Abid commanded to his gunmen.

A smile crossed their faces at the pleasure they were about to enjoy in performing their murderous act. They raised their guns to shoot when suddenly a short sub-machine gun burst from behind a packing case, high up at the back of the warehouse, ripped into both gunmen, permanently wiping the smile from their faces.

Abid, surprised by the sudden turn of events, stared at the direction the shots came from, allowing Mr Brown time to draw his weapon. He shot Abid in the shoulder, sending his gun spinning to the ground. He spun round, aimed through the passenger door window and shot the driver in the head as he fumbled for the gun in his shoulder holster. The force of the bullet knocked him through the lorry door and out on to the warehouse floor.

Abid held his blood-soaked shoulder and cowered as Mr Black advanced towards him, picking up one of the weapons from his own men and thrusting it into his face.

'I always make contingency plans in case anything goes wrong. It's a lesson that I learned the hard way, when the Metropolitan Police Force saw fit to scoff at all my ideas and turfed me out. Unfortunately, you will not have time to learn that lesson, as you will be dead.'

A slim-figured woman stepped out from behind the packing cases and nimbly jumped to the ground, a Heckler and Koch MP5 sub-machine gun cradled comfortably in her arms.

'Come in, my dear,' Mr Black beckoned with an outstretched arm. 'I want Abid to see the lovely young lady that has messed up all his stupid selfish plans.'

Abid stared at her. She certainly was lovely, and with that weapon, deadly.

'Meet an old partner, who has become my newest associate. The delightful … Miss Pink.'

28

Expire

In the Exeter Airport warehouse, Paula stood by the packing case with a wry smile on her face, clasping the weapon that had saved the lives of Mr Black and Mr Brown.

Several weeks earlier, when Mr Black had his first meeting with the men who represented Abid, he had been concerned with his reception. He understood their caution, especially when they found out that he had once been a Metropolitan policeman; he expected that. But their whole attitude towards him had been one of seeing him as merely an insignificant hireling who needed them to supply the cash that would turn his robbery into a profitable venture. Mr Black had dillusions of grandeur about his status, and scoffed at the ill-informed group with which he was about to do business. He was uneasy about these men, and concerned about the possibility of a double-cross. He had now discovered that these fears had been well founded.

For Paula, events had taken a turn for the better since she followed Suzie and Mr Brown back to Mr Black's new barn hideout, after their meeting in Portsmouth. She mistakenly saw Suzie as the rival who had prevented Mike from reuniting with her after his first tour of duty as a mercenary. On her way to their rendezvous at the old docks in Portsmouth, she had hatched a plan to try and get her own back, and concealed from Mike and Sir Joseph the fact that she had arrived in time to follow them.

The following day, she had tailed Mr Black and Mr Brown to the Exeter Airport warehouse, when they visited to check on the location that he was intending to use for the conclusion of his deal. Careful pre-planning always paid dividends, Mr Black maintained. Paula had approached him and taken a chance that he would accept her as a sleeping partner, which he was happy to do, in more ways than one, after discovering that she had some very interesting information with which to barter.

He was delighted, and surprised, to find out the truth about Suzie and her association with Sir Joseph Sterling, and even more surprised to learn that Ryall was still alive, after assuming that he had been blown to kingdom come with the rest of his gang in the limousine.

On his return to the barn, he discovered from Mr Green the alarming news that he had detected interference to his electronics, and that he was certain there was a homing device on one of the women. A quiet search of the surrounding area brought to light confirmation that Ryall was still alive, and the realisation that, because he was nearby, he must now be in partnership with one of his pilots. Miss Ochre, he now knew, was working for the authorities, and Mr Ryall was a thief and a murderer, so it had to be Miss Lilac who was his partner, a fact which disappointed him, but came as no real surprise.

With the knowledge about Suzie, he knew that he had in his grasp all the information he would need to make fools of the authorities once again. Not only would he elude them, but the gold would make him a multi-millionaire, and with that kind of cash they would never be able to touch him. He could buy just about anything, or anyone.

Mr Black put a fatherly arm around Paula's waist. 'You have done very well, my dear,' he assured her. 'And proved yourself to me beyond doubt. Mr Brown will tell you that I reward loyalty, and reward it well.'

'Good. That's why I teamed up with you,' she maintained.

'There are two more guards outside that we must take care of.'

'Yes. They must be wondering what all the shooting is about.'

'Oh, I don't think so, or they would have been in here by now,' Mr Black suggested. 'I'm sure they are well aware that Abid here was likely to kill myself and Mr Brown and take the gold.'

While this was happening inside the warehouse, outside, Ryall and Tanya had crept along to the side of the building.

'What was that? It sounded like shooting,' Tanya said.

'Yeah. Maybe Black has met his match. Someone might have saved me the bother of killing him.'

They kept close to the side of the warehouse and moved to the front, listening to the two guards chattering in a language they did not understand.

'Are you sure this is the right place?' Tanya whispered.

'Yeah. It's the right place all right. They sound Indian to me. They must be the foreign buyer's guards. If they've shot Black, then we'll have to take the gold from them.'

'So, there must be more inside?'

'Probably. These two are wearing suits and carrying hand-guns. They're no match for this weapon,' Ryall confidently predicted, holding the Beretta up. 'Come on. Let's go. Don't go cold on me now.'

Taking a deep breath, Tanya nodded. 'Right. Let's do it.'

The pair rounded the corner and confronted the guards.

'Drop your weapons,' Ryall ordered, waving his gun at them.

Both men immediately reached for their guns and Ryall shot them dead with two short bursts, while Tanya stood and watched, doing nothing.

'That'll warn the others. Come on, we've got to be quick,' Ryall said, making for a door by the side of the shutters.

Inside, Mr Black was about to finish his business and escape with the gold. 'You, my double-crossing friend, must die,' he said to Abid, raising his gun.

At that moment came the gunfire from outside. Mr Black turned his head towards the direction of the sound and hesitated for a second. Abid made a desperate attempt to grab his dropped handgun, but no sooner had his long fingers reached the trigger, than both Mr Black and Paula turned their guns on him. Bullets ripped into him and his blood-soaked body crashed back against a packing case, staining it with red streaks as he slumped to the ground.

'Get in the lorry,' Mr Black told Paula, then pointed at the exit and shouted to Mr Brown. 'Open the shutters,' he said, climbing into the driver's seat.

Punching the red button on the wall, Mr Brown saw Tanya and Ryall appear on the far side of the warehouse, from behind some packing cases. The shutters clanged their way to the top as he fired a shot, missing them both. Paula heard the gunfire and jumped down from the cab, while Mr Black started the engine and backed the truck towards the exit.

With the vehicle between them, Mr Brown dodged back and forth searching for Ryall and Tanya. Meanwhile, Paula stepped over Abid's body, picked up his gun and shoved it in her waistband, then crept along the side of the packing cases.

The truck reversed out of the warehouse, leaving Mr Brown with a clear shot. He fired, hitting Tanya in the arm, knocking her to the ground, the Beretta slipping from her grasp. He turned to shoot at Ryall, but was not quick enough. A line of holes ripped across his chest and his gun fired into the roof when Ryall's machine pistol spat out its lethal burst of bullets. Paula instinctively ducked low as Mr Brown's bullet-ridden body crashed against the shutter button and the doors started their downward descent, mimicking the slide of his body to the floor.

The sounds of gunfire, peppering the air, greeted Mike and Suzie as they ran towards the warehouse. Drawing their guns, they peered around the side of the building in time to see the truck, with Mr Black at the wheel, reverse out through the shutter opening.

Inside, Ryall bent to look at Tanya, who was barely conscious and bleeding badly, before glancing up to see Paula, who appeared from around the packing cases, standing before him. She was wearing a figure-hugging T-shirt, had a gun jammed in the waistband of her trousers, and a pair of dark glasses concealed her eyes. In her left hand was the H&K sub-machine gun pointing directly at him.

Tanya raised her head and looked up with stark surprise. 'I thought you were dead.'

'No. Lover boy here saved me, then wanted me to thank him in bed. Such a shame. It looks like I'm the one important conquest that he's failed to make. I could have gone for you, Ryall, but I lost interest when I saw you hiding in the woods outside Mr Black's barn in a camper van, waiting for your big-busted girlfriend. You should be more careful when you switch the lights on.'

'I did save your life,' claimed Ryall.

'That's true. But I'm equally certain that the only reason I was in such a nasty position in the first place, was thanks to the two of you cooking up that fancy story about me and Mike killing Mr Grey at the motel.'

'That was Ryall's idea,' blurted Tanya, now very anxious to protect herself, whatever the cost.

Ryall gave her an acid glare.

'I could've given Mr Black the information that you were parked outside his barn,' claimed Paula, 'but I didn't. So, I reckon that makes us quits, and I'm sorry about this,' she apologised, pulling the trigger as Ryall made a move to swing his gun towards her. The bullets hit him full in the chest and he was dead by the time he hit the floor.

'And as for you, bitch …' snarled Paula, deliberately shoving the gun into Tanya's face.

Tanya stared with horror at the weapon and collapsed back to the floor. Paula was about to exact her revenge when she looked up and, before the shutters finally closed, saw the gold-laden truck accelerating away without waiting for her.

She ran across and banged the button to raise the shutter doors. As they rose, she ducked low and emerged in time to see the truck, along with the open gold container crashing about in the back, racing down the airport side road.

'Bastard!' she shouted, emptying her sub-machine gun at the fast-disappearing vehicle.

'Paula? Is that you?' asked Suzie, she and Mike stepping out behind her from the side of the warehouse.

'Hello, Suzie. I didn't expect to see you here, you're supposed to be dead as well,' she confessed, standing with her back to them. 'It seems that a lot of apparently dead people are turning up here alive and well today.'

'I think you'd better drop the gun,' Suzie advised.

To emphasise the command she cocked the hammer of her weapon. The sound was enough to cause Paula to drop the sub-machine gun to the ground. She knew when the odds were stacked against her, and with an empty gun there was no point in taking any chances at that moment.

'How come you're here, anyway?' Suzie asked.

'I followed you to Mr Black's hideout and, despite the fact that he tried to have me killed, I knew there must be a lot of money involved. I couldn't resist making him an offer, which he accepted. The rewards were too great. Now Black's getting away with a truckload full of gold. We could soon catch him up. There's enough money in it for both of us. How about it? We could do a deal,' she suggested, continuing to stand with her back towards them.

'Not a hope. The military will be here soon. He won't get away.'

277

'I feel sorry for you, Suzie, after the way that Mike and me had fantastic sex at the motel. I don't suppose he told you about that?' she taunted, playing the game of putting her opponent off while she slowly reached for the weapon in her waistband, masked by her body.

Suzie lowered her gun. Paula, she thought, was unarmed, and anyway, shooting her would have been have been a tough decision to make, especially with Mike standing next to her. Suddenly, Paula swung round with the gun in her hand and two shots rang out, sounding as one.

Overhead, an army Lynx helicopter buzzed past and chased after the escaping lorry, tearing along the runway approach road. Mr Black thrust a sub-machine gun through the window and fired at the pursuing aircraft. The helicopter swayed out of the way and the pilot weaved it from side to side to avoid the bullets randomly sprayed in his direction.

The approach road came to an abrupt end short of the main runway, but Mr Black continued his escape attempt by crashing through a barrier and driving on to a disused dead-end road, which ran parallel to the runway. The helicopter maintained its position behind him, and prepared to land the troops when the truck reached the end of the badly cracked and grass-invaded road, which had previously joined the main runway.

With aeroplanes flying in and out of the airport every few minutes, Mr Black, with no other avenue of escape, was expected to ditch the truck and make a run for it. But he had other ideas. Trapped, and with his only escape route the runway in front of him, he was forced to make a quick decision. Driving on to the runway was a dangerous route to take, but this did not deter the desperate Mr Black, who charged straight through the fencing at the end of the road, headed down the tarmac and drove at an alarming pace towards the main buildings.

Outside the hangars, police and ambulance sirens wailed

through the air on their arrival, and Tanya was attended to by the medics, before being whisked away to hospital.

Mike stood over Paula's prostrate body, wisps of smoke still drifting from the barrel of his gun. 'Suzie may hesitate at shooting you, but not me. You should have known that when it comes to the crunch my instincts take over and remorse comes later. 'Bye Paula. It's a shame things had to come to this.'

Mike helped Suzie to her feet as she clutched a flesh wound in her arm. She knew what Paula had once meant to him and how hard it must have been for him to face his actions. His eyes were glassy with the sadness and regret he felt over her death. Suzie stroked his face. They looked at each other with a feeling of warmth and love passing between them, counteracting the sadness that both felt for the measures Mike had been forced to take.

'Come on,' she encouraged, 'Black is getting away. We can't let that happen, especially not now.'

'You're right,' Mike said, snapping himself into action and dashing back to collect Ryall's stolen RS Turbo. 'Get in. We've got a rat to catch!'

They charged off in pursuit of Mr Black and his truck full of gold bars.

An Airbus A320 came in to land, too near its touchdown point to abort. The aircraft's wing sliced over the top of the renegade truck, hammering down the runway. The helicopter kept back, well away from the flight path of the incoming aircraft, and shadowed the truck alongside the runway. The airwaves were hot with angry traffic controllers shouting at the airport police with incredulity at the stupidity of the truck driver. They demanded that he be removed from the area immediately, before he caused a major catastrophe. Police sirens wailed as four airport security cars charged on to the runway in pursuit of the lorry.

All flights were hurriedly put on temporary hold after the

helicopter and pursuing local police cars were given permission to cross the runway. Mike and Suzie, in their sporty stolen vehicle, followed the police cars on to the taxiway and main apron. Mike put his foot down, sped ahead of the chasing group and raced after the truck. Mr Black, desperately searching for a way out of the airport, turned off the main runway and motored past the terminal building. He saw a small, 'Airport Personnel Only' service road that led from the complex to the outside.

Staff dived for cover when the truck sped down the narrow service entrance, smashing several airport luggage trolleys on the way, before skidding into the airport access road. The container full of gold bars slid to one side when the vehicle slewed round the corner, and sped off towards an area of open fields bordered by the occasional oak tree.

Mike blasted the horn to warn staff of his fast approach, giving them time to back out of the way. The red Ford flashed past and skidded round the corner with Mike performing a handbrake turn to speed after the truck.

With the helicopter now back on his tail, Mr Black shoved the sub-machine gun through the window and began firing again. The pilot pulled the helicopter aside to avoid the fusillade of bullets streaming his way.

Despite his manoeuvres, several shots struck the helicopter. The pilot radioed their situation to his control and asked for permission to return fire with a missile, now they were clear of the airport complex, and before the truck reached a populated area. Permission was granted immediately, and the pilot lined up the lorry and fired with a TOW anti-tank missile.

The projectile screamed towards the vehicle, sparks and clouds of smoke billowing from the rear, and found its target. An almighty explosion blew the rear half of the lorry and container to pieces, sending gold bars flying in all directions. The vehicle zigzagged out of control with the trailer and cabin burning furiously. It weaved its way along the roadway, crunched up the kerbway, motored uncontrollably across a grass verge and smashed into a tree. Seconds later, the petrol tank exploded, showering debris and more gold bars into the air, spewing them across a wide area of the grass.

The helicopter circled once before hovering nearby and landing. Armed troops spilled on to the grass and rushed towards the burning truck. The RS Turbo came to a screeching halt and Mike and Suzie stared at the truck as flames enveloped what was left of the vehicle. The heat was too intense for any of the soldiers to get near; there was nothing they could do but watch it burn.

No one got out.

'It's all been such a waste of many lives,' Mike said, staring at the flames, 'including Paula's. Greed does funny things to people, and relationships.'

'Yes. So does meeting people in motel rooms it seems. What's all this about the pair of you having great sex?' asked Suzie, snapping back into the usual bantering mood they shared.

'Oh, and I suppose you didn't sleep with Mr Black?' he countered.

'Only because I had to. It was all part of the job.'

'Same here,' quipped Mike. 'We had to make sure it looked authentic in case anyone interrupted us.'

Suzie gave him a sideways glance and smiled. After all, it had turned out to be the last moments Mike had alone with Paula. They wandered across to look at the burnt-out lorry.

'So much for Mr Black and his crazy plans. It didn't do him much good, did it?' Mike asked, bending to pick up one of the gold bars that were scattered everywhere. He shoved it into his shirt. 'These things are quite heavy. I wonder what one of them is worth?'

'What do you think you're doing?' Suzie demanded.

'Well, as you were instrumental in saving all that gold, and ending Mr Black's reign of terror and crime, I'll have to thank you by buying a few more silk blouses for you to wear. That'll cost me money. I'm simply trying to offset the expense a little.'

Suzie put her hand in his shirt, pulled the bar out and dropped it to the ground. 'I'm sure Sir Joseph would be more than a bit suspicious if precious booty went missing yet again, after another job that we've been involved with.'

'Yes, perhaps you're right,' Mike said. 'But of course, that's assuming he knows how many of those things were stolen in the first place.'

Suzie gave him a 'don't do it' glance. 'Anyway, you and the silk blouses are all I need,' she declared, as Mike put an arm around her shoulder and walked her back to the red sports car.

'And all I need is you – and the odd block of gold,' he whispered, trying to sit comfortably in the driver's seat with a heavy bar sticking out of his back pocket.